THE MURDER BOOK

THE MURDER BOOK

A Henry Johnstone Mystery

Jane A. Adams

Severn House Large Print
London & New York

This first large print edition published 2017
in Great Britain and the USA by
SEVERN HOUSE PUBLISHERS LTD of
Eardley House, 4 Uxbridge Street, London W8 7SY.
First world regular print edition published 2016 by
Severn House Publishers Ltd.

British Library Cataloguing in Publication Data
A CIP catalogue record for this title is available from the British Library.

ISBN-13: 9780727893161

Severn House Publishers support the Forest Stewardship Council™ [FSC™],
the leading international forest certification organisation. All our titles that
are printed on FSC certified paper carry the FSC logo.

Typeset by Palimpsest Book Production Ltd.,
Falkirk, Stirlingshire, Scotland.
Printed and bound in Great Britain by
T J International, Padstow, Cornwall.

Prologue

Ruby was used to keeping out of the way when her mother had visitors. Sometimes she would sit on the stairs and listen to them talking in the front parlour but she was always ready to run back to her room. Her mother always told her that the visitors must not see Ruby, that she should stay quiet as a mouse and they should not hear her either. She had found that if she sat right at the top of the stairs she could not be seen but she could listen, and sometimes she could smell them too. People, in Ruby's experience, smelt like the jobs they did. The road mender always smelt of his bitumen, the men who were building the shop next door smelt like bricks and mortar and paint, and the coal man always carried the scent of coal around with him. The men who came to see Ruby's mother didn't usually smell of any of those things. If there was any odour at all then it was usually of soap and polish and the grease they put on their hair to keep it smooth and dressed. They left their scent behind them in her mother's room long after they had gone.

And they spoke quietly too, so that when Ruby tried to listen she could rarely hear the words, only the vague sound of the conversation.

These conversations never lasted for long; she would listen for the pause and then know it was

1

time to run to her room. The downstairs of the house had gas lights and there were paraffin lamps for upstairs that they took up to bed with them. When Ruby's mother and her visitors came out of the parlour it would be the signal for Ruby to flee silently back to her room and turn the lamp right down so that there was only a tiny glow. Her mother knew she didn't like sleeping in the dark so she never made her put the light right out, but she did want her to turn it down so no one else could see it under the door. Ruby was good at being very quiet. At not being seen or heard.

That night a man had arrived that smelt of violets and when her mother had gone upstairs with him Ruby had lain in the dark, listening. She knew what sounds to expect and she knew that when they stopped there would be a little more conversation and then the man would leave. Usually her mother would then make tea for them both and she would sit on the end of Ruby's bed and they would chat for a while. Even though she was only seven years old, Ruby had a fair idea of what was going on in the next room. Her grandparents were tenant farmers and she knew what happened when the ram tupped the ewe because her granddad had told her that was how they got lambs in the spring. She had sometimes wondered if her mother would have another baby but so far one had not come along. The men didn't visit when Ruby's father was home; she liked it when her father was home and Ruby had enough sense not to tell him about the visitors.

The man that smelt of violets was new. Her

mother had regulars but this one hadn't been to their house before though Ruby vaguely remembered him speaking to her mother in the street. He'd tapped lightly on the window, Ruby's mother had let him in and they had gone to talk in the parlour. Only a little while later had they come upstairs and now they were in Ruby's mother's bedroom. Ruby closed her eyes and tried to doze but the sounds they were making were all wrong. Ruby sat up, some instinct telling her that whatever was going on in her mother's bedroom was not the usual kind of activity.

Ruby crept out of bed and listened at the bedroom door. The sounds her mother made seemed odd, frightening, like she was gasping for breath. As silently as she could, Ruby opened the door and peered through the gap. The man was still dressed but she could see her mother's clothes were torn. He was on top of her and his hands were around her throat.

For a few seconds Ruby stood and watched, and then she screamed.

'Get off my mother. Get off her now!'

The man turned and looked at her, his hand still at her mother's throat. Ruby ran at him, scratching at his face, scratching at his hands – anything to make him let go. The man hit out at her and Ruby flew across the room and crashed against the wall. Dimly, she was aware that someone else was now in the room but she was too dazed to recognize who it was. She was aware of the sounds of fighting and angry shouts, and when she did manage to open her eyes fully she saw that her mother was still lying on the bed while two men scuffled around her. And then there was silence.

Ruby struggled to get back to her feet but she felt shaky and sick. The room was moving like she was on board her father's boat and the man was coming towards her, the one that smelt of violets, and the other man, that she now recognized as her cousin, Walter, was lying on the floor and there was blood all around him.

A second blow, this time with more than a fist. She died with the scent of violets hanging in the air.

Extract from *The Murder Book*, the commonplace book of Chief Inspector Henry Johnstone.

I have recently re-read my copy of Megrun's La Faune des Cadavres. Despite its being published in Paris in 1894 I still find much to commend about the book. I'm aware that our pathologist, Sydney Smith, believes that some of Megrun's findings are now somewhat outdated, though unfortunately none of our contemporary entomologists seem to have published anything beyond the occasional monograph and what strikes me again about this book is the care taken and the accuracy that the author was striving for. It began with the finding of a child's body, a baby that's been hidden away and found some two years after death. The time of death was worked out purely on the basis of the creatures found to have been living on the little corpse. Megrun was able to establish the passing of two full years from his observations of the pupal remains left behind by the insects that have taken turns to feast there. I am relieved that my French is still just about up to the task of reading this in the original as I'm aware of no translations.

I'm often reminded of Megrun and his study; each time we are called out to a murder scene and find that some well-meaning individual has tidied and cleaned. Megrun's little corpse had been undisturbed for something close to two years. Ideal conditions, I suppose you might say, for the insect life to go through their cycles, breeding and feeding, maturing and breeding again but with no other disturbance either from human or larger animals. Even the rats seem to have left the body alone. Each time we view a scene and examine a body, we have to ask ourselves what has been moved, what might have been disturbed, what creatures have clawed and bitten at body parts and destroyed or impugned the evidence there. I suppose, unless there comes a time when we are permitted to experiment, to leave bodies lying in the ground or in shallow scraped graves, covered in vegetation, or left in the open until nature and decomposition take their course, then much of what we do is likely to be guesswork or reliant on those chance discoveries that, while they are informative are, by their very nature, unusual and out of the normal run of events.

One

He decided to bury them in the yard but left it a full day before he came back. The night they had died he'd let himself out of the house and walked slowly down the street, past little terraced houses and small corner shops. There was building work going on next to the house – the woman had said the shop was being rebuilt and refurbished and that their little cottage was going to be part of the extension. He had hoped to find space, perhaps beneath the floor of the shop, that the builders had left but the doors had been padlocked and he'd been unable to get inside. He had thought of leaving the bodies lying in the bedroom – even thought of calling the police and letting the young man who'd attacked him take the blame. But that would have led to many questions and he knew he was best just keeping out of the way.

And so it was on the following night that he took a spade and a nail bar, borrowed from a gardener's shed, went back to the little cottage and into the yard that separated the shop from the house, where he proceeded to examine the possible burial site. The yard was partly flagged and partly cobbled and there was a mass of bricks and mortar, building sand and debris from the shop next door alongside an old pram and part of a bicycle. In the end the graves were shallow, mere scrapes beneath the lifted flagstones and the displaced cobbles. He had been afraid of the noise he was making and moved as silently as he could. He placed each body on a sheet, dragged it down the stairs then tipped it into the scrape. He wasn't even sure why he was doing this, though it seemed like the decent thing. He'd been shocked by the sight of them lying there – the woman, the young man and the child. Although he was fairly certain that the bodies would soon be discovered – after all, his grave-digging skills were constrained by the rubble in the yard, the hardness of the ground and his attempts to keep the noise as slight as possible, and he knew, anyway, that the builders would soon smell something wrong – some pricking of conscience drove him to make the effort.

Twice he thought he would be discovered. A dog barked, its owner shouted, he heard the sniffing beneath the gate and then, to his relief, the skitter of four paws as it ran back to its master. The second time two drunks, singing at the top of their voices, promenaded down the street only a few feet away from him, beyond the wall. He heard windows open, shouts and threats and drunken responses and he froze, terrified that a fight might start and that he'd be trapped in the yard. But shouting was all it came to; the drunks marched on singing and the window slammed closed.

He covered the bodies with loose earth and then the flags and cobbles and then spread the mess already in the yard across the whole area. He stepped back to inspect his handiwork and

8

decided it would have to do, then he went back through the house, closed the front door behind him and walked away. He half expected a window to open and someone to shout at him but no one did. It was late, this was a street full of working men and women and they had gone to bed, switched out their lights and were sleeping, preparing for the next day's early start. He quickened his pace, eager to put distance between himself and the scene and longing, now, for his bed. It had been a very long and exhausting night.

Two

Mother Jo Cook had waited three weeks to die. She had hung on tenaciously to what was left of her life, fearful that the reaper might catch her before she could reach home.

Home, for Mother Jo, was not so much a place as it was the people gathered there, and when the wagon turned through the gateway at Roman Hole that night in late June, it was the welcome of family that told her it was now all right to die.

So she had herself placed by the fire in her old armchair with her shawl about her shoulders and her favourite rug, hand pegged from scraps, cast across her lap. And she drank the health of all who came to drink it with her.

She drank to all the bairns born in the past

year and all the young folk newly wed or waiting until the harvest to jump the fire. She drank to the young men, still fast on their feet and handy with their fists, and the old ones whose strength lived on in their dreams.

As the dawn broke and pearly skies welcomed the sun, she drank to her own health one last time and died with her old face turned towards the morning light.

That night, they burned her wagon. Painted roses peeled from about her door as the fire reached out and the Worcester plates were smashed upon the steps. Her family, extended to fifty souls or more, ate the spit roast pig that farmer Hanson had gifted and drank and fought and danced and the wagon fire both lit and shadowed them.

'Barbarians! We won't get a stroke of work from any of them tomorrow.'

'They'll work. They know which side their bread's buttered.'

Robert Hanson snorted. His father's gift of the pig had disgusted him enough, without his father's grudging approval being added to it.

His horse skittered sideways, disturbed by the smell of smoke rising from the valley and Robert thoughtlessly jerked on the reins. The horse was a raw-boned, black beast with a hard mouth and a will to match that of its rider, and it rankled with Robert that his father would not trust him with the finer animals in the stable. His father's horse snorted. By contrast, this was an Arab cross, with the small head and short back

10

of its desert mother and the stamina of its English father. A pretty thing by any reckoning, the bay was his father's pride and Robert was allowed nowhere near it.

'That's Samuels' boy,' Hanson senior said, pointing with the handle of his crop. Samuels was his stockman, a man trusted where Robert was not. 'If he works like his old man I'll have no reason to complain.'

'Works?' Robert scowled at his father. 'Gypos don't work. They scrounge. Do just enough to make it look right and then cheat you blind.'

He dodged back, the riding crop having changed direction and flicked his way.

'Samuels is a good man. Knows the beasts and works his time. You'd best remember that. You'll remember too that your great granddad was related to Mother Jo.'

Robert said no more. He glanced contemptuously back down into the valley to where the young man his father had indicated danced with Helen Lee and he frowned all the more. Gypsies! He didn't care what his father said about it – no way were their kind any kin of his.

She had seen him round and about the village, of course, but from the moment she saw him up close Helen knew that Ethan Samuels was no ordinary man. He had eyes as blue as summer and his dark hair, despite his youth, was already streaked with winter grey. Tall and strong, he held her firmly as they danced, his hand burning through the cotton of her dress and his body just a little too close to hers for it to be proper.

11

On the edge of the circle, half hidden in the smoky shadows, Frank watched them. Helen glimpsed him as she turned in Ethan's arms. She smiled provocatively at Frank and saw his expression harden, his jaw clenching tight.

Ethan followed her gaze.

'Has he spoken for you then?' he asked. He pulled her even closer. 'If I'd spoken for you I'd let you dance with no one else. You know that?'

She pulled her gaze back, looking up at him with bright, mischievous eyes. 'He never thought he'd have to speak,' she said. 'Just assumed, did our Frank.'

'Well, he assumed wrong then, didn't he?'

'Did he?' Her smile broadened. 'What's it to you anyway, Ethan Samuels?'

'Don't be *chy* with me, girl. I looked at you, you looked at me. Nothing more to be said, is there?'

Helen laughed. 'Chy?' she said. 'I'm not being *coy* with you, lad. I'm dancing with you, ain't I?'

'That you are, Helen Lee.' He glanced sideways at Frank Church. Frank's hands were clenched now as well as his jaw. 'Much of a fighter, is he?' Ethan asked.

'You'd bare your fists for me, would you?'

'I'd bare more than that.'

She pulled away but only a little, just enough to let him know he'd crossed the line. 'You'll get me talked about,' she said.

'I'll guess you're talked about already,' Ethan said. 'But if he wants to fight, I'll fight him. Like I said, he should have spoken for you and since he's not . . .'

12

Helen allowed him to draw her close once more, catching a disapproving look from her mother as they turned again. 'No, he's not,' she said. 'And he's not much of a fighter anyway.'

Ethan smiled at her and Helen felt her heart melt.

Robert Hanson had turned for home long before his father rode down the hill to join the wake. Elijah had come to say goodbye to his kinswoman. Old habits and old traditions were still too much a part of his being for him to let this moment pass without wishing her a good journey into the afterlife. He handed the horse's reins to his stockman and strode into the circle where the dancers had now ceased to whirl and the fiddlers fallen silent. Someone handed him a glass and he drank deeply to the memory of a woman who had seemed old when Elijah himself had been just a boy.

Dawn was breaking, showing itself in a lightening of the sky and a reddening of the clouds that echoed the smouldering fire.

Mother Jo's sons and grandsons stood beside it, the pyre of Mother Jo's possessions and memories burning down now into ashes and still-glowing wood. Elijah poked with his booted foot at a sliver of painted door, the roses charred and blackened but still just visible in the orange light.

'She was a good woman,' he said quietly.

Harry, her son, nodded. 'But it's best she's gone,' he said, his voice equally soft. 'Times are changing. She couldn't change with them, not no more.'

He nodded respectfully to the boss man and then strode to the centre of the circle, gathering his people about him and waiting until silence fell before he spoke.

'My mam didn't want no one to mourn for her,' he said. 'She had a good life and a long one and she didn't want no tears shed unless they were in friendship. So I'll not wait another year to say this. I'll let her be gone now.'

A murmur of approval whispered through the assembly and Harry took a deep breath in to stop his own near-falling tears, then slowly let it out.

'*Devlesa araklam tume,*' he said. 'It is with God that I found you. *Akana mukav tut le Devesla.* I now leave you to God. I open your way in the new life, Mother, and release you from our sorrow.'

Her grandson came to stand beside his father.

'The sun shine on your soul,' they told her spirit, fancying they saw it rise with the dawn mist. 'And the Earth keep and bless your bones.'

Three

Ethan had the grandmother of all hangovers. He was trying desperately not to let it show, though the careful way he kept his head still even while he walked and the tender-footed steps he took along the rutted farm path might have given a clue to anyone that was watching.

By contrast, his dad strode out as energetically

as usual, though Ethan knew that for every glass he'd sunk last night his dad had matched him with another two.

Neither of them had slept, going straight from the wake to work as dawn brightened the sky. But then the same would be true of most of the workers that morning and Ethan wondered, painfully, how many of them would be feeling as rough as he did. Still, he compensated himself, they'd given the old lady a good send off and everyone had eaten well, and that was something that could not often be said these days – though the pork now sat a little too heavy on his queasy stomach.

It was June 23 of 1928 and depression was biting hard. News of the so-called General Strike of two years before had briefly impinged on the village; its failure had merely reinforced the sense that those with money would always hold the power too. No one in this village would ever have dreamed of withholding their labour. What would be the point? Destitution could bite swiftly and deeply enough without anyone deliberately drawing it down.

The track brought them to the yard at the back of the Hanson place. A gravelled driveway led up to the front door but Ethan had never approached the big house that way. It never occurred to him that he should. The rear yard was enclosed on three sides, the back of the house making up one full wall with stables and stores and tack rooms filling out another two. A low wooden fence with a double gate finished the square but it was rare for the big gates to be closed; too much traffic in the shape of people and carts and horses and machines went in and out that way. The big, cobbled yard with the farmhouse kitchen jutting out into it was the heart of Hanson's farm.

Ethan's boots clacked loudly on the cobbles. The noise did nothing to help his sore and aching head, the sound cracking upward from his feet and shattering through his entire body. His boots were studded with hobnails, the same as all the workers. Boots were an expensive commodity, bought too large to allow for growth, and the leather softened with grease until they moulded to the feet, the soles reinforced with metal cleats and broad tacks. As a child, Ethan had delighted in the way his hobnailed feet could be made to strike sparks on the hard stones and in winter, with a little work, the studs could be polished flat and shined up, perfect for sliding on the frozen pond. But he'd not been a child for long. The adult world impinged long before his adult height was reached or his voice deepened or he'd felt the need to shave.

Hanson senior's horse was being groomed. She was tethered to an iron ring driven deep into the stable wall and Elijah's oldest son was taking care of her himself. Dar Samuels led his son over.

'This is Ethan,' he said.

The young man, about Ethan's own age, looked up with a friendly smile and extended a hand. 'Ted Hanson,' he said. 'But I remember you — we were in class together.'

Ethan nodded. 'You got me blamed for pulling Emma Casey's pigtails.'

Ted laughed. 'God, but you've got a long memory. She got married last spring. Did you know that?'

'Aye, our mam was telling me.' He reached out and laid a gentle hand on the horse's neck. 'It's a fine beast,' he said. 'We were both soft on Emma Casey from what I remember. You weren't at the wake last night,' he added.

'No, Ted was stuck in Lincoln,' Dar Samuels said. 'His dad trusts him with a lot of the business these days.'

Ted Hanson nodded and began to move the burnisher over the horse's flank once more. 'I was sorry to have missed it,' he said. 'Dar, you may as well make a start with Miss Elizabeth's pony. She's coming lame again – still got that swelling. Dad says give it one more try and if you can't fix it we'll just have to call in the vet, but you know how much he doesn't trust him.'

'I'll do that,' Dar said. He gestured to Ethan to follow him.

'He's all right, that one,' he told Ethan as they made off towards the far stall where the little grey belonging to Elijah's daughter was housed. 'He's grown up like his dad. Cares about his animals and his people. Not like that other one. You watch yourself with that Robert – he's a bad 'un.' He paused; glanced sideways at his son. 'You'd do well to mind yourself with that lass too. She's a fly one is Helen Lee.'

'I'm not a kid, you know. I can handle her.'

17

'Maybe you can but there's been an under-standing between her family and Frank Church's from when they were both little mites. It doesn't do to come between families.'

'She doesn't seem so keen.'

'She was keen enough before last night.' He sighed. Ethan had that fixed look on his face that his father knew so well. I'm not hearing you, it said. I'll not listen to something I don't want to hear.

'Look, boy, I'll grant she's pretty enough but you know what they say. Look with your ears when you choose a bride, not just with your eyes.'

'You're saying she's got a reputation? Dad, there's not a girl in the village the women don't talk about. Not a girl married but the old folk count the months until her first child is born.'

His father sighed again. 'Well, you'll make your own mind up, I've no doubt. Look, boy, I've nothing against the girl but it doesn't do to come upsetting the apple cart when things have been expected. The Churches and the Lees want this marriage. They've been friends for years. They're second cousins. It's expected.'

'Maybe Helen has other ideas. Molly didn't marry where you wanted.'

'And your sister's lived to rue it too. Miserable, she is.'

'And I'm sorry for that, but that doesn't mean . . . Anyway, who's talking about marriage? I met the girl just last night.'

His father gave him another sideways look before unlatching the door to the pony's stable. 'Just be careful, lad,' he said. 'You've come home

18

now. This isn't some port you'll stop over long enough to get laid and load your cargo. It doesn't go to upset folk you have to live among.'

Ethan said nothing. If he was honest with himself he knew that his dad was right but he wasn't in the mood just now for being honest. His father's comments brought a flush of guilt and a little shame. That was exactly what he'd done as soon as he'd reached home. Before returning to the village he'd gone in search of an old friend that he knew he might rely upon for . . . well . . .

Mary Fields.

It had cost him a little of his hard-earned pay but he'd thought it well worth it at the time. Now . . . suddenly . . . he wasn't so sure.

They had argued.

But it didn't matter now. He wouldn't be seeing her again, that was for certain.

He leaned back against the stone wall of the pony's stall, watching his dad running expert hands over the little beast then, just for a moment, he closed his eyes, hoping that the pounding in his head might cease. It didn't but he kept them closed a little longer anyway, enjoying the image that came unbidden into his mind, pictured behind his tightly closed lids. It was the face of Helen Lee.

Four

It was four days after the burial that the bodies were discovered. The landlord had told the builders that the woman and child were leaving by the end of the week and that they could move into the yard and start work there. Knock down everything except the privy, they'd been told, flatten the outbuildings and start taking up flags in the yard.

The builders had knocked on her door several times, wanting to let her know what they were going to do but there had been no reply. They duly brought down the wall at the back of the shop and started to clear the rubble away, hauling it into a flatbed lorry outside in the street. The foreman had spoken to the neighbours but no one had seen either woman or child for a couple of days.

'Like as not she's gone to stay with relatives or something,' they were told. And the builders, not knowing any different, had shared this assumption so they moved into the yard as the landlord had instructed them to do. The foreman peered in through the kitchen window and was surprised to see the remains of a loaf and a pat of butter on the kitchen table. He could tell from the state of the house that the woman and child were down on their uppers so he was shocked to see food left for the mice to get. A little uneasy now, he knocked on the back door. The sound echoed through the house but there was no response. Something told him that all was not right but his need to get paid at the end of the week overcame these misgivings and told him that he should just get on with the job and mind his own business. 'You can start on the outhouse,' he told two of his men, 'and Benny, you start to get that rubbish in the yard taken out to the lorry. Use the wheelbarrer, Truby, you give him 'and.'

He went back into the shop to check on the plastering. June it might be, but it had been dank and cold so far and the new plaster was taking the Devil's own time to dry out. He figured they were about three days behind where he wanted to be – not disastrous but enough to be an irritation.

It was about half an hour later when he heard the shout and he went outside to find Truby and Benny staring at a hole in the ground.

'What the bloody 'ell you two lookin at?'

'We just lifted that flag and under the stone . . . I think it's 'er. Mrs Fields.'

'What the 'ell you on about?' The foreman came round to peer at the hole. They all gathered and looked down. A woman's face, her face caked in mud, her nose broken where the flagstone had been dropped down but her eyes open and seeming to be staring back.

Five

'You coming for a drink, George?'

George Fields shook his head. 'Thanks, but I'll be heading off – make it back home tonight if I can. See the wife and bairn.'

His companion laughed. 'Aye, well get off then – safe trip. See you in another week or so.'

George walked swiftly, away from the docks

and through the streets of terraced houses and corner shops and pawn shops and pubs. There was a prevalent joke that a man would return from the boats with money in his pockets on a Friday, buy his missus a fur coat on a Saturday and that the coat would be in hock by the time he went back to sea again. George was of a mind that this was a rumour put around by richer folk who understood nothing of the streets and terraces occupied by what they might term the lower classes, but even he had to own there was some truth in the tale. Many of his shipmates would go home with their pockets lightened by a day in the pub before their wives saw any of the profits.

George paused beneath the street lamp and lit his cigarette. It was still not fully light but the streets were already busy. Working people off for their daily grind. Three little kids ran past him, one wearing hobnailed boots, two barefoot, their shirttails hanging out and muck on their faces even at this hour. Mary would never let their Ruby out without her face washed and her hair combed, George thought. And he was thankful that she'd never gone without shoes or had to do with hand-me-downs. It was a source of pride that their kid had never gone hungry and that Mary never had either even if that did mean George being away from home for weeks at a time. He plucked his watch out of his waistcoat pocket. It was old, battered brass with a worn face but it still told the time. It had been his father's. One day, he had told Mary, he would buy himself a wristwatch. There'd be the money to spare and he would get himself one with a good leather strap. He began to walk towards the centre of Grimsby, intending to grab a bite to eat at Freeman Street market – the traders would have set up but there would still be cheap breakfasts on the go. He could have got food on the dockside and beer too had he gone with his friend, the licensing laws counting for little there, but George was strict about drinking before the evening. His dad had always said it was a slippery slope and George knew how easy it was to slide.

He walked quickly, his feet and legs finding their rhythm on the hard street, his body adjusting to the solid ground after the shifting of the ship's deck. Ten days he'd have now – ten days of Mary and Ruby and home. He had money in his pocket, would soon have a full belly and by this evening . . . By this evening he'd have a woman in a warm bed and all would be right with the world.

Six

Since 1907 it had been the right of any police force in the country to summon the murder detective from Scotland Yard. There were some seven hundred detectives in the metropolitan district but a mere handful spread across the rest of the land, and so far the men of the murder squad had taken their skills to just about every corner of it, but Henry could not remember anybody going to Louth. He had not expected to be called upon for immediate departure; the board in the central office that listed detectives on call had him down as third on 22 June 1928, and that meant he should have had a full day before being expected to get himself to the station with his sergeant and equipment and head north. But as so often worked out, the first on the list, Chief Inspector Protheroe, was on a call and the second, Chief Inspector Savage, was still giving evidence in court, which meant that Chief Inspector Henry Johnstone was next in line for the job.

He had a message sent to his sergeant to meet him at the station in an hour and Henry went home to collect the bag he left ready packed. Henry had no one to say goodbye to and he had bought tickets and was standing on the platform well ahead of time. Tall and slim and quiet, Henry took up a position in the centre of the space where he knew his sergeant would be able to see him. The stream of porters and travellers simply broke around him, as though he were some large stone in a fast-flowing river. Henry was used to people giving him a wide berth; they did so unconsciously but regularly.

Sergeant Mickey Hitchens strode across the concourse towards him, a bag gripped in each hand. One large leather holdall contained Mickey's personal effects, the other, though insignificant looking, was the famous murder bag that all detectives now carried with them when on call. It contained basic Scotland Yard-issue materials for the collection and analysis of a crime scene and also a few Mickey Hitchens extras.

24

'Lincolnshire, then,' Mickey Hitchens said.

'Lincoln tonight, on to Boston and then Louth with the milk train first thing in the morning. It's too late to get a through train tonight. I thought we'd walk up from the station into the old town. From what I remember the White Hart is a good place to stay.'

Mickey dumped his bags on the floor. The crowds of travellers and porters now broke around both of them – two stones in the river. 'What do we know?'

'Three bodies found by builders excavating the yard. Not been in the ground too long from the sound of it. I've given instructions to cover the scene with tarpaulins and leave it in situ until morning. That didn't go down too well but hopefully they'll listen to me.'

Sergeant Hitchens nodded. The announcement their train had arrived came over the tannoy so Mickey hoisted the bags again. 'Don't know that part of the world,' he said. 'I hear it's very flat.'

'Louth is in the Lincolnshire Wolds, not on the fens. It's far from flat.'

'Too far from the sea to go for a paddle then,' Mickey Hitchens commented.

Seven

Behind the cottages that made up Red Row there was an open field. In that field lay the remains of a manor house, sacked at the time of

Cromwell's war. Its foundations were still visible in the grass, together with one small piece of wall rising to about six feet in height. The locals called this ruin 'the castle' and believed it to be much, much older than the civil war. They told stories of the ghosts that resided there, gliding and drifting through the long, ruined hall and visible in the mist that rose most mornings from the damp of the spring-ridden grass.

The field was too wet for cultivation, the whole of the hillside being riddled with underground streams that filtered down through the sandy soil and filled the mill pond, the reservoir for the manse and the dew baths for the sheep. Sometimes the field was used for grazing, but as often it lay empty. Ethan had wondered since boyhood what had possessed the builders of the castle to put it there, where the ground was little more than marsh from October to May, but no one had been able to tell him.

He saw her the evening after the wake, standing in that back field, leaning against the bit of ruined wall and looking carefully the other way pretending, he fancied, to watch the flock of caddie crows rising from where Hanson's men had been ploughing the top field that afternoon.

'Eat up, Ethan,' his mam told him. 'You'll be clemmed after the day you've had and no sleep the last night.'

'I'm OK, Mam. In fact, I think I'll take a walk before I get to bed.'

'A walk? You haven't done enough walking today? You've been on your feet since Lord knows when.'

'I'm not that tired. Not that hungry neither.' He pushed his plate over to where his younger brother and little sister stood, waiting for their turn at the table. He and his dad were the workers in the house, fed first while the rest of the family, his mother included, waited for whatever was left. Ned, his brother, dived on the plate, stuffing the scraps into his mouth even before Ethan stood up. Ethan frowned. When he had gone away from home, in fact, through most of his childhood, the family had abandoned the old pecking order and sat together at table, but he'd come back to find the old ways reinstated and not just in his father's house. It was a sign of poverty returning, though his mam managed to keep the pot filled somehow and even now she was ladling more on to Ethan's abandoned plate and handing the young ones bread to mop up the gravy.

Ethan ran his fingers through his hair in an attempt to tidy it. Too long, his dad said. He tucked in his shirt, trying to neaten himself up. Ethan frowned. 'Do you still have the button tin, Mam? I lost one somewhere. I meant to ask before.'

'Of course I do. Leave the shirt out and I'll find the closest match I can,' she promised him. 'And I'll tighten the others too. You don't want to go losing more.'

'And if you see any rabbits on your walk, bring us a couple back,' his dad said.

'I'll do that,' Ethan promised. He took the heavy walking stick his dad kept in the corner by the door. The field behind the house was one big warren if you moved quietly; it was easy enough to kill a rabbit with the stick. Rabbits and whatever the garden provided were the staples that went into the pot, together with the tares and field beans his mother kept dried in old glass jars stacked in the pantry. The farm workers supplemented their own feed by filching locust beans and linseed cake meant for the cattle, slipping the odd fragment into their pockets to give the kids. Dar believed that it was good for them and the locust beans were sweet.

Ethan glanced back from the doorway, watching his siblings fight over what was left of the rough bread. 'Mam, don't forget to feed yourself,' he said.

Ethan skirted the row of cottages and hauled himself over the wooden fence that separated the gardens from the field. Would she still be there? he wondered. The sky was a clear dark blue, the night threatening but not yet fully arrived. A few more weeks and they'd still be working this late of an evening, though Ethan loved the harvest for all that it was exhausting work, and this year it promised to be a good one. The men would get paid then, their rate depending on what the grain made when it went to market and what cattle Hanson decided to let go rather than feed through winter. Too good a harvest and the price would drop. Too poor a harvest and there would be too little left for domestic use. Too low a price and the wages agreed with the men back in February might not be met; there would be no bonus if the price was high. The owner of the land took care to get his profits first – even a good man like Elijah Hanson.

Ethan himself had made no arrangement with his boss. He'd returned and been taken on because of his dad and Elijah Hanson would be the one to profit from his labour this summer, if there were any profit to be had. Ethan would get his food and board at home and be given breakfast each morning at the farm. If Hanson was pleased with his work there'd be money agreed after the harvest was gone. As an unmarried man with no dependents, Ethan had expected nothing more. The old ways had largely died out elsewhere and many workers in the district – those who had work, and work was painfully scarce – started to have their pay calculated weekly or monthly, though as far as Ethan could tell they were no better off for it.

Ethan could have signed on, of course, but the dole would give him nothing. They might even have means tested his family so they'd have lost the little bit of stuff they had. Then they'd have given Ethan his daily ticket and sent him off to wherever. Twelve miles away, twenty, it didn't matter. If the dole found you work and you didn't go you got nothing, and if your excuse was that it was twenty miles of walking before you even started and another twenty back they'd just tell you to start out sooner. Ethan would rather go back shipboard than deal with any of that, so when Hanson's offer had been made he'd taken it gratefully.

Once in the field, Ethan paused for a moment

29

to work out the best way of approaching the place where Helen stood. Silently, he circled round, looping up into the field towards the ruins so that he'd come upon her, if she was still waiting, without her seeing.

He caught his breath. Helen Lee still stood beside the broken wall, her gaze still fastened on the now-vanished caddy crows and the fading light of the upper field.

'Waiting for someone?'

To his immense satisfaction, he saw her jump.

'Who would I be waiting for?' She smiled at him, recovering quickly from her shock.

'Oh, I don't know. Your dancing partner maybe?'

'There's no music to dance to.' She shifted uneasily and glanced around her. 'I was about to go, anyway.'

'Why? You scared of the castle ghosts?'

She wriggled her shoulders irritably. 'Why should I be scared of ghosts? The vicar says there's no such thing.'

'And he's a wise man, Mr Newell – we all know that.'

She laughed. 'I wouldn't know – I'm chapel meself. I don't go into the church.'

'Ah, and what does the minister say about the castle ghosts?'

'I don't think I've ever discussed it with him.'

Ethan had moved towards her, almost as close as he had when she had danced with him the night before. She put out a hand to stop him, her palm flat against his chest. Ethan felt as though his heart might stop.

'So,' he said, 'you ain't afraid of no ghosts. Ain't afraid to be here alone.'

'I'm not alone now, am I?' The palm against his chest trembled slightly.

Ethan gently covered her hand with his own then, as gently, he moved the hand aside, stepping inside her boundary.

'Ethan. I told you, no closer.'

'I didn't hear you say nothing?'

'I didn't say, I . . .' She stepped away from him, her back now against the old bricks of the castle wall. Her eyes were bright in a face made pale by the twilight, eyes that half laughed but displayed just a little fear. 'You going to give me my hand back?' she asked him and now her voice trembled too.

'I might.' He had followed her backward step, moving once again within the boundary she had set. He could feel the heat coming off her body, see the rise and fall of her breasts, more rapid now with her growing excitement and nervousness. He released his grip on her hand but only lightly, just enough to allow him to slide his own palm over hers and then on to her wrist and the slender swelling of her forearm. She was wearing an old blue cardigan over her dress. Carefully, he slid two fingers beneath the welt of the cuff, circled her arm with his hand and slid the fabric back, relishing the soft skin along its inner side. Then he slid his other arm around her waist, the back of his hand grazing against the wall before he eased her forward, away from the coarse bricks and closer to him.

Closer now than when they danced. He held

her tightly, though after the first moments she didn't struggle. Instead, she raised her face expectantly towards his, not smiling now but her full lips slightly parted, the tip of her tongue moistening them nervously.

Ethan bent his head and kissed Helen Lee.

Eight

It was after eight o'clock when George Fields arrived in Louth. He'd walked the final five miles, impatient with the buses that came past but failed to be going his way. When he had left home three weeks before his wife and child had been living in rooms above an ironmonger's shop off Eastgate but when he got there that evening the lights in both shop and floor above were off and there was no sign of activity. He went round the back to let himself in the rear door only to find that his key didn't fit; someone had changed the lock. Anxious now, he hammered on the door, all sorts of thoughts and ideas rolling around in his head. Perhaps there had been a break-in, perhaps she'd lost her keys and the lock had to be changed, but she should have been home by now. Mary was always keen to have Ruby in bed by about eight; she said the child needed to sleep well if she was going to study hard and Mary was very keen that Ruby should study hard and make something of herself. Do better than they had done. Mary and George Fields were ambitious for their only child.

His hammering on the door had attracted attention. A neighbouring window opened and a woman shouted down.

'George, George, that you? Yer woman's gone, George, moved out just after you went off. Landlord said he didn't want . . . Well, you know. We all warned her George, told her . . .'

George's shoulders sagged. 'For God's sake, Mary,' he muttered quietly, despairingly. 'Where did they go? Did she say where they were going?'

'Sorry, George, but she never told me.'

The window closed, the light went out and George was left standing in the darkness. The euphoria that had carried him through the long day of travelling and walking now dissipated. He knew what the neighbour was saying, why Mary and Ruby had been turned out of yet another home. Landlords didn't like that kind of thing – women carrying on when their men were away – and Mary wasn't always subtle about it. But she'd promised him, last time he was home, that this would be the end of it. And he'd believed her, hadn't he? He'd certainly wanted to but maybe that was just stupidity on his part. They all told him, friends he discarded because they told him, family that had been trying to look out for him, they said, by telling him she was no better than she ought to be, but he'd ignored them all because, God help him, he loved her. Loved her, loved Ruby, with an intensity he'd never felt for anyone else, even knowing what she was and that she would never change

33

whatever she told him, whatever he chose to believe.

George turned away back into the street. In the morning he'd start knocking on doors – someone would know where she was – but in the meantime he was going to have that drink. He wished now he'd gone off with his shipmates, got himself blind drunk and come rolling home the following day like most of them would have done. She would have deserved that, carrying on while he was away again. Slow anger burned inside of him, setting a fire in his hungry belly and reminding him that it was hours since he'd eaten because he'd not wanted to spend any more of his hard-earned money – he'd wanted to wait until he reached home and a good meal and a good woman.

More fool him, George thought. More bloody fool him.

Nine

It was only a short walk along Eastgate from the train station to the police station and Henry and Mickey had arrived with the early train. There were only three people on duty in the police station when Mickey and Henry arrived in Louth – the desk sergeant and a couple of constables. The man who had sent for them would not, it seemed, be available until much later in the morning. Henry Johnstone remained behind to try and get their informant on the telephone and sent Sergeant Hitchens on ahead. He followed about fifteen minutes later.

They had left their personal luggage in the care of the desk sergeant with instructions that it should be sent on to the King's Head Hotel and Henry now followed his directions to the crime scene some ten minutes' walk away, back down Eastgate and past the station and Holy Trinity Church, then towards the canal and the oddly named Ticklepenny walk. It was still early, the town just waking and stretching. The scent of fresh bread drifted across from somewhere, reminding him that they had not eaten that morning but instead left the hotel in Lincoln and come to the small market town as early as possible. He *should* be feeling hungry, Henry thought.

The street they had been directed to was on the outskirts of town, a small terraced row on one side of the street and a shorter row including two shops on the other, one shop on the corner and one next to the crime-scene house. This establishment was empty but they'd been told that refurbishment was taking place in readiness for an extension. The existing shop was separated from a narrow house by a partly broken wall and double gates that led into the yard. He spotted Sergeant Hitchens standing with a group of people Henry assumed must be neighbours. Mickey Hitchens spotted him and came across the road.

'That's the house the dead woman and child lived in.' Sergeant Hitchens nodded at it. 'And that's the yard they were found in.' A police constable stood on guard outside the yard gates and another, looking very young and uncomfortable, next to the house.

Detective Inspector Johnstone introduced himself and one of the gates was opened just enough to let them through.

There were three bodies. A man, a woman and a child, all laid out in separate but shallow graves. When he had sent word that they were to be left alone and undisturbed until he arrived, it had taken some arguments and some harsh words on his part to get the agreement of the local police. It was disrespectful, he was told. It was unkind.

It was necessary, Johnstone had insisted. He needed to see the bodies just as they'd been buried. View the scene as it had been found.

Eventually he had got his way and it was agreed that the bodies would be left in situ.

Overnight, the uncovered graves had been draped with tarpaulins and these weighted down with bricks from the half-demolished wall that surrounded the grave site. After midnight it had rained heavily and the backyard, now almost devoid of flagstones and cobbles, was a rough landscape of churned earth and slimy clay.

The workmen who had originally uncovered the bodies and who had now pulled the sodden tarpaulin aside stood warily next to the broken wall.

'It ain't right,' one of them muttered, 'leaving them in the ground like this.'

Johnstone glanced his way then moved carefully across the mud and crouched down beside

36

the smallest of the bodies. Beyond the broken wall a small crowd had gathered. The two police constables kept them at bay but the bus stop directly across the road provided a legitimate rallying point for the curious. Johnstone wondered how many would actually get on the bus when it arrived. Walking up from the station he had noticed that the buses here in Louth were still emblazoned with the cipher *Silver Queen* even though the company had become part of the Lincolnshire Road Car company the year before and they were now liveried in green. He liked the idea of a fleet of silver queens. Road Cars sounded bland in comparison, though from what he had seen of the area the practicality of the new name would suit better. Louth, he had decided, was peopled with the solid and honest, but it was not an imaginative place.

Sergeant Hitchens crouched beside him. 'The neighbours say the kiddie that lived here was seven,' he said. 'Looks about right. Her name was Ruby Fields.'

Johnstone nodded. Fair hair lay in a muddied and sodden mass. Her features had all but gone, the shallow grave being no protection from the rats, and Henry could tell that the tarpaulin covering the bodies had been even less protection overnight, remembering the notes he had made in his commonplace book. That real crime scenes were rarely as predictable as Megrun's example. The flesh left on the limbs was mottled and grey beneath the coating of clay. She had, he noted, been dressed for bed. Her arms lay at her sides.

Hitchens picked up a bit of stick and scraped some of the earth away from the child's neck. Her head was turned to the right. 'I'm guessing at a broken neck,' he said. 'Angle the head's at is all wrong. And there's what looks like a depressed fracture just behind the temple.'

'The neck injury could have happened after she was put in the ground,' Johnstone cautioned. 'She looks to have been crammed into the grave. Whoever dug this was in a hurry.' He stood up and turned his attention to the other two buried beside the child. The smell of decay was already present but it was not yet particularly rank or foul. He had smelt worse and was reminded always of his army days. He was grateful that the June day was unusually chilly and damp. The woman was fully clothed in a blue dress and a lightweight cardigan. Her dress had a lace collar and a brooch had been pinned, front and centre, where the lobes of the collar met. Her hair was still carefully pinned at the temples and Henry could imagine the tight waves, held in place, neat and delicate. She had made an effort with her appearance, had wanted to look nice . . . for whoever had killed her. 'No stockings,' Johnstone noted, 'and her feet are bare.'

'Neighbours reckon it's Mary Fields,' Hitchens said. 'They got a look at her yesterday when the workmen found them. She's still recognizable if you knew her, I suppose.'

'No wedding ring.'

'Might be in the grave. Might have fallen off.'

'And the man. What do the helpful neighbours say about him?'

'That he's not her husband,' Hitchens said flatly. 'They don't know who he might be but she was a lady with, shall we say, a bit of a reputation and a husband who was working on the boats for weeks at a time. So, plenty of opportunity for playing away. That's what the gossip says.'

Johnstone nodded. The man was lying face down and his hands had been pulled back as though they'd been tied behind him, though there was no ligature present that Johnstone could see. 'And, not seeing his face,' he enquired, 'how do the neighbours come to the conclusion that he isn't the husband?'

'Because the husband is six feet three and built like a brick shithouse, apparently. I doubt this fella's more than five feet seven and he's built more like a whippet than a bull.'

Johnstone got to his feet. Whip thin himself, all sinew and lean muscle, he knew he looked built more for speed than fight. Unlike Hitchens, who was shorter and solid and looked like the boxer that he was. The truth was that Johnstone was more than capable of standing his ground when the need arose and Hitchens equally fleet of foot, though he lacked the stamina of his boss.

'Have them lifted,' he told the workmen. 'Make sure that anything in the graves is kept with the bodies. Wrap the whole lot in sheets and then in tarpaulins and take them to the hospital. They're expecting you.'

'Hospital,' one of the men muttered uncertainly. 'Crowtree?'

'High Holme, I was told,' Johnstone corrected him.

'You means the workhouse infirmary. Not the hospital.'

'Workhouse?' Hitchens asked. 'Thought they went out with Dickens.'

'Not here, apparently,' Johnstone said coldly. He turned and headed out through what was left of the broken wall and turned his attention to the house. This cottage at the end of a terrace had been due to be knocked down. The shop next door had stood empty for the past year but the grocer down the street had bought it a month before and the land next door too. The plan had been to knock down the little house and extend his premises.

One of the workmen had followed Johnstone out.

'The sheets,' he said. 'Where should we get them from, sir?'

Johnstone stared at him. 'You know what sheets are? Where do you usually get them from?'

The man looked disturbed and Hitchens coughed then intervened. 'You go ahead, boss. I'll sort this and catch you up.'

Johnstone frowned but walked slowly on. Hitchens caught him a few minutes later. 'You need to think,' he said gently. 'I doubt any of those men own more than a couple of sheets between them. My dear old mother—'

'Oh, spare me—'

'No, you have to learn. My dear old mother was proud of her linens. When she passed over there were three pairs of unpatched sheets in

40

her linen cupboard and she'd itemized them in her will.'

'Very Shakespearean,' Johnstone said.

'Shakespearean?'

'He left his wife his second-best bed.'

'A rich man then. Having two beds.'

Johnstone looked closely at his companion and realized that Hitchens was laughing. 'Oh,' he said. 'A joke.'

'That was but the sheets were not. I've sent a boy with a note to the Beaumont Hotel. They'll have old linen, I expect.'

'Good. So we talk to the houseowner and the old landlord. The neighbours and anyone that might have anything to say in the local pub. I'll leave that to you,' he added.

'I could take offence at that.'

'But you won't.' Johnstone managed something that might have been a smile.

'I've been told this town has about fifty pubs in it,' Mickey added thoughtfully. 'Doesn't seem like a big enough place, does it?'

'We've not seen all of it yet. I suppose you could make it your mission to count them up. And we'd better go and placate Inspector Carrington first. See what he's got to say and assure him that we want to help, not take over,' Johnstone told him.

'Even if that's not the truth.'

'Even if that's not strictly the truth. Then we arrange for the autopsies to be done. Carrington can advise us on that. He knows the local doctors and it doesn't sound as though the so-called hospital will be anything more than basic, not if it was the workhouse infirmary.'

41

'We might be lucky.'

'We might, but I'd as soon assume not. Then we have some late breakfast. Carrington can advise us about that too. I suppose we should invite him to join us?'

'Might go some way on the placating front if we do. I'd rather have him on side. You know what it's like when the locals really take against us. Can't get bugger all done.'

'True,' Henry Johnstone agreed.

They turned and walked back towards the police station on Eastgate, towards the railway station. It was a pretty place, Johnstone thought, now he had a chance to look at it. Georgian and medieval buildings sat side by side and he glimpsed tiny, still-cobbled streets branching off the main thoroughfare lined with narrow houses and small shops.

'And did the neighbours suggest who our male might be?'

'No, they didn't speculate about that. When I asked them why the woman and kiddie had not been missed they said she occasionally stayed with relatives down in Newark.'

'Was it usual for her to go away suddenly?'

'That I don't know. One woman suggested on the quiet that she'd been having trouble with the rent. When she didn't see them for a day or two she supposed they might have done a flit. She said the landlord was on the verge of evicting them – the deal with the grocer had been signed and he wanted rid of his tenants anyway. Another said she'd taken on the house with the understanding it would be a short let. That she was getting ready to move on.

'So far the husband is top of my list. A woman takes lovers – paying or not – and my money's always going to be on the husband.'

Ten

Acting Chief Inspector Carrington had still not been available when Henry and his sergeant returned to the police station. They were told that he was still not in, that he lived some distance away and that he was just covering until the usual incumbent returned.

'And the usual incumbent is where?' Henry Johnstone asked.

'Kent, sir. His dad passed on. He's gone to see to the funeral and suchlike.'

'I see.' Inspector Johnstone frowned at the unfortunate man and Sergeant Hitchens, fearing a storm, decided to intervene.

'I'll take myself back to the scene after we've had a bite to eat,' he said. 'Most likely he'll have got here by then. Constable, is there somewhere we can get breakfast?'

The constable, relieved to be asked something he could give an answer to, directed them to a cafe down on the market square. 'It ain't smart,' he warned. 'Mostly services the local farmers when they come in for market day but it's good, solid fare. Sticks to·your ribs.' He eyed Chief Inspector Johnstone, clearly of the opinion that he definitely needed something sticking to his ribs.

Mickey Hitchens nodded his thanks and led his inspector away.

'He has a murder enquiry on his hands and he's still not in?'

'This isn't London, guv. It isn't the Met. He's not ruled over by our Mr Wensley.'

'But he's still a serving detective.'

'And the case isn't in his hands, is it? He's shifted responsibility over to me and thee. It all goes pear shaped he can tell the world he called in the experts. It goes well he can tell everyone how right he was to call in the experts. Fella can't lose, can he?'

Henry grimaced. 'And it's only a working woman and her child,' he said. 'Not anyone of importance, it would seem.'

'And whoever the lad might be. But yes. Henry,' he said softly, 'that's what we signed up for. It don't make no difference for us if it's a prostitute or a princess, it's still a dead body that needs speaking for, but it isn't like that for most – you know that. There's not many levellers, not even war and death.'

Henry Johnstone nodded but it was clear he wasn't happy. This Chief Inspector Carrington had well and truly blotted his copybook, Mickey thought. His boss wouldn't give him an easy time of it when they did eventually get to meet.

* * *

An hour later and Mickey was back at the crime scene, Inspector Johnstone having returned to the police station.

The constable had been right, Mickey thought. The food had been good. Fresh eggs and thick slices of fatty bacon and Lincolnshire sausages, heavily flavoured with spice and sage. It did all stick to his ribs and, if he was honest, sat a little heavy on the stomach – though that could have been down to the extra slice or two of bread that Mickey had used to mop his plate and then his boss's plate. Inspector Johnstone hadn't grown up in a house where you ate bread with every meal, including Sunday dinner, but Mickey had never lost the habit. It makes the meat go further, his mum had always said. Mickey smiled to himself, hearing in his head Henry's usual retort about being sick of hearing about Mickey's 'sainted' mother – a woman Henry had actually been very fond of, despite what he might growl in public.

Two young constables stood outside the crime-scene house. One was chatting to the grocer whose building plans had been so dramatically inter-rupted and from what Mickey could observe was in full 'placating the public mode', so Mickey gestured to the other one.

'Upstairs with me, lad,' Sergeant Hitchens instructed the young constable standing by the front door. 'You can give me a hand.'

The constable, who looked no more than about eighteen, exchanged a worried look with his colleague.

'I haven't got all day,' Mickey Hitchens told him. 'Let's be having you.'

Mickey had already done a brief survey of the house and decided that most of his attention should be focused on the bedroom. That was obviously where the killing had taken place. The rest of the house could be looked at later but it was important to get a sequence of events in his head.

He paused at the bedroom door and waited for the young constable to catch him up. 'Now, lad,' he said, 'the first thing you do is take a good long look.'

The constable looked puzzled. 'What are we looking for, sir?' he said.

'What do you see?' Mickey asked him. 'Go on, take a good look but don't go inside yet.'

Mickey bent down to take the camera out of his bag while the constable made a first survey of the room. 'Well?'

'Well, there's blood on the floor. A lot of it over by the bed. And there's blood on the wall on the opposite side of the room.'

'That's a start,' Mickey told him. 'What else do you notice?'

'The bed's untidy, like someone's been . . . Sleeping . . . Or something.'

'Probably more of the something,' Mickey told him. 'Right now we start to look properly. The first thing we do is take a few pictures of the room, just from where we're standing. So we can see the whole scene. Then when we're talking about what might have happened the person we're talking to can see it as well. You got that?'

'Yes, sir.' The young man was looking at the camera. 'Is that yours, sir?'

'No, my lad, this is a rather wonderful specimen of a Kodak vest pocket camera series three. And it is the property of Chief Inspector Henry Johnstone. I just get to use it when there isn't a photographer available.'

'There's Mr Clare down on Eastgate, next to the chapel. Our Elsie had her wedding photo done by him.' The constable was evidently trying to impress, Mickey thought.

'Well, I expect we'll be asking our Mr Clare for the use of his darkroom later on,' Mickey Hitchens told him.

The bedroom curtains were still closed and although a narrow shaft of light filtered in from where they didn't quite join and another from where they didn't quite reach the sill, the room was still dimly lit. Mickey decided he would have to use his small stock of flashbulbs to take the first images.

'We could have opened the curtains,' the constable suggested, blinking hard at his eyes try to readjust after the sudden blasts of light from the flashbulbs.

'And then we would have changed the scene before we photographed it. We don't want to go doing that. You look at the scene as it was and you record it as it was. First rule.'

Mickey Hitchens set the camera down and opened up his bag. 'This here,' he said, 'is what is commonly called the murder bag. We take one with us whenever we go on a murder investigation. It was put together by Bernard Spilsbury and Detective Superintendent Brown after Mr Spilsbury had to go to the Bexhill-on-Sea murder of a woman by the name of Emily Beilby Kaye. It has been a hot month, you see, and there he found Chief Inspector Savage and his men, scooping up lumps of putrefying flesh and dumping them into buckets without a pair of rubber gloves between them.' He glanced up at the younger man's face, noting the pallor and look of shock. Mickey grinned at him. 'Don't you get sick, lad, or you'll be clearing it up yourself. So Mr Spilsbury, he decided something should be done, and so they put this bag together for us to take with rubber gloves and envelopes and jars for storing samples and the fingerprint kit just in case we can't get Mr Cherrill up here.'

'Mr Cherrill?'

'Looks after all the fingerprint records does Mr Cherrill. Keeps tabs on the dabs.' Mickey laughed at his own joke and the constable, obviously trying to please, laughed too.

'So, what now, sir?'

'Now we look more closely. Anything missing, anything that shouldn't be here or might be out of place.'

'Like what?'

Mickey smiled at the younger man. 'Well, son, we won't know until we see it, will we?'

Constable Parkin followed Mickey's close inspection of the room. Mickey could sense the young man's eagerness to discover something that might help the investigation or, at the very least, impress the sergeant. Mickey started at the door and moved slowly towards the window. He drew the curtains back and took a small torch

48

from his pocket. 'Now, let's take a closer look at that bloodstain,' he said.

Both men crouched down on the rough wooden floor and Constable Parkin stared hard at the marks on the wall and floor. 'See,' Mickey said, 'where the poor little mite hit the wall, the blood streaks as she slid down on to the floor. She'd likely be unconscious or semi-conscious at that point and she was bleeding from maybe her mouth or face or even her ear – see the little pool, here?'

Constable Parkin nodded. 'So,' he hazarded, 'she fell sort of on her side with her face on the floor?'

'That would be consistent with the injuries we saw, though of course until the post-mortem is done it's hard to be sure of everything. There's a partial hand print there, look.'

'The killer?' Parkin was excited now.

'No, lad, look at the size of it. The kiddie came round, pushed herself up and her hand dragged in her own blood. You can see the marks of two fingers and that curve is likely to be the side of the hand. So, the likelihood is she pushed herself up, maybe even tried to get up, but by then the killer had finished with her mum and that young man and he came over and finished her off. What we think was the killing blow, on account of it being the deepest, was on the left-hand side of her head, so he struck from that side, maybe from close to where you are now, and she fell again. Look, there's another big patch of blood here and just there,' Mickey paused and pointed at the floor, 'are a few little threads caught in the splinters of the floorboard. Maybe where our killer knelt down to make sure he'd finished the job.'

Constable Parkin gazed at the tiny threads as though they were something magical. 'Do we collect them, sir?'

'Indeed we do. In the bag you'll find a little leather case containing tweezers and beside that there'll be a package of small manila envelopes.'

Parkin scrambled to his feet. 'Walk back the same way we came in. Don't trample around like a bull elephant – you risk standing on potential evidence, my lad.'

He stayed put until the constable had returned and then gently eased the threads free of the floorboard splinters and tucked them into the envelope.

'Now,' Mickey said when he had sealed it. 'You write down what we've found and where we found it and number the envelope as one. Hopefully it will have some friends to join it soon.'

They continued their slow perusal of the floor. Close beside the bed, caught up in a fold of the rug was a small button. Mickey plucked it out with the tweezers. 'From a shirt, by the look of it,' he said. 'It could have come from the husband's shirt, I suppose, but as he's been away at sea that seems less likely, don't you think?'

He dropped the button into another envelope, handed it to Constable Parkin for labelling then shone the torch beneath the bed. 'Just a bit of dust under there,' he said. 'Have another look at that rug, make certain there's nothing else caught up.'

He stood then and looked at the bed itself.

The sheets were stained with urine and the smell was sour and ammoniac. There was a tiny smear of blood on the pillow. The blankets had been kicked aside and Mickey could imagine Mary Fields fighting for her life, her feet scrabbling for purchase against the mattress, her hands scratching at her assailant. Was the blood hers or his? Mickey wondered. Taking a small pair of scissors from the leather case, he cut the bloodstain out of the pillowcase and dropped that into a third envelope.

'It looks as though there's something missing from the bedside table,' Mickey said.

Constable Parkin stood up. 'Oh,' he said. 'Marks in the dust.'

'Lucky for us Mary Fields was not the most house-proud of women. Something with a square base. A lamp, perhaps, or a candlestick.' He glanced quickly around the room.

'The murder weapon?' Constable Parkin asked.

'That is a definite possibility,' Mickey told him. 'We'll check the rest of the house but if we don't find anything that fits that space then the chances are our man took it away with him.'

'Why would he do that?'

'Fingerprints, most likely,' Mickey said. 'He maybe didn't trust himself to wipe it clean enough. He was scared enough that he had to get the murder weapon out of here. So the question is where did he dump it?'

'Canal, maybe. It's close by and there's empty buildings and waste ground.'

Mickey nodded. 'We'll make sure we look for

it. Meantime, you and I will see what else he might have left behind. Fingerprints, lad. We'll see if we can find ourselves some nice, clear dabs.'

Acting Chief Inspector Carrington had finally arrived, profuse in his apologies and calling out for tea to be brought to them both in his office. Inspector Johnstone followed him in and took a seat on the visitor's side of the desk.

He said little until the constable had come in with their tea, Carrington filling the conversational void with talk of his journey in that morning and the shock of having such a terrible event in their little community.

'So,' Detective Chief Inspector Henry Johnstone asked when the constable had left. 'What do we know about the dead woman and her child? And the young man in the third grave?'

Across the desk from Henry, Carrington sipped his tea. 'The woman's full name is Mary Elizabeth Fields. She's been married to George Fields for the last twelve years and they have one child from that marriage – or they had. Ruby Fields, aged seven years. According to neighbours there was a boy too but he died in infancy. George Fields was a canal man before the canal links closed in 1924. A lot of good men lost their jobs that year but after the floods . . .'

'In 1920, I believe,' Henry said.

'That's right, yes. After the floods there was so much silt in the canal basin, so much damage that the industry went into rapid decline. By 1924 they had to give it up. Fields, I understand, then went off to sea, took to the fishing boats sailing out of Immingham and Grimsby but from what my sergeants tell me, from what the neighbours have told them, the work has been slack and the pay has been bad.' He shrugged. 'It is a familiar story around these parts, whether it's in farming or fishing or any other industry you care to name.'

'You *are* remote, here,' Henry said. 'I was surprised at just how far this little town is from anywhere else.'

For a moment Carrington looked offended then he just nodded. 'I suppose for a Londoner it must seem that way,' he said. 'But before the floods we were among the largest of the inland ports in the country. Coasting vessels could travel from the sea ports, via the Louth navigation canal, right into the town.'

Henry let the man talk for a while then he set his cup down with a loud chink upon the saucer. 'I haven't always lived in London,' Henry Johnstone said.

Carrington paused, waiting for him to elaborate. Instead, Inspector Johnstone said, 'And the dead woman?'

'Of course. Of course.' He frowned at Henry, clearly irritated. 'So the woman, Mary Fields, has a record for soliciting. In fact, she has a record both before and after her marriage. It seems that while her husband was away she entertained herself by entertaining men, and from what the neighbours say he couldn't seem to break her of the habit.'

'And his response to this habit?'

53

'It seems that most of the time he closed his eyes to it, or at least that's what they say. Though how any man could do that I don't know.'

'Sometimes women do what they must,' Henry said quietly, 'and their men accept that because they must.' He could see the disgust on Carrington's face. Carrington picked up his cup and sipped more tea as though to wash the taste of that comment away.

'And is the husband known to be violent?' Henry Johnstone asked.

'He has no record of violence. In fact, he has no record at all. The neighbours claim not to know him because the woman and child moved to the house only a week or so ago and he was already away.'

'And yet they seem to know a great deal about the woman.'

'They saw men come and go from the house and drew their own conclusions. It seems one neighbour knows her from where they both lived before. Mrs Ida Cook.'

'And yet this Mrs Cook claims to know nothing about the husband? Despite having lived close to Mrs Fields before?'

Carrington frowned again. 'I don't think she claims to have been close to the woman, only that they lived in the same street. I'm sure your methods will extract more information than our enquiries have done.'

'I'm sure they will. And the child, what is said about her?'

Carrington scowled. 'Nothing is said about her – she was a child. The neighbours say she was always well turned out and clean and that she was fed and went to school. Her teachers say she worked hard – she wasn't exceptionally bright but she had friends as you would expect. What else is there to say about a seven-year-old girl?'

Henry nodded but there was no sense in that nod that he agreed with Carrington and he made no immediate reply.

'It's a truly terrible business,' Carrington said, trying again to fill the silence. 'A ghastly business.' He shifted uncomfortably as Henry Johnstone looked at him again as though suddenly remembering that he was there.

'We must track down her clients, see what they can tell us about this woman.'

Carrington looked uneasy. 'That might not be the best course,' he offered.

'And why would that be?'

'I would have thought that obvious. You risk causing distress to other families. Men might be thoughtless and stupid enough to stray but why should their wives and children suffer for it? I've no doubt respectable men . . .'

'Respectable men, one of whom may have killed Mrs Fields.'

'More likely it was someone she refused to deal with, some workman who lived locally who had too much to drink, maybe broke into the house with the intention of . . .'

'And ordinary labouring men are not respectable, of course,' Henry challenged. 'There was no sign of a break-in. No sign of violence in any other part of the house from what I could see. No, she let her killer in. She took him upstairs.'

'That's as may be, but to suggest in the first

place that any respectable man would have dealings with such a woman and then gone on to kill her, kill her child, kill . . . whoever that young man might have been . . .'

'Murderers come from all classes and cultures. I'm astonished I have to point this out to you.' Chief Inspector Johnstone paused. 'In fact, I'm astonished that you summoned us here at all. It's clear you want our investigation to be superficial, swift and draw conclusions that implicate no one locally. So why call us here?'

Carrington scowled at him. 'It's the right of any police force in the country to request additional help from Scotland Yard.'

'And so it is. It is also the expectation that when that help is requested the officers attending should be able to follow the evidence wherever it leads. And it's not as though you are lacking able investigators locally. You could have sent to Brigg and asked for Superintendent Dolby. He's a sound man and is a scant, what, dozen miles away? Or did you suspect that he might have too much local knowledge?'

'I don't like what you're implying.'

'Neither do I, and I hope I'm proved wrong.'

'And what exactly do you mean by that?'

'I mean that I hope you are correct and no . . . respectable . . . men are involved. But I *will* follow where the evidence leads me, and I *will* speak to anyone that I think might have known this woman or had dealings with her.'

He got up and plucked his hat from the table top. 'Thank you,' he said. 'I'll take up no more of your time. I'm sure you're a very busy man.'

56

Outside, Henry Johnstone shrugged into his dark, broadcloth coat and put on his hat. He might not have handled that as well as Sergeant Hitchens would have liked, Henry thought. Hitchens would have told him that he could have been a little more diplomatic and Henry would have told Hitchens that Carrington reminded him of Brigadier Staines, at which Mickey would have shrugged and grinned. Hitchens and Henry Johnstone had met a scant few months before the war had ended and Brigadier Staines was a man they had both come to hate.

He walked slowly down Broadgate, noticing the shops and listening to the snatches of conversation. A young woman in a blue cloche hat over a neat dark bob smiled at him as he passed and Henry tipped his hat politely. A group of men in heavy jackets and flat tweed caps gossiped outside a pub and Henry paused to listen.

'Mazzled, he were – could barely stand up right. I said to him . . . I said, "You'd best get yourself home before your woman comes out after you with rolling pin. Got a temper on 'er has our Alice."'

Henry walked on. Briefly he found himself following two young women, chatting, he presumed, about a friend. 'But it was such a ghastly colour and then she wanted a matching hat.'

Henry almost smiled at that; it sounded like something his sister might say.

The town looked prosperous and busy. The market square was packed with stalls. Henry decided to get the lie of the land, to walk the area and think.

It was a Wednesday and therefore the market was on. Henry walked between the stalls selling mostly local produce: fruit and vegetables, meat and cheese and a stall selling cheap cloth. Another sold crockery packed into baskets in layers of straw. He glanced at the names on the shopfronts: M.C. Cousins, J.A. Birkett – establishments that looked settled and ancient and belonging. He wandered out of the marketplace and back on to Eastgate, then on to Cannon Street, away from the crowds.

Henry paused outside the Louth Playhouse Cinema and lit a cigarette. His cigarette case was battered, made of old brass and engraved with the initials A and G. It was worn smooth from handling; the rounded edges felt satisfying and soothing in his hand. He tucked it back into his pocket. He noticed that Hitchcock's *Easy Virtue* was playing at the cinema a few weeks after it had finished its run in London. He'd gone to see it with his sister when she'd come up to town. Cynthia made sure she kept an eye on him. She was only two years older but had taken on the role of senior sibling with the same seriousness and intensity that she took on everything else.

'So you're still doing this ghastly job then,' she'd asked him as she had at just about every meeting in the last ten years. It was almost her equivalent of saying hello. She usually followed it up with something like 'I'd have thought you'd seen enough of that during the war', but on that occasion, he remembered, she had resisted. She'd just smiled, kissed him on the cheek, asked him how he had been and told him he looked tired. Then tried her other gambit: 'You know you only have to ask and Albert will find you something in the company – he always tells me to remind you. You'd be more than welcome.' And Henry, as always, wondered if his brother-in-law had actually extended this invitation and what he could possibly offer to a company that manufactured copper tubing anyway. Cynthia had, somewhat surprisingly, married into money and, having produced the heir, the spare and the one that might be useful to be married off somewhere, she had focused her energies on being a capable and welcoming hostess for her husband's many acquaintances and business associates.

She was proud of her little brother, though. He knew this and on those rare occasions that he attended one of the frequent social gatherings she hosted she introduced him as, 'My brother, the murder detective.'

Henry walked slowly back to the crime scene.

Sergeant Hitchens had left, he was told – gone in search of a photography studio in the hope of using their darkroom. He had taken Constable Parkin with him. Henry went on into the house and stood in the narrow hallway.

For a few moments he listened to the silence, street sounds muffled, cars and footsteps and a bus pulling up at the stop across the road. No neighbours with adjoining walls, the little house stood alone connected to the shop next door by the yard an external wall and the gate. He guessed that the premises had been originally built as a single unit, perhaps a flat over the shop for an employee and a home for the owner – this house – next door with the yard, big enough for deliveries or for storage in between.

What must once have been a symbol of prosperity was now damp and dank and run down. He laid a hand against the wall, felt the cold and wet seeping through and knew that if he clawed at the faded wallpaper it would come away in his hand.

Henry turned away and went into the front parlour, noting that this would have been a larger house than most in the terraced row, having a hallway from which the stairs ascended rather than a front door opening straight into the front living room and enclosed stairs rising, usually from behind a door in the middle room. Once this would have been a cherished and proud home; now it was sparsely and cheaply furnished with a single upholstered chair and a couple of what looked like Victorian hall chairs, flat seated and straight backed together with a small, drop leaf table.

It looks like a waiting room, Henry thought.

There were no personal possessions in this room, no pictures of books or photographs. Nothing to give a clue as to the residents. Perhaps she wanted it that way, if this was where she first brought her clients? Perhaps it was simply that they owned so little there was nothing to spare for this formal, underused little room.

He moved out into the hall again and through into the middle room. This, he thought, was where mother and child would have spent their time, here and in the kitchen beyond. The fire had been made up, ready to light, and two chairs and a little stool set beside it. A handful of books sat on the windowsill and there were cheap ornaments and a vase on the mantle. The vase had been stuffed with wild flowers. He recognized pink campion and there were wild rose petals that had fallen on to the tiles.

The kitchen was clean and tidy, the food left out on the table beside two unused cups – one with an mismatched saucer, one without. Had she planned to make supper and tea for herself and child after she'd dealt with her client?

Client, Henry thought. Somehow that sounded better than . . .

But she had opened the door and shown her murderer into the front parlour and then taken him upstairs to her bedroom. And he had killed her and her child and also the young man . . . He must have had a key, Henry thought. So a friend or a relative. Or possibly someone who had lived in this house before?

Henry went up the stairs and into what was obviously the child's bedroom. Clothes hung on a hook behind the door and a pair of shoes had been placed beneath a chair, a doll on the bed and a rag rug beside it. Another hand-pegged rug, larger this time, had been cast across the foot of the bed to be used as an extra covering.

Everything pointed to the child being well-cared-for despite the evident poverty. Where would they have gone to, Henry wondered, after they left this temporary place?

The larger bedroom at the front of the house was evidently the crime scene. He had earlier seen the blood on the floor and the wall but now the curtains were open and the violence of the scene was clearer. He could visualize where the young man had lain and where the child had been sent crashing against the wall. Another rag rug on the floor by the bed had been kicked aside and the bedclothes were pulled back, the sheets rumpled. There was no blood on the bed itself, which lent credence to the idea that the woman had been strangled or suffocated. The room and the house were very quiet. He wondered what would have been heard that night had there been anyone outside. Had the woman screamed? Had the child cried out? Was that what had brought the young man running in or was he already there? Had there been some arrangement that he should come round and check on the woman and child and let himself in?

There had been two cups on the table in the kitchen; for the woman and child? Or for the woman and the young man?

Henry turned away and went back downstairs and then out into the street. He knew that the local police and Mickey would have spoken to the neighbours but he also knew that it was worth him questioning them again. Mickey's approach elicited one kind of response and his, sometimes, quite another. The difference in attitude, appearance and even accent meant that people often gave a different kind of answer. It was useful to know this.

After a quick word with the constable on duty Henry proceeded to knock on doors.

* * *

George Fields had woken with a hangover. For a short while he hadn't known where he was – curled in the doorway of a derelict building at the bottom of Thames Street. He must have crossed the canal, George realized. It was a miracle he'd not ended up in the damn thing. He was on the outskirts of town and freezing cold on an early morning that, though it promised sunshine, was still very chilly. June, he'd been told, had been a difficult month. Hot days but chilly nights and some very cold rain. He was grateful that he'd not been rained on.

His first thought was that he had been robbed. He had no concept of how he'd arrived or exactly where he was but a quick check of his pockets and duffel assured him that he still had his pay and his possessions. He remembered, then, finding out that his wife and daughter had left, not knowing where they had gone and the crushing disappointment he had felt. Disappointment because he realized that the landlord had moved them on because Mary had been at it again. At which point he'd gone and got drunk.

George took a deep breath. His watch told him that it was eleven in the morning. He must have been out for hours and a quick check of how much money he had left reinforced the fact that he had drunk heavily. He dimly remembered being thrown out of the last pub and staggering off. He had been lucky; he'd ended up here, out of everyone's way and invisible and he'd not been rolled; thankfully he still had his money.

Painfully, George got to his feet and looked around. He was down by the canal. He'd been sleeping in one of the warehouse doorways, abandoned now since the canal had gone out of use. It made sense that he had found his way here. It had been where he'd worked for a long time and where he met Mary.

He'd have to find them, George thought. Whatever Mary was, she was still his wife. He still loved her and nothing in the world would persuade him to abandon Ruby. Thinking about his child seemed to fill him up, his belly, his chest, his heart flooded to bursting point. He would ask around – someone would know when and where they'd gone – and then he'd have it out with her once and for all. Tell Mary it would have to stop. He'd said it before but he meant it now. Ruby was getting older and this could not go on. He'd even do what she wanted and head south to where she had family in Newark and in Nottingham. She'd been trying to persuade him to move down there, get work closer to where she'd grown up. He was now of a mind that this would not be a bad idea; if she had her family around her she might be more inclined to behave. And it was certainly no good for Ruby the way this was going – a few weeks in this house, a few more in these rooms, a few days in some other dank, dark lodging house. What kind of life was that for a little girl?

George tidied himself up as best he could and headed back into town, back towards his last address. He would talk to their old neighbours, find the landlord and see where his wife and child had gone, but first he needed something to eat, something to sober him up. Then he'd find

Mary and Ruby tell them that life was going to change from now on.

The story of the murder was all over town but George had not heard it, at first being too concerned with getting some food inside him. By early afternoon, though, he was back at the rooms where he'd lived with his wife a few weeks before and he was banging on doors asking for news. The neighbours said she'd left in the night. Typical, George thought. One thought she'd gone to Brigg, another off to Lincoln. One said she may have gone to stay with her brother – she'd talked about doing that. The butcher said she owed him money, as did the grocers on the corner, and George assured both he would settle with them later, though he knew it would eat heavily into what he'd brought home. He almost dreaded meeting up with the landlord – no doubt Mary owed him too. Then, on the corner, he heard two women gossiping about a murder – three murders. A family, they said. George paused to question them. A woman and a child and a man, they told him. The police had come up from London – a murder detective and his sergeant.

'Where?' George asked them. 'Do you know who it was, only . . .'

'A family, that's all we heard. A man and a woman and a little child. Who would do something like that?'

A man, woman and child: alarm bells rang in George's head but he told himself it could not be Mary – she would never have a man living with her. He made his way to the street the women had mentioned and stood at the end of it, not daring to go and speak to the policeman on duty outside the house. He went into the shop on the corner to ask there but beyond being told the woman owed them money they could tell him nothing.

'Her name?' George asked. 'You must know her name.'

The woman behind the counter looked puzzled. 'And why would you want to know?' She sighed; another customer had come in and this one might actually want to buy something. In the act of dismissing George, she said, 'Fields – Mary, I think. Had a little girl called Ruby, sweet little thing.' Turning to her new customer, she dismissed George from her mind. George reeled out of the shop. At 3.15 on the afternoon of 26 June his universe tumbled around him.

Eleven

It was as well, Henry thought as the waiter showed him to his seat, that he had insisted the bodies be left untouched and that his orders had been followed. All too often he and his colleagues arrived at a scene days or on occasion even weeks after the murder had been discovered. The trail had gone cold or the scene tidied up by well-meaning neighbours who were trying to save the family more upset or even by the local constable on one memorable occasion.

Taking his seat at the table, Henry ordered a whisky and then settled down to wait for his sergeant to arrive. He took his book from his pocket and opened it at the page marked by a blue ribbon. It was worn and faded but had been his bookmark now for twelve years. He uncapped his Waterman fountain pen, running his fingers across the name inscribed on the barrel – a name that was not his own. The he began to write in what Mickey termed his 'Murder Book'.

The woman, Mary Fields, lay on her back, head at an angle, and my immediate assumption is death by strangulation. Despite the mud and stones still partly covering the body it was still possible to tell that she was dressed either for going out or for receiving guests. This, by all accounts, was not a wealthy woman – she worked for what she had and there are hints from the neighbours that she supplemented her income as many in her situation have done before. Was she expecting a man on the night she died?

Note: inspect the clothes carefully. He paused. He had already sent a note to the hospital that they were to be dried and kept.

The child was killed by a blow to the head. I would be very surprised if we unearth any other cause. Her skull was all but caved in and the damage must have been massive and instant. The angle of the neck might indicate a fracture but might simply be an artefact of the burial. The post-mortem will tell us more, I hope.

She was dressed for bed.

Did she know about her mother's visitor? Was she used to men coming to the house late at night? The neighbours will tell us eventually but it strikes me that this is a street where the curtains are closed early and the families retreat to the middle room at night. I doubt there will be many sitting in the front parlour. If this street is anything like the ones I know in the working-class districts of London the front room will be used on high days and holidays and for special visitors.

Did the dead woman use the front parlour for her business? Sergeant Hitchens will tell me that when he has finished with his inspection of the scene.

Henry glanced up from his writing and looked towards the door but there was still no sign of his sergeant. The waiter, noticing the movement, came over and asked if he was ready to order.

'In a moment,' Henry told him, 'when my colleague arrives.'

The waiter withdrew but his curiosity was palpable. Henry doubted there was anyone in this part of town who didn't know who he was and why he was there or who had not passed judgement about the situation.

He returned to his writing.

The young man seems like an anomaly. From what I could observe he was dressed in a working man's clothes and his hands were calloused. He was buried in the shallowest grave and closest to the gate, as though the murderer might either have less interest in him or might simply have become exhausted by the carrying and the

68

digging. It was possible to see evidence of a blow to the head, across the right temple. This body, at first glance, seems also to have been in the worst condition. The rats had got to his face and to some of his fingers, whereas the woman and child had been more thoroughly covered by, according to the workmen who found them, an old carpet and a stack of wood and cobbles. It seems they noticed that the rubbish in the yard had been moved two or three days ago but thought nothing of it at the time. This observation, however, may be helpful in pinpointing the time of the murder or at least of the burials.

He glanced up again as a chair was drawn out and his sergeant plonked himself down with a deep sigh.

Henry closed his book and put away his pen. 'Tell me what you found,' he said.

'I think we should order first,' Mickey Hitchens replied. 'I'm famished and you've not eaten since morning.' He nodded towards the empty glass. 'Whisky won't satisfy. You need meat.'

Henry Johnstone sat back in his chair and observed as his sergeant interrogated the waiter and made the decisions.

'What have you ordered?' he asked.

'Supposedly a local delicacy. Stuffed chine of beef. Constable Parkin suggested we give it a go. He's been assisting me. Bright boy. And you'll eat it,' he added sternly.

Henry Johnstone allowed himself a smile. 'You're a mother hen, you know that, Mickey?'

'Someone has to be. Now.' He had hung his jacket on the back of his chair and now felt in the pocket and withdrew his own notebook. The murder bag, Henry noted, had been parked beneath the table. Mickey laid the notebook down open at a sketch of the bedroom.

'The way I read the scene,' he said, 'this is where the bodies lay.'

'They were all killed in the same room? I saw no blood elsewhere in the house.'

'It looks that way and it looks as though they were left for a time too.'

A polite cough caused Mickey to close the book and sweep it aside. Their food had arrived, carried by a disapproving waiter. He set plates down in front of both men and took drinks from a young woman who had followed him over.

'Molly, I'll be serving the gentlemen,' Henry heard him tell her quietly as they moved away.

Mickey smiled wryly. 'Let's eat and then find somewhere we can talk in peace,' he said. 'There's a pub down the road with a snug that looks like a likely spot.'

Henry nodded and picked up his fork. He prodded at the meat, suddenly aware that he was in fact really hungry. He was also aware of Mickey watching him, a look of quiet satisfaction on his face.

'It's good,' Henry said. Hunger always took him by surprise.

'And you'll have pudding too,' Mickey told him. 'Something to soak up the beer we'll be drinking later.'

It was almost another hour by the time they took up their position in the snug. It was clear from the looks of the other customers and the quiet gossip that went on behind their backs that everybody knew who they were. Two men who'd been occupying the snug before they arrived quickly departed and they had the small space to themselves. Mickey pulled up a second table and took the photographs out of the bag. 'The way I read it is this,' he said. 'The woman had a visitor and she took him upstairs into her room. The bed was messed up, signs of probable sexual activity. But I'm guessing he got violent with her pretty quickly and maybe the kiddie heard, came in worried about her mum and this mystery visitor attacked her. There's blood on the wall like he shoved or even threw little Ruby against it then she slid down. And there's more blood on the floor, next to the wall, like he hit her again and her head maybe slapped into the floor. I went up to the mortuary and took some initial pictures.' He handed the second bundle of pictures to Henry. 'The doc sent word he'll be ready for you bright and early. I told him you'd be there for eight.' Mickey grinned. 'I get the feeling he didn't think it would be that early.'

Mickey paused as Henry shuffled through the photographs. The bodies had been stripped naked and the wounds were now clear. Henry was satisfied to see that the bodies had not yet been washed.

'His assistant wasn't happy when I told him to leave the mud on and not to wash the blood away,' Mickey Hitchens said. 'Reckoned it was disrespectful. I told him it was more disrespectful if that meant that we couldn't find out who killed them because he'd washed the evidence down

71

the drain. He shut up after that but you can expect a few grumbles in the morning.'

'The child's head and shoulder.' He pointed at the photo. 'Looks like the hair's matted with blood and what looks like bruising on the shoulder, but if she's been left lying on her side it might just as easily be post-mortem lividity.'

'Then we will have to do what Sydney Smith advises and get the doctor to take sections of the bruising.'

'That's if your doctor here knows how to identify the difference.'

'We'll have to hope the best, won't we?'

Mickey nodded. 'Mary Fields would appear to have been strangled. The finger marks on the throat are well-developed – the post-mortem should verify that. The young man, on the other hand, appears to have been hit with something hard and heavy, probably what was also used on the child. At first sight it looks like something with hard edges and angles to it and possibly a pattern of ridges. There was something missing from the bedside table, something with a square profile. Might be a candlestick, maybe a lamp base. Whatever it was, there is substantial damage to the skull and what looked like defensive wounds on the arms.'

Henry returned to the photographs of the crime scene and pointed to the bloodstains by the side of the bed. 'So we are presuming this is where the young man lay.'

'That's the way I read it anyway,' Mickey said.

Henry Johnstone nodded thoughtfully. Sergeant Hitchens was good at reading a scene and Henry

72

doubted he'd be very far wrong. 'As you know, I came back to the scene after I'd finished with Inspector Carrington and I spoke to the neighbours again and to the officers who'd done the initial interviews. Carrington, I think, regrets calling us in.'

'Been here the last few weeks,' Mickey said. 'I think he's just offended that a murder should happen on his watch. So how did you get on with the neighbours? Anything new?'

'Mostly they just confirmed what we had already learnt. Mary Fields, thirty years old, described as quiet, and most emphasized the little girl was always clean and neat and well fed. I get the feeling that mattered to most of the neighbours more than what Mrs Fields might get up to while her husband was away. It seemed the mother and child have only lived there for a short time so we need to look at previous addresses. I've done an initial interview with her previous landlord but it needs to be followed up.'

'Addresses?'

'The family had very little money. He was having trouble getting work and she was making ends meet the best way she knew how. No landlord wants a prostitute on the premises or a woman with a reputation. It reflects badly on him. So my guess was that they had moved often and into cheaper and cheaper accommodation and I was proved right. The last place they lived was only a few streets away and they had rented rooms above the shop. They'd been there almost four months. The landlord states that she owed him money, that she paid a part of it two days

73

before they left and that she and the child had then done a flit. He knew where she'd gone, of course. This isn't that big a town. And he'd been round to her new place, said he demanded she pay him and the neighbours remember that he made a bit of a scene. She paid off some more of her debt and he went away. He told me he was prepared to leave it at that but I don't believe him. It's my belief that he'd have gone back and had payment either in cash or in kind.'

'Reckon him for a suspect?'

Henry Johnstone shook his head. 'No, I reckon him for a bully who makes a lot of noise in public but wouldn't have the stomach for three murders. Too messy, too personal, but we'll look into his dealings with the Fields anyway.'

'So they went from the flat to a house. A step up?'

'A house that was due to be demolished. You've seen the damp in the kitchen and the rotting floorboards in the hall, so no, not a step up – the landlord was probably just glad to get a few weeks' rent out of the place before he pulled it down to extend to the shop next door. The family would have been moving on again.'

'And the husband?'

'By all accounts at sea but expected back any day.'

'Which shouldn't be too hard to prove, one way or another.' Mickey picked up his pint and sank half of it. 'Drink up,' he said. 'We've got a lot of thinking to do.'

Henry Johnstone obediently took a few swallows then set his glass back down. Mickey Hitchens shook his head despairingly. 'From what I heard

74

there's no other family round here. The woman wasn't local – blew in from Lincoln and Newark before that, worked at a hotel in her teens and then met her husband when he was still on the canals. Tough life no matter how you look at it.'

Henry Johnstone nodded. 'And a brutal end to it. Fingerprints?'

'A whole collection of them – she wasn't much for dusting. I took sample prints from the three deceased and I'll get the glass on the prints and do comparisons when I get back to my room tonight. See what we can eliminate.'

'That's good. Anything else?'

'A few sample fibres and a button. Probably from a shirt and torn off in the struggle. If you take the fibres and the button with you tomorrow you might be able to borrow a microscope and do a comparison, but from what I saw it was nothing the woman or the child was wearing. There were no shirts in the drawers or wardrobe that the button might have come from and it seems unlikely it had laid there since the husband went away, so it could prove important. Do we know who the boy is yet?'

'Not certainly, but one of the neighbours thinks that a cousin of George Fields used to call round quite a lot and sometimes stayed overnight. Walter Fields, nineteen years old or thereabouts, who did something for the local bus company. They think he might have been a mechanic. There was no identification on the body?'

'A bit of loose change in his pocket hand-kerchief.'

'The neighbours think he had his own key.'

'There was no key on the body and I didn't find one anywhere else in the house. The killer may have taken it and used it to get back into the house when he moved the bodies.'

Henry shuffled thoughtfully through the photographs and Mickey, giving up on his boss, went to get himself another pint. Henry looked at the faces of the three victims. The child was seven, Henry remembered, but looked much younger. Decomposition had already begun to slacken the features and affect the skin. He wondered if a photograph existed of Ruby Fields or of her mother. Perhaps there was a wedding picture of the mother or perhaps a school photograph of Ruby. And the young man . . . Henry could see that he might be about nineteen from what was left of his face but the side of his skull had been so badly battered, there'd been a blow across the eye and his temple had been disfigured on one side, which made it hard to guess what he might once have looked like. The attack had been vicious, furious. Whoever had attacked him had intended to kill.

Henry thought about it. Had the killer gone with the intention of killing the child and the young man or only the woman? The killing of the child might simply have been a chance event if she had interrupted him, the young man an even more chance encounter, perhaps.

Not that it really mattered, Henry considered. All three were dead and the only recompense Henry could think of was to have their killer hanged.

Twelve

Another man might have gone straight to the constable outside the house and declared himself, but George was suspicious of the police and at that point had been overwhelmed with emotion. He'd staggered away back down towards the canal and for a time stood on the towpath on the point of throwing himself in. He told himself that they could be wrong, that the woman might have got the name wrong, but in his heart of hearts he knew there was little chance of that. George was possessed of few coping mechanisms and after a time he decided on the easiest one and found the nearest pub.

He had stayed there, drinking steadily until chucking out time. A few of the locals had recognized him and passed the time of day with him and, later in the evening, he had been aware of many looks cast his way as those with news of the murders and of his relationship to the victims spread word to those who did not. A couple of men bought him a drink and one tried to offer awkward condolences but most had taken one look at him and, deciding that he was not in the mood for conversation, had left him alone.

When the landlord called time, George drained his glass and upended it on the table in front of him. Conversation and amiable goodbyes paused as George announced, by the turning of the glass, that he was up for a fight.

'Time to go, gentlemen,' the landlord said firmly. 'An' any of you'n hanging around outside will be barred.'

George was the last to leave. The landlord took one arm and his barman the other. They lifted him to his feet before escorting him to the door and depositing him on the pavement outside. George staggered and then turned, took a wild swing at those who dared to put him out and met the closing door with his fist. He fell backwards on to the pavement and lay there looking up at the sky.

When he finally got back on to his feet the street was empty, his fellow drinkers having taken the landlord at his word and disappeared, but George was still looking for a fight. He was angry with the world but he couldn't thump the world and he couldn't beat seven shades out of the man who'd done for his Mary and his Ruby but he still wanted to hit something. He made his way more by instinct than thought to the little house where his family had died. A constable still stood by the door and he turned to look at George as he staggered into the street.

'On your way home, sir?' George could see the young constable reaching for his truncheon, clearly having taken one look at this drunken man and decided that trouble was brewing.

Home, George thought. Somewhere at the back of his mind he remembered how he had felt when they had reached port, the anticipation of coming back to his family. To his wife. And now some bastard had taken that away from him.

George managed a single punch which made contact with the constable's eye just before the truncheon made contact with George's head and the second constable, that he had not noticed, leapt out of the shadows and floored him with a rugby tackle. George went down heavy.

Thirteen

The infirmary, newly refurbished, he had been told, stood at the rear of the red brick workhouse building, joined to the main block by a covered walkway.

Henry arrived promptly at a few minutes before eight o'clock and was satisfied to find that the surgeon was waiting for him and the body laid out.

He was even further reassured to see familiar volumes on the shelves of the mortuary.

'You have studied the work of Sydney Smith?'

'Of course. I may be responsible for a country practice but I like to keep abreast of developments. I'm called on to perform post-mortems several times in any given week here or in Lincoln or even Boston, and I've actually sat in the public gallery of the Old Bailey and seen the man in action.'

Henry nodded, reassured. 'You've witnessed Spilsbury too?'

'Unfortunately not. I'm told he's something of a showman?'

'He likes to perform, that's true. But a perform-ance often helps the jury to understand the science so I've no objection to that. He brings equipment into the court, demonstrates the whys and wherefores of the evidence. Sometimes that helps.'

Doctor Fielding waited for an explanation of the 'sometimes' but when none was forthcoming he moved over to where Ruby's body lay. 'I thought we might start with the child,' he said. He beckoned to a young man who had been standing in the doorway. 'Mr Brant is studying medicine,' he said. 'He'll be recording events and assisting if necessary.'

Henry nodded and came close to the marble slab on which the small body lay.

The doctor described the age and length and weight of the child and then he and Henry began their examination.

'There is a contusion to the side of the head,' Henry noted, 'and the skull has what looks like a depressed fracture.'

'Likely the killing blow. When I've shaved the hair we'll get a better picture. I've done a preliminary examination of the young man and my first impression is that the killing blows for both were caused by the same weapon but—'

'We must be careful not to get ahead of ourselves.'

'Indeed. The child was in generally good health, adequately nourished and clean. There is extensive bruising to the right shoulder and this continues on to the back – as you will see in a moment.'

'Definitely bruising?' Henry asked.

The doctor laughed. 'As you'll see when we turn the body, there are signs that the child was left in a slumped position, probably against a wall. The blood has pooled and settled in the extremities. It's easy to distinguish from the bruising in this instance.'

Henry nodded, satisfied. It was good, he thought, to find someone knowledgeable right out in the sticks like this. He reprimanded himself for being prejudiced. The doctor, as though reading his mind, nodded. 'I was a war surgeon,' he said. 'I learnt more about the inside of the human body than I ever wished to know. It seemed like a good idea to refine what I had learnt and keep my knowledge up to date.'

'Where did you serve?' Henry asked. Mickey had told him that it was a question most folk found obvious and were surprised when it didn't come up.

'Too many places. One field hospital looks very much like another after a while.'

Henry looked at the man with more interest. The answer was very much like his own would have been. He began to think he might like Dr Fielding.

Fourteen

The first that Inspector Johnstone knew about George Fields' arrest was when he returned to the police station after the post-mortem. He was not pleased that he had been kept in the dark about it.

'Apparently,' Mickey Hitchens told him, 'he turned up at the house, blotto, swung for the constable and the constable swung for him. There was, you could say, an exchange of blows, but I think our Mr Fields came off worst. He was put in a cell and left to sleep it off. Constable Parkin has a right shiner.'

'And no one informed us because?'

'To be fair, I don't think Constable Parkin realized who he was,' Mickey Hitchens said. 'And the man was in no fit state to give his name.'

'And no one thought there was a connection to be made?' Henry Johnstone said coldly.

Mickey, used to his boss's moods, merely shrugged. 'I'm told he's fit for interview now,' he said.

'Then have him brought up.'

The interview room was tiny. There was barely space for the small table and three wooden chairs that looked as though they had come from a schoolroom. Mickey sat but Henry stood, frowning at the door as they waited for George Fields to be brought in.

'How did the post-mortem go?'

'Efficiently enough. The man had sense enough to follow Sydney Smith's instructions and did a good enough job. Confirmed most of what we thought. And the employer came in and verified the cousin's identity.'

'So the young man is definitely Walter Fields then.' He paused. George Fields could be heard making a racket in the hallway, shouting over another voice which was clearly a police officer trying to remonstrate with him. 'Did he live with Mrs Fields and the girl?'

82

'Apparently not, just checked in on them from time to time. He had a room close by the bus depot. We'll talk to his landlady later this afternoon.'

The door opened and George Fields was ushered in, a policeman hanging on each arm. He was persuaded to sit down though the chair was nearly knocked over in the process. Bleary-eyed, bruised and filthy from where he'd rolled in the gutter, George Fields stared defiantly at them.

'If you quieten down there, Mr Fields, we can have ourselves a bit of a chat,' Mickey said.

'And who the hell are you?'

'We,' Henry Johnstone said quietly, 'are the men who are going to find who did this to your family. Our condolences, Mr Fields. Now, if you are willing to be quiet then our colleagues here can let you go and we can talk like civilized people.'

For a moment it looked as though George Fields wanted to do anything but sit quietly and talk, then he slumped in his chair and cradled his head in his hands.

'Grief and a hangover,' Mickey said. 'Not a good combination in anybody's book. Constable, you can maybe get the man a cup of tea.'

'He chucked the last one at the wall, sir,' the constable objected.

'Yes, but maybe he's in a better frame of mind now so fetch him another one.'

The constable left and Mickey turned his attention back to George Fields, his boss stood quietly in the corner of the tiny little room. Out of the corner of his eye Mickey could see him fiddling with his cigarette case. 'Now then,' Mickey said, leaning back in the child-sized wooden chair, his shoulders overhanging on both sides and his feet planted firmly, compensating for the lack of an accommodating seat. 'Now then,' he repeated, 'what the hell were you doing throwing a punch at a young police constable in the middle of the night? He ain't the one that did for your wife and child. Guarding the crime scene, that's all he were doing. And he gets a black eye for his trouble.'

'I'd had a drink or two. What of it?'

'And from what the landlord told us you were spoiling for a fight. Picked on the wrong man, didn't you?'

'Couldn'a get hold of the right bastard, could I. Ifn' I had you would have had another body to be dealing with.'

'And you'd have been hanged when another should have done,' Henry said.

'So what, you'll not get him. He'll be someone you can't touch, someone they'll all protect. What does someone like my Mary matter or my Ruby? What do they matter to people like you?'

'You know what they say about your wife?' Mickey asked.

He nodded. 'And I know it's the truth.'

'And how did that make you feel?'

'How the hell do you think it made me feel?'

'You must have been furious with her?'

George Fields lifted his head and looked Mickey straight in the eye. 'I was shipboard until yesterday. I never touched my Mary; never raised a hand to her even though I sometimes wanted to. She'd promised me it had all stopped.'

84

'They say a leopard can't change its spots,' Mickey observed.

George Fields looked away.

The door opened and the constable brought a cup of tea. He set it down cautiously in front of George.

'You can go,' Mickey told him. 'Mr Fields will cause us no more trouble, isn't that right, Mr Fields?'

The constable left reluctantly and Mickey shifted in his chair, more uncomfortable by the minute. 'And what do you know about the men who visited your wife?' Mickey asked. 'Picky, was she? Prefer the ones who were able to pay more? Respectable men?'

George Fields didn't move. His fists rested on the table either side of his cup of tea and he stared Mickey in the face. Henry would not have taken bets at that moment on the tea not following the stare but finally George slumped again, his shoulders sagging. He wiped his face with shaking hands. 'She was a good mother and a good wife,' he said. 'But there was never enough coming in. She wanted Ruby to have the best and so did I but I never wanted Mary to do what she did. She said she were careful, she said she'd only do with nobs, with the men who could afford to pay and wouldn't make trouble. And she promised she'd finished with it anyway. Promised she weren't doing that no more.'

'So she lied to you, or perhaps you never really believed her.'

'I wanted to. I really truly wanted to. I hoped she meant it.'

'And knowing she lied to you? What did that make you want to do? You must have guessed she was telling you what you wanted to hear – who's to say you didn't arrange something? Arrange for someone to keep an eye on her and when you found out she'd broken her word . . .'

The fists were back, slamming down on the table top. The cup rattled and tea spilt into the saucer. Mickey remained impassive and Henry continued to turn his cigarette case in his hand as though contemplating the possibility of a smoke.

'Who was she seeing?' Mickey persisted. 'She must have told you, or maybe you got your Walter to keep an eye on her? Maybe that's what he was doing when he went round that night – seeing who had come visiting. Maybe there was even a thought of blackmail involved? He thought he'd find out and touch them up for a bit of cash?'

Henry watched as the colour drained from George's face and he realized that up until this moment he hadn't known about his young cousin's death. 'Walter? What do you mean about Walter?'

'They found three bodies when they dug up that yard,' Mickey told him. 'Your wife, your child and a young man we now believe was Walter Fields.'

The man had looked sick before, Henry thought, but now he looked on the verge of fainting. There was no colour left in his face and even his lips were blue. For a moment Henry wondered if he had a heart condition, then George took a couple of deep breaths and though the colour didn't fully return he looked a little more normal.

'Three of them? There were three of them? I heard there were three bodies found but I thought . . . I mean, I were only thinking of my Mary and my little girl. Everything else went out of my mind. Someone killed all three of them?'

'Three bodies found.' Mickey shifted in his seat again. 'The way I read the scene is that your Walter came in, saw what was going on and tried to intervene. From the look of their injuries, Walter and Ruby were struck with an object that had a ridge and a heavy base. Can you think of anything in the house that might fit that description?'

George's eyes widened and Henry could see the horror in them as he imagined the scene. 'Mary had a candlestick by the bed. Pewter but with a weighted base. Lead in the base. The base was like a square and ridged round the edge. It was a heavy thing.'

'And Walter. Would he be likely to intervene if he saw something wrong? Is that something he'd be likely to do?'

George nodded. 'I asked him to keep an eye on them – not in the way you said, just to make sure they were all right. He used to drop in to make sure they were all right.' He took a deep breath. 'I need to know, my Ruby, had she been . . . you know.'

'She'd not been interfered with, no.'

George nodded, thankful for that small mercy. But she was still dead, Henry thought.

* * *

Inspector Johnstone gave instructions that George Fields was to be held as there was still the small question of Constable Parkin's black eye to be dealt with. Whatever his state of mind and provocation, George Fields had still assaulted a police officer.

Still burning that he had not been informed immediately of Fields' arrest and irritated, despite Sergeant Hitchens best attempts to mollify him, Henry went in search of Chief Inspector Carrington and found the man had just arrived.

'Just how long does it take you to get here in the morning?' Henry Johnstone snapped.

'I beg your pardon?'

'I asked how long it takes you to get here in the morning. How far you have to travel, because it seems to me that it would be more appropriate to have a man living locally.'

'I don't see how that is any of your concern.'

'It's my concern because you summoned me here. It's my concern because a murder investigation is going on and you seem to be utterly detached from the process.'

'I summoned you here because I could not be anything *but* detached from the process, as you say. I am fulfilling my obligations to the victims by bringing in so-called experts from London.'

'Chief Inspector,' Mickey Hitchens' voice, nonchalant and calm, drifted through from the front office. 'I think our appointment with the landlord was at eleven-fifteen a.m.?'

Henry Johnstone looked at his watch. A silver Longines, it had been a gift from his sister and was undoubtedly the most expensive thing he

88

owned. It was just after eleven o'clock. He saw Carrington observing the watch – no doubt assessing the price of it – and turned on his heel and left before the other officer could say anything more.

'The landlord's name is Joseph Penning,' Mickey told him. 'Owns half-a-dozen properties in the town and more elsewhere. His upper-class lets he does through the agency of a Mr Mountain, who owns an estate agency and deals with the customers who have some money to spend and therefore some choice in the matter. The lower end of his business is taken care of by a man called Sump, who doesn't appear to be available at the moment having been sent off to Lincoln late yesterday, apparently to deal with some dispute over rents.'

'And is this Sump a person of interest for us?'

'In the ordinary run of things, probably. In this case, probably not. He's been out of town for the past week, came back the day before yesterday and was sent out again yesterday afternoon so it's unlikely he was directly involved. That doesn't rule out indirect involvement, of course, and it doesn't rule out him having an arrangement with Mrs Fields either.'

'And so we are seeing the landlord himself?'

'We are. I told him to meet us at the house. It seemed appropriate.'

Henry Johnstone nodded. Everywhere had its slum landlords and they were not a breed that he was fond of.

Joseph Penning was pacing the street outside

the house when they arrived and looking ostentatiously at his wristwatch. Henry glanced at his own and noticed that it was just on the quarter hour. Constable Parkin was back on duty and Henry wondered if he'd managed to get any sleep. His right eye was an impressive mess of black and purple. Henry ignored the landlord and went first to speak to the constable.

'You need to learn to duck, lad,' Mickey told him, standing back and waiting for his boss to return his attention to the matter in hand. The landlord did not have Mickey's patience.

'I thought we agreed to meet at eleven fifteen,' he said. 'My time is of value, Inspector.'

Inspector Johnstone turned slowly and looked at the man. Nothing was said but it was Joseph Penning who flushed red, shuffled uncomfortably and apologized.

Mickey Hitchens hid a grin.

'Shall we go inside?' Henry Johnstone asked.

'In there?' Joseph Penning looked very uneasy.

'It is still your house, is it not? Until the end of the month, I believe. That's if the grocer still intends to expand his premises?'

Constable Parkin opened the door and Inspector Johnstone led the way, going straight upstairs and giving the landlord no option but to follow. Mickey hung back on the landing and watched the other two men as they paused in the doorway.

Henry Johnstone pointed. 'Your tenant, Mary Fields, was strangled on the bed. Her daughter was thrown against the wall – you can see the blood – and her head was then smashed open. The young man who came to their aid – well, you can see his life ended on the floor beside the bed. We understand that Mary Fields had . . . visitors. Men. I'm assuming you know about that.'

'I didn't *know* about anything. I'm told there were rumours but the woman was not known to me I was just trying to be a Good Samaritan by giving her and her little girl somewhere to live.'

'A place with rotten floors and damp walls that was to be demolished in few days' time?'

'By which time her husband would be home and they could agree to do something else, go somewhere else. It was better than being on the streets, I'm sure you'll agree to that. Or throwing themselves on parish care and risking the child being taken away from her.'

Henry Johnstone nodded but whether he agreed or not was a moot point. 'So what did you know about her?'

'I knew very little. One of my other tenants came to me and said there was a woman looking for a place to live. She had a little girl and she'd had to leave her previous place in a hurry but she had a deposit for this one. My tenant knew that this would be empty for a few weeks, the woman was desperate and, if I'm honest, probably knew I wouldn't turn down the opportunity to make a few quid out of it. There, I'm being upfront with you, sir. So I agreed for Sump to meet Mrs Fields here and if he decided she was deserving we should go ahead provided she had the deposit and . . .'

'References?'

Joseph Penning did not reply.

'And did this tenant of yours explain how she came to be in such dire need? And as we know that she left her previous lodgings with rent unpaid, how do you think she raised a deposit?'

'All I know is that she had the money. I left it at that. If I'd known she was going to be so much trouble I would never have agreed to it.'

'Trouble? Because she got herself killed?'

'No, I didn't mean that. I meant her reputation.'

'Which you claim to have known nothing about,' Henry pointed out.

Joseph Penning shifted uncomfortably. 'You can't help but hear things,' he said.

'And did you visit Mary Fields at night? Did Sump?'

Joseph Penning drew himself up to his full height, still only reaching the level of Henry Johnstone's chest, his face flushed with outrage. 'I am a respectable businessman with a wife and family.'

'As, I'm sure, were most of those who came to see Mrs Fields. By all accounts she tried to be careful. She relied on the business of so-called respectable men.'

'I take it you're finished with me, Inspector.' Joseph Penning replaced his hat and turned away from the door.

'Would you like to take a guess, perhaps, as to whom Mary Fields' clients might have been?'

'Clients? A businessman might be said to have clients. A solicitor might be said to have clients. A prostitute . . .'

'Whatever label you'd like to apply,' Henry Johnstone said. 'I'm interested only in names.'

'And you'll find no one willing to guess at them,' Joseph Penning said.

Mickey Hitchens watched as the man stamped his way down the stairs and out of the house. 'He's right, you know,' Mickey told his boss. 'No one is going to implicate their friends or their neighbours just to find the killer of a prostitute and her kiddie and cousin.'

'Then we'll have to follow the leads of what they *don't* say, what they don't tell us,' Henry replied.

Henry and Mickey left shortly afterwards to go and speak to the previous landlord, Mr Paul Tring, who had been responsible for evicting Mary and Ruby from their former rooms. He had agreed to meet them in the shop he owned, over which the little family had lodged. Henry had spoken briefly to him the previous day. Tring sold hardware, hammers, nails, tin baths and candles from a corner shop a few streets away from where Mary and Ruby had died. His own family, he told them, now lived in small terraced house in the same street as the shop but the rooms above had once been theirs.

'She seemed like a nice enough woman,' he said. 'And her man worked hard, was away a lot. Then I started to see them sneaking round the back at night. Men, you know, after just one thing.' He tidied his already tidy counter, clearly embarrassed. 'I didn't wish her and the lass any harm – certainly not this – but I didn't want it over my shop. Selling herself, and the child in the house too. And I didn't want my wife and my

kids seeing and thinking that I might have . . .
well, you know.'

'And did you?' Mickey asked.

'No, I most certainly did not!'

'And did you recognize any of these visitors?
Did your neighbours put a name to any of them?'

Tring shook his head but he wouldn't meet
Mickey's eyes. He looked at Inspector Johnstone.
'Well-dressed, not from round here. Not working
men.'

It was clear they were going to learn very little
more from Tring. 'Maybe we should speak to your
wife or your near neighbours,' Henry Johnstone
said. 'In streets like this there is always someone
to see and the women keep their eyes open. In
my experience women don't miss much. So if
you think of anything please let us know.'

The shop bell chimed and an elderly woman,
still in her apron and slippers, came in. Mickey
and Henry left and the woman looked curiously
after them.

'You reckon he knows anything?' Mickey said.

'I think he can guess at a lot, and I think he
might tell us if he thinks we really will go and
talk to his wife.'

'Are we going to do that?'

'Maybe later, when he's had a chance to think
about it. Perhaps we'll just show up tonight,
when all the family's there and see what his wife
has to say.'

Mickey Hitchens laughed.

Fifteen

Dar Samuels had always told stories. It was in the blood, he'd say. His father had told stories and his grandmother before that. It was the way you kept the past alive.

The family had gathered around the fire after supper. It might be June but it was still cold in the evenings, the weather still not having caught up with the calendar, and as the fire was used for cooking it was kept in most of the time with the big pot full of stew hanging above it.

Three chairs had been fetched from beside the table and the younger kids, Ned and Alice, sat on the rag rug in front of the hearth.

'There was once a vicar,' Dar Samuels said. 'His name was Emsworth. The Reverend Emsworth, and he was called out one night to one of his parishioners that was sick and about to die. It was a bleak, dark night but the Reverend Emsworth was a good man, not like some, and even on a night with the wind blowing fit to burst and the rain coming in slantwise, when the boy arrived with a message saying that old mother Clark was about to pop her clogs he wasn't the sort to just think he would wait till morning. So he gathered his things together and told the housekeeper to make sure the boy what had brought the message was fed and he'd set off alone towards Binbrook to give the old lady what comfort he could.

'Now to go by road would have taken him an hour longer, maybe more, and he'd been told the woman wouldn't last, so he set off across the fields carrying his bag and with his coat pulled tight around him and a shawl around his head. All the time he was walking he had the sense of someone watching him but every time he looked around the rain was so thick and the wind was so strong, blowing it into his eyes, that he couldn't see a thing. And as he walked he said a little prayer, like the man of God should do, asking the good Lord to protect him.'

Ethan laughed then; his dad was certainly not a religious man, neither was he a great believer in the righteousness of vicars.

'So after a little while, this Reverend Emsworth began to feel a presence beside him, walking along pace for pace, and it seemed to him that the rain had slackened off and the wind grew less and the feeling of him being watched? Well, it was still there but it didn't seem to matter any more. So he reached old mother Clark, gave the final blessings and then she died.

'Now, it must have been two, three years later when he was summoned to Lincoln, into the castle to shrive a man what was to be 'anged next day and when they showed him into the cell the young man said, "I know you."

'Well, this Reverend Emsworth, he reckoned he had a good memory for faces but he knew he'd never seen this young man in his life before and told him so. And the young man said, "No, you never did see me but I saw you. One night I saw you walking in the rain, struggling up the hills with a bag in your hand and a shawl around your head all bundled up against the rain. I planned to rob you. So I followed you but then I saw this other bloke come out of nowhere, walking up the hill by the side of you. Big bugger, he was, built like a brick outhouse, so I followed for a bit, see if he might go away but he never did."

'And this Reverend Emsworth, he remembered that night and how he'd certainly felt another presence walking beside him after he prayed to God. And he figured it must have been one of them there angels come down to help and he told the young man so.

'Next day he saw the man hanged for the thief and murderer that he was. Directly he must have gone home and he must have thanked his lucky stars that he wasn't another victim, robbed and left dead in the mud.'

There was a knock at the cottage door and Ted Hanson let himself in, calling out a greeting.

'Come along in, boy,' Dar Samuels said, standing up but otherwise dropping all ceremony. This was his place and he considered Ted to be a good lad.

Ted closed the door and nodded to Ethan's mum, who was hustling the children upstairs to bed.

'I won't be stopping,' he said, 'I've just got in from Louth and the horse in foal will be arriving tomorrow. Dad will want you to check them over so I thought I'd let you know. Come to drop the papers in too.' He placed a bundle of newspapers, the *Lincolnshire Echo* and the *Louth Standard*,

97

on the kitchen table. Ted had always made a practice of buying extra and bringing them along to Dar. He knew Dar liked to keep up with the news and so he always saved the papers that came to the big house as well as supplementing them whenever he went into town.

Dar thanked him. 'So what's happening out there in the big world?' he asked.

'Drama like you wouldn't believe, Dar. Triple murder in Louth. A woman and a bairn and the young man they reckon is a cousin. Brutal, it is.'

He indicated one of the papers and Dar Samuels got up to take a look.

'Three slain in Louth horror,' he read. 'Horror unearthed in backyard. Strangled and beaten. Police name the victim as Mary Fields, her seven-year-old daughter Ruby and her husband's cousin, Walter . . .' He read on in silence and Ethan watched as his mother went over to join her husband, looking over his shoulder.

A chill weight seemed to have dropped into Ethan's belly and he felt the colour drain from his face.

He was suddenly aware that his little sister had appeared at the top of the stairs. Grateful of the distraction, he turned to her. 'Come on, sweetheart, you're meant to be in bed.' He climbed the stairs towards her and realized she was crying. 'What is it, lovely? What's the matter then?'

Alice pointed towards their parents. 'I heard,' she whispered, 'someone killed a little girl like me.'

Ethan hugged his little sister. 'It happened a

long way away,' he said. 'Nothing like that will happen here, I promise you. Ma and Dar and me will look after you. You and Ned.'

She cuddled into him for a moment and then allowed him to lead her back up to bed. Ethan tucked her in and kissed her forehead. Then he went back downstairs.

'Alice heard what you read out. She was upset.'

'Upsetting news,' Dar said. 'What bastard would kill a child?'

'I'd best be off,' Ted Hanson said.' See you in the morning, Dar.'

When he had gone Ethan picked up the newspaper and read the article, recalling the last time he had seen Mary Fields.

They had argued.

She had wanted more money than he'd been prepared to give.

Ethan recalled the anger he had felt. And now she was dead.

'It's a bad business,' his father said.

Ethan nodded. 'I . . . I knew her slightly,' he confessed. 'Her husband and I, we were shipboard together for a while.'

'I'm sorry to hear that,' Dar nodded. 'Makes it worse when it's someone you know.'

And murder detectives had been called up from London, Ethan thought. Self-consciously he fingered the buttons on his shirt, a suspicion growing in his mind that he might have lost the button there, in Mary's room.

Sixteen

Mickey had been dispatched to Grimsby early that morning to interview those who had served with George Fields on his last trip. He returned late afternoon and they retired to The Wheatsheaf to compare notes.

'George Fields is a well-thought-of man,' Mickey Hitchens said. 'He's reckoned to be a good worker and gets on with everyone shipboard. Not a trouble-maker. He's got into the odd fight but nothing that anyone takes as serious.'

'And what were these fights about?'

Mickey consulted his notes but Henry Johnstone knew this was just for the look of it. Mickey already had the information in his head. 'One time he was trying to break up an argument, witnesses say everyone was three sheets to the wind, George Fields included. Someone hit George by accident and George lashed out – hit back. End result, six of them were fined. End of story. Second time it seems someone insulted his wife. Said she was no better than she ought to be. You know, I've never understood that expression.'

Henry Johnstone nodded thoughtfully. 'And George Fields did what?'

'Broke his nose for him. Apparently everyone shut up after that.'

'But nobody stopped thinking it, I presume.'

'Joe Peck, master of the *Miriam Sanders*, after

a bit of pushing admitted that they all knew about Mary Fields and thought her husband a damn fool for putting up with it. Most of his shipmates said they'd ha' beaten seven shades out of her and then left had it been their wife, and no doubt beat more than seven shades out of the men that went with her, but everyone agreed that George wasn't the type.'

'And was he seen as less of a man for that?'

'By some, certainly. But they all agree that there was no better man to have with you in a force nine and no better man to have your back in a fight. It seems they reckoned his only weakness was that wife of his.'

'And his daughter?'

'Everyone reckons he doted on her. The master thinks it was little Ruby that kept the two of them together and even those who had no time for Mary Fields admitted she was a good mother, apart from her, shall we say, professional activities.'

'So what was to stop him taking Ruby and leaving her?' Henry Johnstone wondered.

'Love is a mysterious thing,' Mickey Hitchens pronounced. 'Besides, how many lone fathers do you know of? He'd not have been seen as a fit parent on his own. And how would he have earned a living with a kiddie in tow? I think I'll get another beer. You want one?'

Henry Johnstone shook his head; he was still only halfway down his own pint. 'No female relatives who could have taken the child in?'

'Not that anyone knew about. George certainly had none and Mary's are not local.'

'Mary Fields is reported to have a brother that

she stayed with sometimes but no one seems to know where.'

'A fiction, maybe? A cover story?' Mickey took himself off to the bar and Henry was left to his thoughts. They had adjourned to the corner of the snug that they had occupied before, and as had happened before, everyone else had vacated the space and left them to it. Henry thought about what Mickey had told him. He found he couldn't quite understand how a man like George Fields put up with his wife running around with other men and taking money for it. Were their straits really so desperate? More to the point, wasn't he afraid of catching something? Henry considered that Mickey was probably right and that love was a strange thing. He couldn't imagine putting up with what George Fields had put up with but for that matter he couldn't imagine loving anyone that much.

Mickey came back to the table and sat the beer down. 'And you – what have you been doing while I've been interviewing sailors?'

Henry smiled briefly. 'Making a nuisance of myself,' he said. 'I spoke to the neighbours again, both from close to the crime scene and from their previous rooms. I also found two more addresses, one a lodging house they stayed in for two weeks and the second a couple of rooms above a shop just off the marketplace. They left the lodging house because it appears the landlord was interested in taking his rent in kind and had a wife that objected to his plans. Their previous residence seems to have been more permanent. An elderly lady, Mrs Fry, employed Mary as a maid and general companion for about eighteen months. Ruby was about four years old at the time and the old lady took a fancy to the family. George did odd jobs for her and even drove and maintained her car for her.'

'Sounds a far cry from where they ended up.'

'Oh, it was. I visited the house. It's a largish place up on the Crowtree Lane, set well back and with an old coach house off to one side. The Fields lived above what had been the stables. The car was parked in the loosebox beneath.'

'And how did this idyll end?'

'Badly. About two years ago, when the old lady died, her family decided that the Fields would have to go and so off they went. It seems that Mrs Fry had left them a small bequest but the family contested it. The family solicitor persuaded them that it was not in their best interests to pursue the matter when George Fields threatened to talk to the local newspapers.'

'Blackmail?'

'Or simply looking for justice.'

Mickey nodded. 'How did you find out about Mrs Fry?'

'One of the neighbours, Mrs Brenda Simpson, had a daughter, Mable, who was a friend of Ruby's, and the children apparently talked about the big house where Ruby used to live. Mrs Simpson was curious, asked the child about it and then talked to Mary. She said that Mary was very bitter about the situation.'

'I'm not surprised. It must have seemed like a complete injustice. So, did you speak to the family?'

'No. The family were unavailable but I have

103

an appointment with the son in the morning. He is a solicitor, apparently. But this probably has no bearing at all on the murders.'

'The death of Mrs Fry led to circumstances that put the family on another road – one that led to their vulnerability and eventually their murder,' Mickey said.

'I doubt the family could have foreseen that.' Henry shrugged. 'Anyway, we'll speak to the son tomorrow and get a better picture of what went on, I hope. I have a couple of names – possible clients of Mrs Fields. One is a councillor and another is an estate agent. Both "respectable men". You're seeing both tomorrow afternoon while I go back to London. The Symington case. My evidence is due. Oh, and George Fields comes up before the magistrate in the morning.'

Mickey nodded. 'Drink up,' he said. It seems that we're making progress.'

Henry nodded. 'I discovered something else,' he said. 'Mary sometimes went off overnight when George was away. She left Ruby with a neighbour, telling her she'd been offered a bit of work in a hotel but she was always cagey with the details. Eventually the neighbour got suspicious of what was really going on and said she'd not be a party to it. It seems that Mary Fields was a good enough mother that she was fussy who she'd leave Ruby with and she seems to have stopped her overnight trips.'

'And started meeting her men in her own home instead. I'm not sure that's an improvement.'

No, Henry thought as Mickey went off to get another beer. It probably wasn't at that.

Seventeen

People would talk, people always had, and Ethan knew to expect it, even if he and Helen tried to keep their interest in one another as quiet as they could. In a small community such as theirs, though, there was no such thing as secrecy. Everyone, man, woman and small child, knew that Ethan Samuels was sweet on Helen Lee – sweet enough that it should become a worry among the old folks. Ethan's father tried again to convince his son to let this go and his mother added her voice to his concern. Helen's parents would have forbidden her from leaving the house of an evening had there been a way, but Helen Lee had been a headstrong child and was now a determined woman. Had her mother locked the door, she would have climbed from the window. Had she barred the way against her returning home, she would have slept out in a neighbour's barn. Such, her parents knew, was Helen.

The village held its collective breath and waited on Frank Church to come to his senses and challenge the unruly pair. After all, the Churches and the Lees had agreed, hadn't they, that their two should wed?

Frank should be a man about it. Show the girl he cared enough to fight for her, or was it, some asked in whispers, that he feared Ethan's fists

– the boy known from youth as one always ready for a scrap. The man he had become, they all assumed, no different.

'Come to church with me,' Ethan pleaded.

'You know I can't,' Helen told him. 'Me mam's been chapel all her life. She can't be doing with all that wordy stuff.'

'But if you come to church . . . we can walk out after. Our mam'll follow us, keep it right.'

Helen laughed, astounded. 'Ethan Samuels, we've been meeting without a chaperone these past days and you've not minded. In fact,' she poked him playfully in the ribs, 'it seemed to me you'd go to any lengths to snatch a bit of time alone.'

'And so I would, but Helen . . . I want to make this proper. To walk out with you like I'm meant to. Meeting in holes and corners – it's not enough.'

'You speaking for me?'

He circled his arm about her waist. 'I thought I did that the night we danced together.'

'Oh, did you now?' Half-heartedly, she tried to push him away.

'So, come to church with me. This Sunday.'

'Ethan, I can't. Mam'd go spare – you know what she thinks about the vicar and his kind.'

'And what kind's that then?' Ethan was amused, knowing already what she'd say.

'Have you got no shame, Ethan, lad? Making me say? Me mam reckons if he and his like wore their trousers the same way round as their collars there'd be a lot less bastards thrown on the parish care.'

106

Ethan laughed, delighted. 'Oh, such language, Helen Lee. What would your mam say about that? Anyway, I reckon she don't think too highly of the minister either. You know, they reckon he has a woman in Louth. A widow, so they say.'

'Oh, you!' She wriggled from his grasp and then leaned back against him, her head resting on his chest.

Ethan held his breath, hardly believing what life had blessed him with. He stroked her dark hair – soft waves shot through with fiery red. 'I love you, Helen. I want you always to be with me, and if Frank Church isn't man enough to put up a fight then it's right he should be the loser.'

Helen pulled away again, not just putting a physical space between them but, this time, something more than that. Ethan felt bereft. He sensed he had crossed some boundary.

'Frank is a good man,' she told him softly. 'And Ethan, I feel bad about what we're doing.'

'But you don't love him.'

She didn't reply.

'Do you? Now, Helen, you tell me you do and I'll not believe you. I'll know you're telling me lies.'

Slowly, she shook her head. 'I don't love him,' she said. 'Ethan, I love you.'

If the village had been holding its breath waiting for Frank Church to act, then his mother had almost run out of air. He had left home that morning with her words burning his ears. They

107

were still burning when he reached the farm, so he knew that he'd remained the major topic of conversation, even if the only one to hear had been the pots and kettles.

'You'll wait till she disgraces you before you do aught?'

'Mam, leave it be. Helen won't do anything she shouldn't.'

'You believe that? I never thought I'd bred fools for sons.'

'Mam, let it go.' *Did* he believe that? Or did he lay awake at night wondering what Ethan and Helen had got up to? Helen, the woman he was supposed to marry and who, as yet, he'd not even kissed. Truth was Frank was at a loss as to what to do. Had it been a simple matter of knocking Ethan flat on his back, Frank would have given it his best – though he was wise enough to know that he'd never beaten Ethan in a fight when they were both kids and he was unlikely to do so now.

But no. Frank had seen the light in Helen's eyes. Light that faded when she looked at him. Light *he* had never kindled in anyone's gaze, not once, not ever. How the hell do you knock that flat? That look, that light?

Frank didn't have a clue. But he knew he was going to be forced into doing something. It wasn't just his mam and dad that talked about the goings-on between Ethan Samuels and Helen Lee. The whole village was talking and Frank was being taken for a blind fool.

It was seven days since Mother Jo had died, ten days since Ethan had come home – less than two short weeks to turn Frank's ordered world upside down. Truth was Frank had done nothing because he didn't have a notion what to do. Had he made their union official, had it been agreed that he was walking out with Helen already and that a date had been set for their wedding, he might have felt easier about challenging any man. As it was, it had been his family and hers that had the understanding. Frank had just taken it for granted that it would be as they said. Sure, he'd been friendly enough with Helen, treated her nice, and they'd got along well enough since their school days. His mam and dad had been joined as the result of a similar understanding and their parents before that. Helen's too, for that matter. You could go back generations and barely had there been a false step, a miss in such a tradition of 'understandings'; agreement often reached almost as soon as the children involved came into the world. And it had worked, Frank thought. Folk wed that had known one another their whole lives. They knew what was expected and what to expect and Frank had, somehow, just come to assume it would be the same for him and Helen Lee.

Nothing had prepared him for Ethan or that light in Helen's eyes.

That both Ethan and Frank now worked for Elijah Hanson was not that strange. Hanson was the biggest landowner and therefore the major employer thereabouts. Frank understood this but it made it all the harder for him that he should be brought into daily contact with

Ethan. Harder still that Ethan was just the same as he had always been, friendly and seemingly open. The fact that he was attempting to hide his relations with Frank's woman made this feel all the worse.

Frank wished, fervently, that he'd just clear off back to sea.

He almost wished that Ethan would take Helen with him.

Today, when he arrived, Ethan was already working in the yard. Dar Samuels was busy with the doctoring of Robert Hanson's brute of a horse. Ethan was holding its bridle, one hand on its back, trying to keep the beast calm enough to accept his father's ministrations.

Despite himself, Frank was drawn to see what they were doing. Dar Samuels' skills with horse-flesh were legendary and Ethan, following his dad about from the moment he could toddle, was not so far behind himself.

'God alive, how did he do that!' Frank stared, horrified at the four-inch gash on the horse's flank. It gaped wide, laid open like someone had sliced it.

'You should have seen it an hour ago,' Dar Samuels told him. 'Bleeding like some quack had set a leech to it. As to how, you'd have to ask his master that one.'

'It took Dar till now to staunch it,' Ethan added. His jaw, Frank noted, was set tight, his anger held in but barely controlled. 'The missus tells us Master Robert rode into the yard and fell from the saddle. *Blocker*, he was. Blind drunk and so mazzled he couldn't tell them where he'd been all night. Mister Hanson kicked him off the bed and sent for Dar to come quick.'

Frank nodded. He recognized the poultice that Dar was packing into the wound. Honey and fresh spider web with a mix of mould, scraped from the wooden dividers in the horse boxes. Workers often used that on cuts that wouldn't heal; sometimes a smear of honey too, when they could get it.

Breakfast would be on the table. He could smell the bacon through the open door. 'I'll tell the missus to keep yours by,' he said as he went on his way And it occurred to him, even as he said it, that much as he resented Ethan, the thought that he might miss out on this one guaranteed meal of the day somehow came out above the anger he might be keeping stored up against him. No one should inflict hunger upon another.

His dad, Frank thought, would have understood the sense of that. His mother, made as she was of sterner stuff, would have clipped his ear for being a muddle-headed lumx.

But, Frank thought, glancing back over his shoulder at the two men working with such care to sooth the temperamental beast, she was in the right in the main. He made up his mind then and there that he would wait on Ethan Samuels when evening came and that he'd have it out with him once and for all. Then, at least, he might get some little peace at home.

Eighteen

Even if the husband was not guilty of murder, he had certainly been guilty of assault, and Henry sat quietly at the back of the magistrate's court as George Fields was presented before them. Somewhat to his surprise, young Constable Parkin, eye more purple than black now, spoke up in favour of clemency.

'He was drunk, sir, but he was also distressed. He'd just returned from time at sea and come home to a murdered wife and child. And a cousin, sir. He weren't thinking clear when he thumped me.'

The magistrates conferred and George Fields, it was decided, would be let off with a fine.

'You are a fortunate man,' the magistrate in charge told him.

An interesting definition of being fortunate, Henry thought.

George Fields paid his fine and found Inspector Johnstone waiting for him outside.

'There's a cafe in the market square; sells a good breakfast if you'll allow me to buy you one.'

George Fields eyed him warily. 'In return for what?'

'A little of your time and a few questions. I could have both easily enough at the police station but I thought breakfast and teas would make it a more civilized interview.'

George Fields nodded and they walked on together.

'The fine will hurt,' Henry said.

'I'm beyond hurting. I've no one to spend it on now, have I?'

'You still have to live.'

'Do I?' He shook his head before Henry could respond. 'Don't fret, Inspector. I thought of that the night I thumped that young constable. I stood beside the water and I thought what it would be like just to go under. But I passed it by. I've still things that must be done before I go and meet my maker.'

'What things?' Henry asked. 'Mr Fields, I have to warn you against . . .'

'Against finding the ba— bugger that did this to them and doing the same to him?'

'Against that, yes.'

George Fields laughed softly. 'And what would you do in my place, Inspector?'

'I would trust to the law to deal with it.'

'Then you're a fool.'

Henry let it pass. They had reached the cafe and he ordered for both of them. George had chosen a table in the shadows, his back to the wall so he could watch the door, leaving Henry to sit with his back to it. Looking at George Fields, Henry understood that this had been deliberate, that he knew how uncomfortable this would make him. It seemed at once spiteful and perceptive and Henry considered the man anew.

'You knew that your wife would never change,' he said quietly.

'Sometimes we all hope for a miracle,' George

113

Fields said. 'Sometimes we believe we've already been in receipt of one and for a while that closes our eyes to the rest.'

'And your miracle was?'

'A woman who loved me and gave me a child.'

'And the rest.'

'As I said, the rest I ignored. Tried to, anyway. I didn't kill her, Inspector. I was nowhere near on the night she died and even if temper had got the better of me and I'd . . . I'd done something, I'd never have hurt our Ruby. Never.'

Breakfast arrived and George seized his knife and fork and dug in with enthusiasm. Henry, debating whether or not he was actually hungry, thought he should at least make an effort – Mickey's voice was in his head telling him that his body needed fuel if his brain was to work. For a few minutes the two men ate in silence and then, as George paused to take a slurp of tea, Henry asked, 'Your cousin – you said you asked him to keep an eye on her. Did that include taking note of who came to visit her?'

George glared but then nodded.

'And how did he know when she might be . . . entertaining?'

George went back to shovelling food and Henry waited. Patience, he thought, would be the key to getting this man to tell him what he knew. Push him and he'd clam up, storm out and tell Henry nothing more.

George devoured his food long before Henry and Henry, taking a final bite of sausage, pushed his plate across. 'Finish it,' he said.

'No wonder you're so bloody thin.' George

114

pushed his own plate away and started on what was left of Henry's breakfast.

'And how did your cousin know when . . .'

George Fields gave him a look that caused Henry to pause. He drank his tea and waited again.

'Because,' George said finally, 'she was so bloody predictable. Tuesday nights and Thursdays, those were her work nights. She kept it to two nights a week, said it made her more exclusive. Exclusive! Like she was anything more than a bloody tart. Then it moved to Tuesday and Thursday and Friday, that's what Walter was telling me. I mean, fucking hell, Inspector – she told me she'd stopped doing all that and here she is, doing it, with Ruby in the house. Doing . . . that.'

'You must have been very angry.'

'Angry doesn't even come close. I told Walter I was going to have it out with her good and proper when I got home this time. I told him.'

'How did you tell him? You've been away at sea?'

'We put into port, all along the coast – land the catch at whatever port is closest. These days *we* follow the fish and the trade – can't be waiting for it to come to us. Other times we haul a bit of cargo. Three weeks ago we was down London way, your neck of the woods. Last week, up at Bridlington. We headed back down this way after that. I can send letters. Walter sends me messages at the Seamens' Missions or the Sally Army. I tell him where we plan to be next and he sends . . . sent them there.'

Henry nodded. 'And the last letter you received?'

115

'At Bridlington. I got a letter there and sent him word from there for when I'd be coming home.'

'And Mary, did she write? Did you write to her?'

'She got our Ruby to write for her. Mary never quite got the hang of it, you know. She could read a bit, write enough to fill in her name when she had to but . . .'

'I see.' Henry nodded. 'And you kept these letters? From Walter and from Ruby and Mary?'

'Of course I did.'

'I'd like to see them.'

'None of your damned business.'

'Someone killed your wife and child. It looks as though Walter tried to intervene so they killed him too. That makes everything in your life and everything that happened in theirs my business, Mr Fields.'

George Fields stared at him and for a moment Henry thought he was spoiling for another fight. 'You'll come off worst,' he said. 'And I won't be as generous before the magistrate as Constable Parkin was this morning.'

George Fields slumped in his chair. 'I'll want them back,' he said.

'Of course you will, and I'll give you a receipt. I'll catch who did this, Mr Fields.'

'If I don't get to them first.'

'If you do I'll see you hang for it.'

'You think I care? You think I'd let you take me? No, this time I'd give myself to the water, Inspector. I wouldn't hesitate.'

George plunged a hand into a deep pocket inside

116

his coat. A poacher's pocket, Henry thought, and brought out a bundle wrapped in oilskin. He laid it almost reverently on the table between them and laid his hand on top. 'I know every one of these by heart,' he said. 'I'll know if any go missing. Don't make an enemy of me, Inspector. I've got nothing to lose now.'

Henry made no comment. He wrote a receipt for the letters and handed it over, taking the bundle and packing it into his own pocket. George Fields left then and Henry finished his tea before following.

He returned to his lodgings to collect his luggage and to speak to Mickey Hitchens. He found his sergeant poring over fingerprints.

'Anything useful?'

'Nothing you'd call conclusive. But if I eventually have anyone to compare them to I've five clear dabs that didn't belong to the family. You?'

'Letters written between the Fields and between George Fields and his cousin. I'll read them on the train. Don't take any crap from Carrington or anyone else. I'll be back late tomorrow or maybe the day after.'

Mickey nodded. It was an inconvenience when a court date broke into an investigation but it was also an inevitability at times. 'Any names that come up in the letters, send me a telegram or telephone the station and leave a message. I'll keep checking in.'

Henry nodded. 'Meantime, keep the pressure on the neighbours. They know more than they think they do. Apparently she saw clients on

117

Tuesdays and Thursdays and had just expanded her business to take Fridays too.'

'And you think the husband is in the clear?'

'I'm not so sure, Mickey. Obviously he didn't do the deed but that doesn't mean he didn't arrange for it to be done. I think he's genuinely distressed but that doesn't mean he's an innocent man. And he says he intends to track down the killer; could be misdirection but, if he's innocent, I believe he means what he says.'

'Men often say as much.'

'And a few mean it. If he's guilty then, as I say, it might either be misdirection or he might be minded to get the one person who could betray him – whoever did the actual murders – out of the picture. If he's innocent then he may know more about the men who paid for his wife than he wants to admit. Either way, he needs watching.'

Mickey nodded. 'I'll see you in a couple of days,' he said.

Nineteen

The day had passed almost without incident. Frank had been sent with the wagon and team of draft horses to get in the last of the hay from the Glebe fields a couple of miles distant. A crew had been working the past two days to get this in ahead of the change in the weather that Dar Samuels had predicted. Dar Samuels' skill at reading the signs was almost as accurate as his

118

skill in treating the beasts. He'd been right the week before, though then, as now, the skies had been clear and polished and as blue as Derby-glazed china. The field had been cut and was almost dried. Dar had warned of rain: Elijah Hanson would have taken note of it, but both he and Ted were away and Robert refused to take heed. Rain had soaked through the newly mown hay and they had all but lost hope of it drying out again before the rot set in.

Elijah was not minded to lose the field now; five days of sun and turning it had taken to repair the damage and even now he was worried it would come in frowsty and be ruined for use as winter feed.

Frank, trusted almost as much as Elijah trusted Dar, had been sent to supervise.

The day had been spent shuttling wagon loads back and forth from the Glebe field and, as Frank brought the last load into the yard, the first of the rain began to fall – leaden summer rain, dripping heavy from a seeming clear sky, though by the time they had all set to and dragged a tarpaulin to cover this final load the clouds had gathered, moiling and writhing, blotting the sun and bringing an early dark.

'That's the last of it?' Elijah Hanson asked, sheltering with Frank under the eaves of the barn.

'The last load and just in time,' Frank told him. 'It's not come in too bad considering the soaking it had.'

Elijah nodded. 'It'll keep like that till morning,' he said. 'Though see it's shifted first thing. And be sure it's turned daily until you're sure there's no mouldering.' He paused and took the watch from the pocket of his tightly stretched waistcoat. 'Get yourself off home,' he instructed. 'It's almost your time.'

Frank nodded his thanks and watched as Elijah made a dash for the kitchens. Across the yard he could see Ethan setting the draft horses to rights and hanging the harness on the pegs to dry. He'd be a while, Frank guessed. Ethan was far too conscientious – and too worried about losing work – to leave the harness uncleaned or the beasts uncared for. His resolve to have it out with Ethan that evening now somewhat dampened by the prospect of waiting in the rain, Frank almost decided to head for home and face another evening of his mother's nagging.

But no, the decision had been made and Frank would not go another day before seeing it through.

Grabbing an old sack from the barn and using it to keep the worst of the rain off his neck and shoulders, Frank set off down the rutted track, its hills and hollows already torrents and waterfalls. He took shelter beneath the ancient beech tree, just out of sight of the Hanson house, and settled down to wait.

The wait was perhaps only a quarter hour but it felt like forever. The sky was almost black with the rain and Frank was soaked through. The tree afforded shelter from the worst of it but rain dripped through the gaps in the canopy and saturated leaves unburdened themselves upon Frank's neck and head and shoulders. The sacking, soaked and useless now, he dropped on to the ground, reminding himself that he must collect it and return it to the barn the next day. He leaned back against the bowl of the tree and waited with as much patience as he could muster, peering through rain that fell so fast and straight he could barely make out more than a few yards distant. His one compensation was the thought that the rain would put paid to any plans Ethan and Helen might have of meeting up tonight.

So heavy was the rain that Ethan took him almost by surprise, the man emerging from the murk and dark. He walked fast, his head down, jacket pulled tight and held closed by a tightly clenched fist.

Frank took a deep but not particularly calming breath.

'Ethan.' Satisfied, he saw Ethan start in surprise.

'Frank! What the hell you doing standing here? You'll catch your death.'

'Like you'd care about that. Ethan, we need to talk. Now.'

'Jesus, lad, but you choose your time, don't you? Can't this wait?'

Ethan was shivering. The rain had carried an unseasonal chill as it often did in these parts and the wind had risen, whipping the rain so it lashed at Ethan's face.

'No,' Frank told him. 'It can't wait. Seems to me I've hesitated long enough before I spoke.'

Ethan nodded. He released his tight hold on the jacket and stepped under the shelter of the tree. 'You're entitled to say your piece,' he said. 'In your place I'd have done more than that and sooner than this.'

Frank opened his mouth then closed it again, suddenly at a loss as to what to say.

Ethan waited. 'We never meant to hurt no one, Frank. But I love her and I'm not planning on giving her up.'

'Love her!' Frank finally found his voice. 'You love her! Ethan, what the hell do you think I feel for her? It's been understood – most of our lives it's been understood that she'd be mine. I've cared for her, cherished her, been willing to wait till our kin reckoned the time was right before I asked her to set the date and then you come along and knock all our plans flat. Ethan, I don't know what life you've led since you went away but you're back here now and round here we don't take another's woman without so much as a by your leave. How do I know – any of us know – that you won't play with her feelings, destroy everything we've planned for and then clear off again just when the mood takes you. It's Helen I'm thinking of, not just me. Helen and our kin.'

'If I left here, Frank, she'd be going with me.'

'So you'd take her from her people. From all she knows and then what? Leave her while you clear off back to sea? What does Helen know about the rest of the world? Her family are here, her life is here, all she knows is here. I'm here . . .'

'And you just presumed it would all be right between you? That a lass like Helen might not want more than what the old folk decided?'

'And I suppose you can offer her so much more,' Frank retorted angrily. 'The great Ethan

122

Samuels, who hasn't even got a proper position! What you going to do, Ethan, drag her to the hiring fairs next spring? You think Master Hanson will want a man working on his land that upset the rest of the village?' Frank, in fact, had no notion what Elijah Hanson would make of all this or if he'd even care, but he saw a moment of confusion in Ethan's eyes. He pushed his advantage home.

'You'll pull her down with you, Ethan Samuels. You'll see her starve, will you, dragged about the country looking for work? No place to belong, no kin.' Even as he said the words it occurred to him that this was, in fact, just the way their families had lived for generations gone by. The way some, like Mother Jo, still lived, following the harvest and the horse fairs. Truth was Dar Samuels himself had dealt in horseflesh in better times. He told himself that didn't matter. Ethan had nothing to give.

'You think I'd do aught to harm her?'

Frank stepped close. 'Seems to me you already have. Seems to me you give no thought you might be ruining the girl you're supposed to love.'

'Ruin her!' Ethan's fist was raised and drawn back. 'You accusing me of what, Frank Church?'

'People talk,' Frank began but he knew the time for words was over. He ducked under the first of Ethan's blows and came up, fists raised, ready for the fight. Ethan struck again, through Frank's guard and catching him on the jaw. Frank sprawled his length into the mud.

'Stay down and we'll call it quits,' Ethan said. 'I'll make believe you never said what you did.'

But Frank, though slow to anger, was riled now, as much with himself for providing Ethan such an easy target as with Ethan himself. He struggled to his feet, slipping in the mud as he charged forward, fists flailing. He made contact with something soft but his anger carried him on and he did no damage. He wheeled; Ethan stood beneath the tree, both fists raised and a look on his face that told Frank that Ethan would give no further quarter. Frank gritted his teeth and lowered his head, bringing his guard up properly this time. He thought of Helen Lee and asked himself what was he really fighting for? Did he really want this woman who no longer wanted him? Had she ever truly wanted him?

Frank didn't know. He put the thought aside. The truth was he was hurting and it wasn't just his bruised jaw or his equally damaged pride. It was the knowledge, dawning just that little bit too late, that, lazy and tardy as he'd been in telling her so, he knew what Ethan felt for Helen because he felt it too.

Frank charged. Ethan was ready for him but Frank was determined he wasn't going to have this all his own way. The ground, slick with mud, slid away from them. They circled, struggling to keep their footing on the shifting ground. Blows landed, balance was lost and Ethan bled from a cut above his eye. It seemed to glow with an almost unnatural redness against the mud that coated the rest of his face.

Frank's jaw pained him. Lightning bolts of hurt where Ethan's fist had made contact for a second time. Frank lunged, Ethan sidestepped and a tree root brought him down. Frank piled on top, all thought of dignity or fair fight now gone. They brawled like school kids upon the sodden ground, pinching and grasping and punching, Ethan thought, like girls in a cat fight in the schoolyard.

Then a strong hand grasped him by the collar and lifted him back on to reluctant feet.

'What in God's name do the pair of you think you're doing?'

Dar Samuels had stayed late to check on Robert's wounded horse. He bent again to drag a sorry-looking Frank upright.

'Look at the pair of you. Like your mam don't have enough work without you ripping and miring your clothes. You too, Frank. You should be ashamed, both of you. I don't suppose I need to ask what this was over?'

The two younger men eyed one another resentfully. Both slimed with mud and oozing blood from knuckles, faces and, in Frank's case, the lobe of his right ear, they looked a sorry sight.

Frank mumbled what might have been an embarrassed good night and strode away as rapidly as his aching limbs would allow him. Ethan was left to face his father.

'He said things,' he mumbled. 'About me and Helen. About how folk thought . . . Dad, he said I'd be the ruin of her.'

'And have you thought he might be right?' Dar Samuels shook his head. 'Enough of this,' he said. 'It's going to be sorted. Tonight. We're sick of the lot of you, truth be told. No more sense than . . .' He turned and strode away. Ethan limped after him, more than a little ashamed and conscious, also, that Frank's technique had improved somewhat since the last time they'd come to blows.

Twenty

Mickey had spent the early part of Thursday afternoon searching the crime scene once again. It had occurred to him that if letters had been sent one way then there must be corresponding letters going in the opposite direction. George Fields had evidently written to his wife, even if she couldn't read his correspondence very well.

But a search of cupboards and drawers and even beneath loose floorboards turned up very little – certainly no letters. There were postcards from someone called Kathleen who had been visiting York and sent a picture of the Minster and the Shambles and a Valentine's card, clumsily written from Mary to her husband. There were school reports for little Ruby and a photograph of the family taken on a beach promenade. On the reverse was the name of a photographer in Cleethorpes and a date for July of 1926. Mickey was familiar with such photographers, springing out on the unwary and taking a snap then handing out their card in the hope that you'd come along and buy it. Truth be told, Mickey had succumbed on occasion when he'd been at Margate or Southend with his mother and sister.

He studied the small picture. George looked

tidier than he had after his night in a police cell but was eminently recognizable. Mary was a pretty woman with soft, fair hair looped up beneath a summer hat and Ruby's curls dropped on to her shoulders. She was smiling at the camera. George was surprised to find the picture in a drawer and not in a frame and out on display, but then there was very little on display in the house. Only the vase he had noticed in the kitchen, a couple of cheap ornaments that might well have been won at a travelling fair and an antimacassar on the back of the chair in the front parlour.

This house, he thought, was a joyless place.

He checked his watch, found that he had an hour before the first of his afternoon appointments and went over to where Walter Fields had lodged a few streets away just north of Kidgate. The landlady let him in.

'He was a nice, polite boy,' she said as she guided him up the stairs. Never came home stinking of the booze like some I could mention. And he cared for that little girl. It was always Ruby this, Ruby that . . .'

She opened a door at the top of the stairs. 'I've not touched anything but I did want to know. I'll need to be letting his room again. I can't afford to let it sit empty, not for long. You do understand.'

'I understand,' Mickey told her. 'We're trying to contact the family. I don't suppose . . .'

'Not an address, no. I don't know much about him, if I'm truthful. His dad were on the barges, like that cousin of his, George Fields.' She sniffed as though George had earned her disapproval. 'Little better than the gypsies if you ask me but the boy was a hard worker, I'll give him that.'

She stood aside. 'I'll let you get on, then. And if you can tell me when I can pack his things away and let the room again I'd be grateful. I've got my advert ready, I put a card in the shop window and—'

'Thank you again,' Mickey said. He entered the room and closed the door.

It wasn't much of a room, Mickey thought, though he'd stayed in worse in his younger days and slept in much worse in the war. The room was sparsely furnished. A single bed under the window, a chest of drawers with peeling paint and an old wardrobe lacking a door. Mickey checked his watch again. Forty-five minutes to go – plenty of time for the search of a room like this. Mickey doubted there'd be very much to find.

A half hour later Mickey was on his way to see Mrs Fry's son, the solicitor, though it was interesting to note that the solicitor handling his mother's estate, the one who had dissuaded the family from contesting the will, was a partner in the same firm. I'll bet that leads to some interesting conversations, Mickey thought.

He'd found little in Walter's room beyond another postcard from the mysterious Kathleen – also of York – and a small collection of letters, some from George Fields and some from Walter's family. They had been tucked into the pocket of a heavy overcoat along with a small amount of cash.

Stashing his finds into his own pocket, Mickey left. He had ten minutes to get to his first appointment with Mrs Fry's son. The first of the 'respectable men' on his boss's list.

Henry Johnstone sat on the train and began to read through the letters George Fields had loaned to him. About half were from Mary and Ruby and the rest from Walter. These looked longer and more detailed so Henry put them aside. He'd been fortunate enough to find an empty carriage though he expected that would change after the change of train at Boston for Lincoln. He felt irritated by the need to go back to London for what was likely to be a brief appearance at court to give evidence in a case of armed robbery that had ended in a death. The gunman's associates were now witnesses for the prosecution. Henry doubted this would reduce their prison terms but Haydn Symmonds was still insistent that he was an innocent party and would not change his plea. They'd even brought in his mother and sisters to try and persuade the recalcitrant nineteen-year-old, his mother hoping that an admission of guilt might save him from the gallows.

'It was manslaughter,' she had insisted. 'Not murder. He didn't intend to kill anyone. He just wanted to put the frighteners on the man.'

Henry doubted her son would see his twentieth birthday.

He settled back in his seat and opened the first of George's precious letters. The envelope was addressed to a seamen's mission at Whitby and Ruby had included a picture, drawn on a scrap of notepaper. It depicted a little girl standing in a garden of many petalled flowers. *Dear daddy, I love you. Come home soon*, she had written across the back in a surprisingly neat hand.

The letter was from Mary but written by Ruby and it covered a little over a sheet of cheap paper.

Dear George,

We are both in good health and keeping happy. Ruby is doing well at school and has been able to borrow some more books from the library shelf. Her teacher, Miss Edwards, says that her reading is coming on really well, she tries hard with her numbers and her copy book is kept neat.

We had a postcard from your auntie Kathleen from York where she has gone visiting her Lillian and she plans to stop there for about another week depending on when Lillian drops. They are hoping for another little boy, I think.

The conductor opened the carriage door at that moment and Henry produced his ticket to be clipped.

The man smiled at the sight of the child's drawing. 'From your little one, is it, sir?'

He departed without waiting for a reply and Henry waited for him to slide the carriage door closed before he continued to read.

She went on to write about their neighbours and the price of meat and bread and random thoughts about buying new ribbons to trim her hat seeing as she was unlikely to be able to afford a new one.

We walked up into Hubbard's Hills Sunday last and saw the Richardsons that we used to live near once upon a time.

Take care of yourself, keep warm, my dear, and know that Ruby and I do really love you.
Your ever loving wife and

Here an attempt at writing daughter had been made but Ruby's spelling had clearly not been equal to the task. The word had been crossed through and *little girl* had been substituted.

Mary had written her name in uncertain letters and Ruby had printed hers beneath, finishing the letter with kisses.

Henry replaced the letter in the envelope and opened the next. He could understand why these missals were so precious to George Fields.

Twenty-One

Edmund Fry had kept Sergeant Hitchens waiting after their appointed time – a move not designed to endear him to Mickey.

The solicitor's office was just off the market-place and through the window of the reception area Mickey could see the clock on St James's Church. This was an expensive office in an expensive location, Mickey thought, but he wondered if there could possibly be enough trade for such an obviously costly legal service in a small market town such as this. He'd noticed another solicitor's offices close beside Mountains, the estate agency, as he'd walked here. It looked to be a more modest operation that he assumed must deal with property matters and the wills of ordinary citizens. Fry and May, in whose reception he was now seated, looked like a much more financially serious concern.

'Do you know how much longer Mr Fry will be?' Mickey asked the stern woman who guarded the reception as the church clock struck the quarter hour.

'Mr Fry is in a meeting with a client,' she told him firmly, eyeing Mickey with disfavour, her gaze taking in his slightly unkempt hair – a few weeks late for the barbers – and his well-worn pinstriped suit. Mickey withdrew his watch from the pocket of his dark blue waistcoat and studied it ostentatiously. The woman just tutted as though disapproving of a silver pocket watch when the rest of the world had moved on and attached their timepieces to their wrists.

Mickey closed the hunter and smoothed the case between his fingers before replacing it. The watch had been his father's. It was plain, unadorned and satin smooth from all the years of wear and love and he didn't take kindly to those who sought to belittle it.

At last the door to Fry's office opened and a woman emerged, accompanied by the solicitor.

She wore a dark blue coat that Mickey recognized as the latest fashion in the cocoon shape. It matched her cloche hat. It looked, to Mickey's eye, like slub silk and covered a grey dress with a pleated skirt. Her shoes were crocodile leather, elaborately buckled and matched the envelope bag she carried. She glanced in puzzlement at Sergeant Hitchens; evidently he was not the usual type of figure to be observed in Fry and May's reception room. She held up her wrist and peered at the tiny watch on its slender leather strap. A silver watch, Mickey noted, but the material was the only thing it might have had in common with his own. Hers was new, gleaming with jewelled shoulders, and she wore a wedding ring together with an impressive engagement ring that bulged beneath her glove as she drew it on.

Mickey stood politely. He would have tipped his hat had it not already been removed. He waited for Fry to see his client to the door and then said coldly, 'I believe we had an appointment on the hour.'

'And I believe I had a client to attend to.' Fry smiled as though utterly unaware of Mickey's tone. 'Please, come on through. I expected the Chief Inspector?'

'He had to return to London to attend on a court case. You'll have to make do with me.'

Fry nodded as though accepting that Mickey was a poor substitute.

The office was panelled in old and carefully polished wood. Fry sat behind an old and equally carefully polished desk. He indicated the visitor's chair, flat seated and straight backed, that had been set on the other side of the desk.

'Sit down, Sergeant, and tell me what you want. I have another appointment in,' he paused and looked at the clock on the opposite wall, behind Mickey's head, 'ten minutes.'

'You'd have had a full half hour if you'd kept to your time,' Mickey growled at it.

'Sergeant Hitchens, I don't have to speak to you at all. Consider yourself lucky.'

133

Sharp words rose in Mickey's throat and sat on the tip of his tongue but he bit them back. 'I've come about Mrs Mary Fields,' he said. 'A lady known to you, I believe. She worked for your mother.'

He looked anew at Fry and wondered now if that could be true. The solicitor didn't look much more than perhaps thirty-five.

'My grandmother,' Fry corrected him, confirming Mickey's doubts, 'who was unwise enough to employ the woman as a maid companion. Mary Fields inveigled herself into the old woman's favour and then sought to benefit from her will when she died. It was a ridiculous state of affairs.'

'Not so unusual, surely, for an employer to want to reward a faithful servant? Especially these days when less women want to go into service.'

'Mary Fields and her brat had lived at my grandmother's house for a scant two years. No one would say that she had any claim of any sort on an old woman who put a roof over their heads and paid far above the established rate. And then employed the husband – a loutish layabout with no skills to recommend him and with no capacity for morality. A family that should never have been allowed to live close to never mind in the same house as such a respectable gentlewoman. If I'd known earlier I would have acted – you can be certain of that.'

'And why didn't you know?'

'Because I was away. Working in Manchester. I rarely came back.'

'And no one bothered to tell you? Or was no one else concerned?'

134

Edmund Fry steepled his fingers together and stared at Mickey Hitchens over their tips. 'Mary Fields was a whore. For all I know her husband acted as her panderer. It would have been only a matter of time before the child followed where the mother led.'

'Ruby Fields was only seven when she died. A bit young for you to be predicting her future, don't you think? And by all accounts, when Mary was working for your grandmother she behaved herself. She valued her position and didn't want anything upsetting the apple cart.' This last was an assumption on Mickey's part but from the look of distaste on Fry's face he either disagreed or simply couldn't comprehend that being true.

'Women like that never change, Sergeant. You must see them all the time in your work.'

'Prostitutes? Oh, yes, I meet a lot of those. Enough that I've learnt that there's rarely a simple story. But for you to be making that kind of judgement, Mr Fry, do I assume that you've a lot of experience that way?'

Fry was on his feet. 'I'd like you to leave now, Sergeant.'

'Maybe. Maybe I still have a couple of minutes of your time left.'

'I'll have you thrown out.'

'Who by? Your secretary has a good glare but I doubt she's the strength to pick me up and chuck me out the door. And I doubt you'll be up for the task. So sit down, Mr Fry, answer my questions and I'll be gone and you can get back to earning money.'

'I'll be sure to make a complaint.'

'Then you'll need to send it to Mr Wensley at the Yard,' Mickey told him. 'Now, tell me, Mr Fry, did you ever meet Mrs Fields away from your grandmother's house? Did you partake of her particular services? Or maybe you know the names of some of the men that did, seeing as how you know so much about what kind of woman she was?'

Mickey left shortly afterwards. He'd received no answer to his questions, beyond more of Fry's indignant threats and posturing, but Mickey was unworried. He was pretty certain that Fry had either been a customer of Mary Fields or he had a pretty good idea of someone who had. Or he'd been one whose custom she had rejected.

Whatever the answer, Mickey felt he'd set a fire under the man and that fire would spread.

He walked jauntily on to meet his next appointment – a man the neighbours had named as definitely being one of Mary Fields' late-night visitors.

Twenty-Two

Ethan had been sent with the wagon to pick up supplies of seed cake from Market Rasen some eight miles away. Most of the day he'd be gone and, to be truthful, Ethan was glad of the break. He'd felt trapped, hemmed in by the sense of disapproval that closed about him in the village and, it had to be admitted, the mundanity of the tasks on the farm. He'd never been bothered before as he was now that one day was much the same as the next, the work hard and the tasks a cycle of fetching and carrying and reaping and sowing and caring for the beasts. That part alone Ethan rejoiced in. He had his dad's talent with animals and they came to him readily and eagerly, looked for his hands on them and settled at the sound of his voice. Only the day before he'd heard Elijah say to Dar that Ethan was made in his father's mould and Hanson was glad of it – that he knew Dar's work would continue even after he had gone. Such praise would have been like a song in his ears if they'd not been so filled with the sound of Helen's voice.

He'd not set eyes on her apart from a glimpse on the Sunday when he'd seen her with her family on the way to chapel.

Ethan, his own family set to attend the church, could not even have the satisfaction of gazing upon her during the sermon.

After the fight with Frank they'd both been made to promise to their families that they would keep apart from one another. A week, Dar had said. Just give themselves and others time to settle into the new order of things. Hard as it had been, Ethan could see the sense in that. Tempers had to cool and he knew that his father and Helen's mother hoped that passions might cool too so, even knowing that would never happen, he had kept his word and not sought her out. Neither had Helen looked to come to him. Ethan was both disappointed and relieved. The close confines of village life made it impossible to keep it secret even if they'd run across one another by merest chance, and he'd not dishonour his kin by breaking his word.

Ethan just counted the days until the week was up.

Helen . . . Helen had other ideas.

He'd walked beside the horses on the steep rise from the village and not mounted to his seat in the cart until they'd reached the relative flat of the Walesby road. He always took care to spare the animals an added burden. The day was still cool, the sun not fully up and the mist still rising from the dew-damp ground. He walked slowly, enjoying the freshness of a morning that promised to turn into a baking hot day. And then, as he led the wagon round the first bend, she was there, sitting on a gate and swinging her legs like a child.

'Helen? Helen, what the devil are you doing here?' He looked around, expecting Frank's mother or his own to push through the nearest hedgerow and confront them.

'Is that a way to greet your girl?' She jumped down and waited for him to draw level.

'You'll be missed. They'll know.'

'Oh, and how will they know? I've been sent on an errand, taking a remedy up to my auntie's place.'

'And that, as I recall, is way over in the other direction from here.'

'I saw the wagon, saw you with it. I thought maybe if I take the long way around we might snatch an hour.'

138

'Helen.' Oh, God, Ethan thought. She was standing so close now, so close he could feel the warmth coming off her body and smell the sprigs of lavender she'd woven into the faded lace collar of her dress. His arm circled her waist and he drew her still closer, only realizing when his lips were on hers just what his body seemed to have done without his bidding. He should let her go. Now, back away, tell her it was only a couple more days and then they could go back to the way it had been before. No, better than before. They would be able to meet without comment. Would be able to . . . 'Helen, we mustn't do . . .'

'Do what, Ethan?' Her lips were parted and he could feel the thumping of her heart, too fast, too eager. Or was that his own heart he could feel?

'Ethan?' Her question hung upon the still, warm air and Ethan knew what was coming, what she was asking him without the words, what . . .

'Oh, God, Helen, I want you so damned much.'

There was a glimmer of fright in her eyes as she looked at him and in the way she passed the very tip of her tongue across her lips. The faintest glimmer of fear in the way she caught her breath and her heart beat even faster – it seemed to Ethan that between them they now had only the one.

Not saying a word, Ethan took her hand and led her through the field gate. It occurred to him that the horses might wander, that someone might see the cart, but that was only the reasoning, sensible fragment of his mind chattering unheeded in the background. The rest . . . the rest was filled with the look and the scent and the feel of Helen Lee and would give attention to nothing else.

He led her by the hand, laid her down on the sun-warmed grass close by the hedge and, with a hand more practised than Helen's, he unfastened her dress and slipped it down while she still fumbled with the buttons on his shirt. She'd come prepared, he realized, and she was naked beneath.

Helen paused, noting the odd button on Ethan's shirt. He tensed. 'I lost one,' he said. Mam had found the closest she had.

Helen smiled at him, undid the button then moved on to the next. Ethan caught her hand and kissed the fingertips. 'Are you certain? Sweetheart, I'm not prepared, you know . . .'

'I'm sure,' she said, and Ethan moved his hands across her naked skin, taking her breasts in his hands and stroking the hardening nipples, and there, in an open field on a late June day, he made love to Helen Lee.

Twenty-Three

George had watched as Sergeant Hitchens left May and Fry, the solicitors and he followed at a distance as he walked back towards the marketplace. Mickey Hitchens was walking fast and had the look of a man who had just scored points and was well satisfied with the outcome.

George wondered what he had discovered and the anger in him rose up to choke him once more.

If it hadn't been for Fry they'd have been settled, able to make a proper life for themselves and get good references from the old lady. She'd promised them. Said, once she knew her time was running out, that she'd lodge the references with her solicitor so that Mary could get a good job elsewhere just like old Mrs Fry's cook had done.

True, their situation was a little different from that of Gabrielle, her cook, a woman who'd served her for so many years they had almost grown old together, but there were many modest households these days that would want a maid of all work and a handyman and would tolerate a child. Mrs Fry had already made enquiries.

On the day of the funeral, after they had paid their respects at the church, Gabrielle had left with her new employer, an old friend of Mrs Fry who had promised that she would have work and a home with them. Dammit, George thought, Mrs Fry had practically left Gabrielle to them in her will. She'd promised to do something to help him and Mary and she probably had, but that bastard grandson of hers just had to stick his nose in and spread stories about Mary.

The irony of it all was that Mary had told Edmund Fry that she didn't do that sort of thing any more. Not even for a member of her employer's family.

George almost wished that she'd given in to him. Given him what he wanted so they'd have been left alone. But he knew, in his heart of hearts, that this would just have given Fry ammunition to use against them. He'd have ruined their lives no matter what.

Sergeant Hitchens appeared to have reached his destination. A private house this time. George didn't know who might be living there but it looked solid and prosperous and moneyed. He found a place from where he could watch and settled down to wait.

Edmund Fry stood by the window of his office and watched Sergeant Hitchens walk away past the church and turn the corner out of sight. He was interested to see the figure of George Fields suddenly appear and follow.

A knock on his door announced the presence of his partner, Charles May. He'd lied about waiting for another client to arrive.

'Police gone, old boy?'

'The sergeant. The chief inspector has been recalled to London.'

'What, for good? They lost interest damned quickly.'

'No, he'll be back in a day or two. Got to give evidence or something. The sergeant wants some manners. Nasty little man.'

His partner came over and stood beside him at the window. 'They'll be gone soon enough,' he said. 'Don't you fret, old man. The police will soon give it up as a bad job. Carrington reckons they'll make a lot of noise and then head back for the city.'

'And he'd know, I suppose.'

'Well, he is one of them, isn't he? A bona

fide chief inspector. A man with ambitions to boot.'

'An acting chief inspector,' Fry reminded him.

'Not for long though, don't cha know? A quiet word here, a few strings pulled there. He's a decent enough fellow, don't cha think?'

'I hardly know the man. I leave the politicking to you.'

'And very wise to do so.' May slapped Fry on the back and left.

Twenty-Four

In contrast to Edmund Fry, Mr Charles South admitted very quickly that he had known Mary Fields: 'In the, er, biblical sense . . .'

Mickey frowned at his attempt at humour and Charles South sunk further into his chair.

'And you were a regular customer?'

South, a man with red cheeks and a balding head, nodded uncomfortably, not looking at Mickey. 'Twice a month for the past year,' he said. 'Excepting those weeks when her husband was home. I must tell you, those were hard weeks. So very hard. She was a lovely woman. A very kind, gentle woman.'

Mickey raised an inquisitional eyebrow but Charles South was finding the pattern on the Persian rug far more interesting and didn't look up.

'Can you tell me how . . . how you found me?'

'You were recognized,' Mickey told him. 'Quite a while ago apparently. No one said anything until now and they only told me on account of me being a policeman and your kind, gentle woman being very dead.'

Charles South shuddered and Mickey realized that the man was weeping.

'So how did you meet her?'

'At first, it was at the house of a family friend. I live with my sisters, you see. We none of us ever married. We used to visit a Mrs Celia Fry. Mary was working for her together with her husband and little Ruby. Sweet little Ruby. How could anyone . . . anyone . . .'

'And did your . . . relationship begin then?'

South shook his head vehemently. 'No, oh no. She was a respectable woman. Driven to all this, she was. Driven to it by the cruelty of others. By that grandson of Celia's. Now there's a bad apple. A real rotter.'

How old was Charles South? Mickey wondered. He guessed at sixty or even older. A soft, marshmallow of a man from the look of him and he'd certainly had a soft spot for the dead woman. 'And so you began to . . .'

'I began our relationship.' South seized on the word Mickey had used. 'And that's what it was. We'd talk before and again after. I said things to Mary that I'd never, ever said to anyone.' He paused. 'I don't want my sisters to know. They'd be shocked and embarrassed. We'd have to leave here and they do so love this house.'

Mickey was not going to make any promises. 'Did you know of anyone else who . . .'

144

'I didn't want to. You have to understand that. Look, I'm sure this sounds foolish to a man like you but for two evenings a month I could pretend. I could make believe that I loved and was loved. That I had someone who . . . who made me feel as though I mattered. She wasn't like a common whore. Mary never walked the streets, she never . . . sold herself like that. She did me a favour. She made me happy and if I could make her life a little easier by offering a little money then, then . . .'

'And when did you last see her?'

'Ten days ago. I saw her ten days ago. I arrived just after eight o'clock in the evening and left just before midnight. My sisters were asleep by the time I returned. They thought I'd been visiting a friend. That's what I told them. That's what I always told them.'

No, he had no idea who would want to hurt her or who else she was seeing.

The clock struck the hour and South looked up nervously. 'My sisters will be back, Sergeant. Please.'

Mickey took his leave. The earlier euphoria had evaporated. He'd enjoyed goading Fry but there had been no pleasure in questioning Charles South.

One more to go, Mickey thought. And this one was a councillor. Mickey didn't expect that it would be an easy interview.

Out of the corner of his eye he caught a glimpse of movement and as he turned the corner he looked back and saw George Fields standing on the opposite side of the road from Charles South's house.

Mickey retraced his steps.

'Mr Fields.'

'Sergeant.'

'Stay away, Mr Fields. One thing I can tell you is that he's not your man. Not unless I've become a complete ass when it comes to judging people. He knew her, that's all. He liked her, thought she was a good sort.'

'And did Fry think she was a good sort?' George asked harshly.

'You don't need me to answer that,' Mickey told him. 'Now come away and stay away, from here and from Fry. You'll only do more harm.'

George Fields stared at him. 'Or what?' he said.

'Or I'll have you arrested for breach of the peace.'

'I've breached no peace.'

'No, but you will, so let's say I just pre-empt that?'

George Fields looked as though he might take a swing for Mickey. 'Don't even think of it,' Mickey said.

George turned on his heel and strode away.

Mickey's final appointment was even less useful than he'd expected it to be. The man would tell him nothing except that he'd not seen Mary Fields in months, that it had been a one-off incident and that he'd been miles away on the night she died anyway, staying with a relative in Lincoln.

On requesting the name and address of this relative, Mickey was instead given the name of his solicitor and told to leave.

Mickey left.

He checked the street but there was no sign of George Fields.

Twenty-Five

Ethan had been in fear all day and all through that night. What if they had been seen? What if Helen had been away too long and her mother guessed that she had not gone straight to her aunt's?

Ethan had been convinced that the guilt he felt was written large upon his forehead for all to see. One look at his face, Ethan thought, and anyone, from the smallest child in the village to the most venerable elder, would see what they had done.

That night, walking home with Dar, he was aware of his father looking at him, scrutinizing him in a way that gave Ethan considerable unease and seemed to confirm the worst of his fears. He must look so guilt-ridden, so blemished, that his father must surely challenge him.

It was only later, much, much later, that Ethan was to realize what had really given him away. His father had read in his eyes that look of exultation, of excitement and joy that Ethan could not, with the best of wills, manage to suppress. Dar knew that look and that joy. Dar could well remember the time, now long passed, when he'd been Ethan's age and when love and desire had eaten into him with that same acid intensity. Had eaten its way inside of him and beamed out through his love-struck gaze.

Dar said nothing. In fact, he spoke little to his son that evening but Ethan was too preoccupied to notice and too wrapped up in his own thoughts to be any more than relieved that his father had not challenged him. He retired early to his bed and dreamed of Helen Lee.

The next morning he rose to find his father already gone, called to another farm to tend to the birth of a foal. He walked alone to Hanson's farm, watching all the way, half expecting to see her in wait for him and uncertain what he'd do should that be so.

Twenty-Six

It wasn't easy for Frank and Ethan to avoid one another but they managed it well enough. It was avoidance characterized not by lack of contact but by a lack of meaningful exchange even if they were both in the same room. At breakfast in the farmhouse kitchen they sat apart from one another, chatted amiably enough with others and, should the collective conversation call for a direct response, would deliver it politely but swiftly.

They valued their jobs too highly to let their differences impinge upon the work, and when

148

Hanson had need of them to cooperate, they did so. A neutral observer would merely have thought them two quiet, industrious men who each knew their task well enough for words to be superfluous.

Ethan had experience enough to know how to play the game. Control enough to know that, though he had won, nothing would be gained from rubbing his opponent's nose in that victory. Helen, on the other hand, though she had not one malicious bone in her body had, Ethan came to realize, few wise or restraining ones either. Helen was passionate. There was no other word he could use. It seemed to Ethan she would lie in wait for him at every opportunity and turn and, though he was flattered by the attention and blessed each encounter as golden, he wished she would learn to be more circumspect in her outward display.

'I'm to marry you, Ethan Samuels, and I'm happy in that. I don't care if the whole world knows. Isn't it a good thing I want to be with you any minute I can?'

'A good thing, yes. But a possible thing? Not when I'm working, Helen, and not when Frank's about.' Or anyone that might see and comment on it, he thought, though he was learning that with Helen some things were best left unsaid.

But it seemed to Ethan that even recognizing her faults made her more precious to him. Helen knew no restraint. She laughed and teased and kissed him so eagerly that it was all he could do to keep control. She asked him questions about his travels, never tiring of his stories of the big wide world; Helen who had gone no more than ten miles in any direction from their valley. Helen demanded knowledge even as she demanded love. She listened with wonder to the tales he told and the knowledge he had gathered. She wished herself 'out there' and even when he reminded her that he was back here because 'out there' could also be a bitterly cold place, she just shook her head in bafflement.

'I'd be with you,' she told him. 'The two of us, Ethan. We could go anywhere, do anything. I know it.'

And a part of Ethan knew it too. Or wanted to.

'You'd miss your family,' he argued. 'You'd miss this place. Helen, you'd want to come back home.'

'Home is where you are, Ethan,' she told him. 'You are my home.'

And she meant it too. Ethan knew it even as he told himself it was unreasonable. She loved him with a passion unqualified by reason or thought and Ethan almost cursed the self-knowledge that prevented him from doing the same. What was reason? What was restraint? What was knowledge when tallied against such unconditional love?

Then she came to him in the barn that day and brought disaster so close Ethan could feel it breathing in his ear.

'Helen? Are you mad? Go away, girl. I've work to do and if Hanson catches you here there'll be hell to pay.'

'I'm here on an errand for Mrs Hanson,' she told him grandly. 'I've a reason to be here, Ethan.'

150

'In the house mebbe but not in the barn. Even the missus doesn't come in here when the men are working. Get off home, Helen. Go now.'

'You *ordering* me about, Ethan Samuels?' She pouted and then giggled, brown eyes shining with mischief. Sometimes, Ethan thought, she seemed more like a child of seventeen than a woman of the same years. 'Helen, please. If anyone sees I'll lose my job and get Dar into deep trouble too. Please, Helen.'

She sighed but nodded. 'I'll go then. I'm sorry,' she apologized. 'I know you're right but I so wanted to see you.'

'And you will. Tonight. But not here. Not now.'

To his relief she turned to go, peering round the door to make sure no one would see her leave. Then, to his alarm, she swung around and grabbed him by the shirt, pulling him off balance so that Ethan almost fell against her. He grabbed her tightly, as much in surprise as in desire, and then pulled back in fear at the sound behind her.

Frank stood in the doorway. Staring hard.

'She was just leaving.' Ethan straightened up and let go of Helen. Her top button had come undone and her hair had collected a wisp or two of straw where she'd brushed against the stacked hay. Inwardly, Ethan groaned. The look on Frank's face betrayed all too clearly what he must be thinking.

'Give you pleasure, does it?' Frank demanded. 'Coming here, acting like a little whore?'

'Like a what?'

Wrong thing to say, Ethan thought.

151

Helen went for Frank, her nails raking across his face. 'Don't you dare call me that, Frank Church.'

Ethan grabbed her and dragged her away. 'That wasn't called for, Frank. We've done nothing.'

'That's not how it looks.'

'Well, how it looks is not the way it is. She were just about to leave.'

'She should never have come.'

'No, she shouldn't ha', but I can't do nowt about that now.'

Helen shook free of him. 'You two stop talking about me like I wasn't here,' she said.

Frank ignored her. 'I'd just about come to terms,' he spat vehemently, 'just about forced me head around the fact that she's gone so far as I'm concerned. Not mine nor ever going to be. But no, you have to rub me bloody nose in it, don't you? Have to behave like a bloody furriner, and her! I never thought her would lower herself so far as this.'

'You what, Frank Church? You talk about me like I'm . . .' Helen, incandescent with fresh rage, flew at him again. Then she fell back, the colour draining from her face.

Ethan groaned. Elijah Hanson, flanked by his two sons, had appeared at Frank's shoulder.

Hanson jerked his chin towards Helen. 'Out,' he said. 'Get home.'

Helen, all fight gone, ducked through the door and ran.

Ethan squared his shoulders and prepared for the worst. Ted was watching proceedings with a look of grave concern upon his honest face.

Robert, in contrast, was smirking at Frank and Ethan's discomfort.

'I don't employ you to entertain your women in my barn,' Elijah Hanson told Ethan. 'Neither do I pay you to pick your fights on my time. I've played fair with you both, chosen not to listen to the gossip and looked the other way until now and, to give credit where it's due, you've neither of you let me down by allowing such foolishness to have a place in your work time. But now!'

'It weren't Frank's fault,' Ethan began. 'He walked in and . . .'

'Give you leave to speak, did I?' Hanson growled.

Robert's smirk expanded into a grin. Ethan would have given anything to wipe it from his face. He closed his eyes and shook his head. 'No, sir,' he said.

'Get shut of the pair of them,' Robert said then yelped as his dad backhanded him, catching his knuckles across Robert's nose so that blood oozed slowly from one nostril.

'I didn't ask you neither,' Hanson said. He took a step closer to Ethan and peered hard into his face. Ethan met his gaze squarely, but not for long. The enormity of what was happening had been reinforced by Robert's words. If he lost *his* position it would be bad enough but Frank *needed* this job. Frank could not just go back to sea as Ethan could. Frank knew nothing else and Frank, Ethan was honest enough to admit, was the innocent in this. He dropped his gaze and stared hard at his booted feet.

'My fault,' he mumbled softly. 'I'm sorry, Mr Hanson, sir.'

'You thank your stars, my boy, that I hold your feyther in high regard and that I need all the hands I can get for the harvest. But mark this, boy. You put one step wrong and I'll have you *ran tanned* out of the valley and that fool of a lass with you. You hearing me?'

'I'm hearing you,' Ethan told him. 'It won't happen again. I swear.'

'Damned right it won't.'

Hanson senior turned on his heel and strode away, calling his sons to heel after him. Ted paused to clap Frank on the shoulder; his gaze, though, strayed to Ethan and the small nod of sympathy cut Ethan to the quick. Robert, smirk back on his face, despite his oozing nose, paused to jeer at the pair of them. 'Bloody gypos,' he said. 'If I had my way he'd be shot of the lot of you. Plenty of men want jobs, you just remember that.'

Ethan closed his eyes and leaned back against the wall. He felt drained of everything. Energy, patience, hope. He felt rather than heard Frank slip quietly away, his thoughts turning to Helen. He knew Hanson senior would go calling on her kin later and that her mam was quick with both her tongue and her hand. Grown up as she was, Helen still lived under her parents' roof so she wasn't too big she could avoid a beating. Ethan allowed a moment of sympathy to sit alongside his annoyance and fear.

All in all, though he too would have words – only words – with Helen next time they met, he could not find it in his heart to blame her overmuch. He understood how she felt and what had drawn her there that day. They were putting everyone in a bad position, Ethan knew, and that could not go on, but his feelings for Helen were as lacking in control as were hers for him. Helen pulled him like a spring tide is pulled by the moon and he could not resist.

Twenty-Seven

Henry had arrived at court to be told that Symmonds had finally lodged a guilty plea and he was not required. He went into the central office and made his report then prepared to catch the train north once again. Symmonds' sudden change of mind puzzled him and he requested permission to see the man.

Symmonds was now in the condemned man's cell. He looked up as Henry entered the cell but did not stand or even seem to react.

'You remember me?' Henry asked.

'Of course I do.'

'I've just returned to London – been called from a murder I'm investigating, expecting to have to give evidence against you in court, and now I find that you've changed your plea.'

'If I've caused you inconvenience, then I'm sorry for it.' Symmonds looked away from Henry. He'd been reading a newspaper, examining the racing pages, Henry noticed in some surprise. It seemed of more interest to Haydn Symmonds than his visitor.

'What changed your mind?' Henry asked him. 'All the evidence was in place, witnesses and accomplices all testified to you being there and yet you continued to deny your guilt. So, I'm asking you, what changed your mind?'

Haydn Symmonds looked up again but Henry could see the irritation in his eyes. Symmonds placed a finger on the newspaper as though to mark his place then finally awarded Henry his full attention.

He sighed. 'You reckon I'd have had my day in court and then be found guilty,' he said.

'I think there's no doubt of that.'

'So there's your answer.'

'No, that was true before and you were adamant you'd go through with it. That you would stick with your plea of innocence no matter what.' Henry came closer, leaned on the table and glanced down at the newspaper Symmonds had been reading. 'What changed your mind?' he asked again.

'The way you see it, I was going to hang anyway.'

'I thought that was the most likely outcome.'

'You see, I always knew that would come about. That they'd stretch my neck along with the others.'

'The others. Your accomplices?'

Haydn Symmonds nodded. 'It's all going to end up the same, ain't it? All of us dead. Them pair, they figured they could sell me out and get off without it being a hanging matter, but I knew. I knew the truth of it, didn't I?'

Henry frowned. 'You knew that turning king's

156

evidence wouldn't be enough to save them. Is that what you mean?'

'Yes, that's what I mean. I was mad at them, see. They thought they could put all the blame on me and walk away. I weren't having that. I might know I was guilty as hell but I weren't going to say so, not to give them no satisfaction from it. Then I hear they've come to court and the judge put on his black cap and condemned them anyway.'

'So I heard.'

'So, nothing more to fight for, is there? I can't win but neither can that pair of lying bastards.'

'They didn't lie, though, did they?' Henry reminded him. 'You were guilty.'

Haydn Symmonds had lost interest now. His attention turned back to the racing form.

Henry, understanding that he would receive no further enlightenment, left him to it.

He took the opportunity of going home and packing fresh shirts and then made his way back to the station and caught the next train. Haydn Symmonds troubled him – not because he was about to hang but because he had provided Henry with no clear answers.

Henry opened his book and uncapped his pen. So, he mused . . .

What does cause a man to confess? For some it is the unbearable weight of guilt. They have committed an act they know to be unjust or barbaric and it is better to confess than try to live with the guilt.

For others, a partial confession is as far as they might be prepared to go. They say 'Officer,

I stole this but not that. I did this but resisted that' as though there are set boundaries to the guilt they are prepared to accept and that which they are not. As though this somehow impinges upon their very identity.

In his book on criminal psychology, Dr Hans Gross, if I may paraphrase him, says that a confession is only of value if all evidentiary material, including possible motive, matches that which is confessed. The inner workings of the miscreant's mind must tally with that of the external and objective evidence. In other words, the accused must accept the accusation, have acknowledged it on some internal level. What Gross calls the inner life of the accused must be brought into focus to match that of the external, objective life.

I have spent many a long hour in the interrogation room striving to make that match with suspects who will argue that black is white and night is day and can be shown any measure of clock or sunlight and still be adamant that it is dark outside. And while they maintain that accord, that difference between the inner life and the external world, there is nothing to be done to shift them no matter what evidence there may be to the contrary.

It takes time to find the chink through which the light can filter. To break through into the inner world and so have an impact upon it.

I was not fully satisfied with the reasons Symmonds gave for a change of plea but I am curious as to what altered. Who found the key to Symmonds' inner kingdom and how? Was it, as he said, that he waited for the others to be found guilty, that he needed the satisfaction of knowing that before he could admit to his own guilt?

What will provide the key to the inner kingdom of whoever killed Mary Fields and her family? Will there be a confession or will the discovery come through some minor mistake; the button or the fibres or the candlestick, should we manage to find that?

Perhaps we should be asking a different question. What, aside from financial gain, drove Mary Fields to sell herself when she had a husband and a child who loved her and whom, by all accounts, she loved too? Was it simply a need for money or was it something stronger, more personal? Some inner sense that the world owed her more or that life had cheated her in some way?

That certainly does seem to have been true in Symmonds' case. He was quite open about his motive when questioned. He wanted money and he wanted to prove that he could do something outside the mundane, the ordinary. He chose, unwisely and unskilfully, to rob a bank – alongside others who were equally unskilful and unwise.

It occurs to me that that might have been his issue with acknowledging his guilt. That to do so would have tarred him with the same brush as his confederates. Symmonds wanted to be set apart, to be acknowledged as better than the ordinary.

Did Mary Fields want the same acknowledgement?

159

Did her killer?

Did she do something, say something that made the man she was with afraid of exposure? Or was it simply that she let the wrong man into her home? A man who wished to kill and who thought that the likes of Mary Fields mattered less because of what she was?

Closing his notebook, he prepared to re-read the letters George had given to him, setting aside the ones from Ruby and Mary and focusing on those sent by the now-deceased Walter.

Walter Fields wrote with a flowing, confident and very neat hand, and Henry sensed a degree of intelligence there. He had spoken briefly with Walter's boss at the Road Car company and the man had spoken highly of him. He worked hard, showed aptitude and was expected to move from general maintenance to fully fledged engineer given time, but the man knew nothing of Walter outside of work and he seemed to have had no close friends at the company.

They had known nothing of Mary Fields beyond the fact that Walter had said he had relatives in Louth that he liked to visit regularly.

Dear George, Walter wrote, *I wish I could give you better news. Mary and Ruby are both well but she has not been behaving as she should. I'm sorry to say that your woman won't be told, won't be advised and says she will do as she wishes and that I am not her husband and therefore should not try to tell her what to do.*

I know that the neighbours are gossiping. I'm worried that she will be forced to move on again.

This had been written, Henry noted, before

160

they had moved to what would be their final home.

I've tried to get names out of her but she won't say and I've kept watch as best I can. There was one man that I know works at an estate agency near the market and another that I think manages a hotel. I think his name is Williams but she keeps telling me that she will do what she wants and that you don't earn enough to keep her and Ruby. She says she loves you but that she can't go on living hand to mouth like the rest of us do.

She keeps saying she wants to go back home to Newark and be with her people and I think that might be for the best, George. Your woman isn't going to change any time soon and at least there'd be other people to keep an eye on her there.

She keeps asking me if I'll look after Ruby because she's been offered some hotel work some- where but she won't tell me where and I keep telling her how can I look after our Ruby when I have to work? I can hardly take her back to my lodging house, can I? And if I stay with her in your rooms how is that going to look to everyone?

I'm sorry, George but I don't want to look like one of Mary's men. I'm sorry to have to be so blunt about it but once someone gets a reputation it rubs off all over the place and I have to tell you that I'm worried for our little Ruby. Mary don't seem to understand or she don't want to.

I got in the habit of just popping in when she's got one of them with her, to make sure she's all right. George, I hate to do this. I go in and I stand there just listening and making sure that she's all right but I hate it, George, and I'm telling you now: you come home and take care of your Mary and Ruby and find some work somewhere else, even if that means going down south, because you can't expect me to keep doing this no more.

Henry folded the letter. The others were in a similar vein though some also talked about other, neutral events, such as a film he had seen or a girl he had chatted to at Hubbard's Hills when he'd walked out there one Sunday.

It was, Henry thought, a strange and unbearable responsibility for a nineteen-year-old boy to have been given. It did explain how he came to be in the house that night, though.

Henry put the letters back into his pocket, found his cigarette case and lit a cigarette. He stroked the initials crudely engraved upon the case. The A and the G. He had been nineteen when he'd died too. In a fox hole, drowning in his own blood.

Twenty-Eight

July had started hot and dry. The parched land sizzled beneath a heat haze and Dar predicted an early harvest.

'Though,' he warned, 'we'd best be quick about it when the time comes. Once the heat breaks the rains will come hard.'

Squinting up at a pale blue sky, the sun a vicious ball of yellow fire that scorched his skin

162

and dried the moisture from his mouth and eyes, Ethan found that hard to believe. But Dar's record was impeccable.

'You told the boss?'

Dar nodded slowly. 'I told him and he wanted me to pass summat on to you.'

Ethan's belly knotted. 'What?' he asked warily.

'Nothing bad, boy. He wanted you to know he'll take you on proper like after the harvest and there's a little place out Towes way he thought you and the lass might want. I know the place he means. Just the one room down and the same up, but it's got a bit of good land to the side of it and it'll start you off better than you've either of you the right to hope.'

'He's offering that?' Ethan was astonished.

'He's offering and I've accepted for you. Tell the lass when you see her if her mam hasn't told her first. Like I say, it's over towards Towes, a good walk from anywhere, but it's still Hanson's ground. He's looking to expand his stock, make better use of some land he's bought out that way and he likes the way you have with the beasts.'

'He said that?'

'Don't let it go to your head, lad,' Dar warned. Then he nodded and Ethan saw the gleam of pride in his eyes. 'He said that,' Dar conceded, 'so I got to thinking.'

He paused and Ethan waited. He sensed something important was about to happen. More important even than the news his dad had just imparted. They kept pace with one another, father and son, tramping the hard baked and heavily rutted way up to Hanson's farm. Finally Dar

163

paused beneath the tree where Ethan and Frank had fought on that rainy evening.

'Your mam and me, we got nothing much to give as a wedding gift,' he said. 'Your mam and Helen's have got their heads together and there'll be a few bits of stuff to set you up and Hanson's putting some sticks of furniture in the place, just to get you going. So I thought it was time you had this.'

Dar reached into the pack he'd been carrying and took out a faded green book.

Ethan recognized it at once.

'No, Dar. No. I couldn't be taking that.'

'I want you to, boy.' Dar flicked through the yellowed pages. 'Look, lad, I've written me own notes and observations on the spare pages and in the margins. It's a good book and my dad gave it to me way back like. Time now to pass it on.'

Reverently, Ethan took the little book into his hands and stared down at it, feeling as though he'd been handed some holy relic. Apart from the family Bible, in which were recorded the births and deaths and marriages of generations of his kin, and the Book of Common Prayer that his mother took to church, this was the only book they owned. '*Clater's Farrier*,' he read. He turned the pages, gazing, as though for the first time, at the pages dedicated to the care of horses and the tricks of the dealers and the home remedies and cures for all manner of ailments, both in man and beast and at the little notes, written in Dar's tight, clear hand.

'Oh, Dar.' He felt tears pricking at his lids and

164

blinked them away. More came and he wiped the back of his hand across his eyes, not caring now if his father saw.

'I'll cherish it,' he said. 'Always, Dar.'

His father nodded and turned back on to the path. Ethan buried the precious book deep in his own pack and followed on, then falling into step beside him. Nothing more was said on the way but Ethan's heart sang. He had the woman he loved promised to him. He had a place for them to live and work at a time when employment was scarce as gold. More than that, it was as though his dad had finally acknowledged that he was a man. An almost equal, or at least someone with the potential to become so.

Ethan looked up, rejoicing at the light blue sky, and thought of Helen Lee.

Twenty-Nine

The previous summer, Ted had persuaded his father to buy a car. Elijah Hanson had been reluctant at first but Ted had convinced him of the time it would save and Robert, for once in agreement with his brother, voiced the belief that it could only add to his father's status as landowner.

Between them, they had persuaded Elijah to purchase an Austin seven. In blue.

Most of its life was spent in the end stables, the block no longer used for the draft horses

Elijah now housed at the Glebe farm. It was covered with a tarpaulin, polished weekly whether it had been used or not, and Ted took it out for a spin twice a month or so.

It *had* proved its usefulness, Elijah admitted. Faster than a horse and a lot dryer though the winter ice had proved too much for its hard tyres and they'd been just as trapped when the snow fell as they ever had with simple horsepower.

That July day, though, when Ethan and his father arrived at the farm, they were surprised to see the car out in the yard and Ted tinkering with something under the bonnet.

'You off somewhere?' Ethan asked him casually. No one stood on ceremony with Ted Hanson. Ethan respected him, certainly, but it was still hard to separate the boy he'd gone to school with and the boss's son.

Ted grinned. 'Off to Louth,' he said. 'So is dad and so's Dar, once he's finished breakfast.'

'I am?' Dar eyed the vehicle with suspicion. 'In that?'

Ted laughed. 'You trust yourself to old Herbert and the carrier's cart,' he said. 'I'm a far better driver. I promise you that.'

'Only when I've no option and I don't doubt you're a better driver. Herbert don't take a lot of beating.'

Ethan laughed. Herbert Deal had been one of the first in the district to motorize, trading his carrier's cart for something resembling a bus. It transported, as the cart had done, people and goods, letters and parcels. Even the odd cage of

166

chickens. Herbert drove the vehicle like he'd driven his horses. Badly.

'What's at Louth today?' Ethan asked.

'Dad's had word of a mare he might buy. Wants Dar to give it the once-over. She's in foal, apparently, but there's been a difference of opinion as to when she's likely to drop. The vetinry's inspected her and says one thing; seller insists another so . . .'

Ethan nodded. Dar would adjudicate and Dar would, like as not, be right though, Ethan knew, he'd manage to be right in such a way as to put no one's nose out of joint. Dar was expert in such diplomacy.

'Is the mare for Miss Elizabeth?' Ethan asked. 'She's outgrowing her pony.'

'Elizabeth is growing like a weed,' Ted agreed about his sister. 'And she's a good horsewoman. Dad reckons she'll soon be ready for something a bit more demanding. By the time the foal's weaned Elizabeth will have got to know the dam and hopefully they'll make a good pair.' He slammed down the bonnet of the car with a satisfied nod. 'All set. Best get yourselves fed; boss is eager to be off.'

'Put Robert's nose out of joint all right,' Ethan commented softly as they walked away, 'if the master favours his girl with a new beast. You know how he feels about that animal of his.'

Dar snorted. 'Me, I'd not trust him with anything what can feel,' he said. 'Mister Robert doesn't give a damn for anything.' He shook his head. 'He's a throwback, that one. Like his great granddad.'

Ethan glanced with interest at his father. Like as not Dar was too young to recall Robert's great grandfather, but the village memory, that collective river of knowledge, flowed strongly in Dar's veins and Ethan had no doubt his father knew the truth of the matter.

Ethan was disappointed when Dar clamped his jaw tightly shut but not surprised. They had reached the kitchen door and the sounds of frying bacon, cutlery against plates and the hum of conversation reached them through the opening. This was not a conversation to be carried on inside.

Ethan smiled. Hanson was a good man to work for, he thought. Kept the old ways and it was as well, he thought, that it would be Ted and not Robert who would inherit. The likes of Robert were just ruin to good land.

The morning passed quietly. The first harvest had already begun but Elijah had left a string of tasks for both Frank and Ethan which would keep them close to the house for most of the morning.

Ethan was surprised at first; this time of year all hands, from those of the smallest child to the oldest of elders was needed to bring the harvest home and to have two able-bodied men tied up elsewhere was a strange thing.

It only occurred to him later that Elijah Hanson had a purpose in mind. That he had arranged this time for Frank and Ethan to make their peace with each other and, as they worked their way through the tasks Elijah had set them, it seemed

168

to Ethan that a truce if not a peace had been reached between them.

'I wish you both well, you know,' Frank said slowly, his hands busy with the harness he was stitching and his eyes, too, fastened on the task.

'Thank you for that,' Ethan told him. 'We never meant to hurt no one, Helen and me.'

'Can't control what your heart tells you to do,' Frank said. 'My fault, anyway. If I wanted the lass I should have shouted louder, shouldn't I?'

Ethan made no answer, knowing none was expected. Their wedding would now be a scant few weeks away and Ethan felt each second drag as though it was itself a minute; every minute like an hour.

A shout and a curse brought him from his thoughts. 'What the hell was that?'

Frank set the harness aside. 'Robert,' he said. 'Missus said he'd not come home last night.'

Together, they went out into the yard. Robert was in the field adjoining the farm. Obviously drunk and barely able to keep in the saddle, he wheeled his horse and set it to take another run at the fence – an uphill run, challenging even for a well-trained and ridden hunter. Too much for a badly ridden beast with self-preservation uppermost in its equine brain.

Robert beat about the horse's neck and head with his crop. He dragged at the bit, pulling its head this way and that. He urged it on with curses and with heels and yet held it back with his tugging and tearing at the reins, seeming not to notice the contradiction.

'What the hell?' Frank began, but Ethan, furious

at Robert's treatment of the much-abused beast and incensed by the sheer stupidity of the man, had begun to run.

'Ethan!' Frank warned. 'You aint goin' to do no good like that. You get back here and I'll fetch the missus.'

But Ethan either didn't hear or didn't want to. He vaulted the gate, raced to where the horse wheeled and turned, refusing the jump despite his master's curses.

There was blood on the crop, Ethan saw as he drew close. Blood close to the horse's eyes and running down the neck. Robert clung to the reins and saddle and a handful of mane. How he kept his seat at all amazed Ethan.

'Whadda you want, Samuels?' Roberts shouted. 'You get outta my bloody way.'

Ethan ignored him. He reached for the reins and found himself on the receiving end of the riding crop. It cut across his cheek.

'You want more, Samuels?' Robert laughed high and loud. 'Think that little tart of yours would like her man so much with a scarred face?' He leaned from the saddle, towards Ethan, and said in a loud and spit-laden whisper, 'From what I hear, though, she ain't that particular.'

Ethan grabbed him and pulled him from the saddle. He landed with a dull thud and a sharp crack. The riding crop was in Ethan's hand now and he brought it down hard on Robert's face. Once, twice, three times, satisfied to see the blood well and seep from the wounds he was inflicting. It occurred to him in a vague sort of way as strange that Robert did not bring up his hands to defend himself, but then Frank was pulling him away, dragging at Ethan's hair in an effort to keep hold as Ethan's fury, bent only on Robert's destruction, continued to rain down on the face and neck of his fallen enemy.

'Ethan! Ethan! For God's sake.'

Something permeated Ethan's consciousness and he let his hand fall to his sides, then turned to look into Frank's horrified face.

'You killed him, boy,' Frank whispered softly. 'You fucking killed him.'

Ethan blinked. He'd never heard Frank curse. Frank didn't curse. What was so wrong that it made Frank curse?

'Look at him,' Frank insisted. 'Ethan, look what you done. You gone and killed him.'

Ethan looked. Robert's face was a pulp of blood and broken bone and the sudden awareness of pain in his own knuckles told Ethan that he'd followed through with his fists. The broken crop lay on the ground beside Robert's hand.

His stomach heaved and vomit, sour and acrid, rose in his throat.

'Oh my God, what have I done?'

Frank was shaking him.

'Never mind what you done, it's what you're going to do. They'll hang you, lad. Hang you without another thought.'

Ethan swallowed but the vomit continued to rise. 'Hang me?'

'You bloody killed him. They'll say it's murder, Ethan.'

'But I . . .'

'He hit his head, didn't you hear the crack?'

'I . . .' Dimly, Ethan recalled the noise of Robert's fall. 'But I didn't mean . . .'

'No? Beat seven shades out of him while he lie there? You think they'll believe you didn't mean to do it?'

'But you said he'd hit his head. That was an accident, Frank.'

'And if it'd stayed at that, just a fall, I'd have said the bloody horse threw him. No one would have thought no different. But I can't say the horse picked up the crop and set about him and even I can tell the difference between fists and hooves. Hell, man, what were you thinking?'

'I wasn't . . . wasn't thinking. God, Frank, what am I to do?'

'Get the hell out, that's what you'll do. Just get the hell away.'

'Away? But Helen, but . . .'

Ethan stared at Frank Church and he knew that Helen was lost to him. This place was lost to him. This time, these hopes. Everything. 'No,' he whispered. 'I can't go. I can't leave her.'

'If you stay then the last memory she'll have of you will be you twisting in the wind. You want that for her?'

'Maybe he's not dead. Maybe he's not.'

Frank sighed and knelt down beside the body. He put his fingers to Robert's throat and then to his wrist. 'If you can find a pulse, boy, you're better than I am. Ethan, you've got to go.'

It occurred to Ethan that Frank was lying, that he was only saying that Robert was dead in order to get rid of him, but as he went closer and knelt beside the man with the pulped and mangled

172

face, he found he could not bear to touch it. He stared hard at the chest but there was no sign of the rising and fall. No sign of breath bubbled between the bruised and swollen lips, though, to be truthful, his eyes were so filled with tears he could not have trusted them to see.

'Ethan,' Frank was pleading. They'd soon be missed. There was little time and they could only trust to luck that no one in the house had heard the noise. Luck and the fact that the field dropped away from the yard and gave some shelter. The sounds that had been clear when they'd first heard them were muffled only because they were at the end of the yard.

Ethan nodded and took off at a run. He stopped to gather up his jacket and his pack and then he was gone, cutting between the fields, following the shortcuts he knew from a life of living in the valley, unsure of his direction but knowing that Frank was right and he had no choice.

He had killed a man and he would hang for it.

He would run, he told himself. Run until he'd reached a place of safety and one day he would send for Helen. She'd come to him, he knew she would. She'd walk through fire and water just to be with him.

And when he could run no more, he dropped to his knees in the dirt and wept as though his heart would break.

Frank stood beside the prone form of Robert Hanson and he watched. And as he watched he understood that he had lied. Robert Hanson wasn't dead, not quite, not yet. If Frank ran now, got help, had him taken to the farm and called a doctor, might there be some chance?

Frank watched as the life ebbed from Robert – the last spark began to fade. It took longer than he'd expected, though, Frank thought. It was difficult to judge the passage of time in such circumstances. He knew the sun had moved from one tree to the next, to the next, to the next. And then, just before, just at that last moment before the glow went out, just before Frank was sure it had been extinguished for ever, Frank drew back his foot and, with all the strength and hatred he could muster, he kicked Robert Hanson in the head.

Thirty

The lies came with surprising ease. Frank was unsure how much time had passed by the time he ran back to the farm to report Robert's death. No more than half an hour, he guessed, but by the time he'd run back up the hill, across the yard and burst through the kitchen door he had wound himself into such a state of distress that he did not have to pretend.

We killed him, Frank thought. Killed him between us and they'll know. Won't they? Won't they know?

'Frank? What on earth? Oh my Lord, what is it?'

Mrs Hanson stared, seeing the blood on his

clothes and the sweat on his face. 'Frank,' she commanded. 'Sit down and let me see.'

'It ain't me, missus. It's the boy. Robert. It's Robert.'

That stopped her in her tracks, and Frank saw in her eyes that she had almost been waiting for that news. She had lived knowing that Robert would come to grief and Frank's heart sank. If Ethan had just let him fall and then let him alone . . .

But the fall hadn't killed him, had it? Frank reminded himself. It wasn't the fall, it was the beating Ethan had given him when he was already on the ground. That and the final kick Frank had delivered. That and the time Frank had waited.

Margaret Hanson had stopped staring at him and begun to move again, calling Jenny who worked in the kitchen to bring water and bandages and shouting at Miss Elizabeth to get someone to go for the doctor.

'I'll go,' Frank told her. Suddenly he didn't want to go back into the field, didn't want to see again what he had left there. 'I'll get the doctor. But missus, don't you go. Send someone else. Please.'

She drew herself up, her stern look admonishing him. 'Frank Church, I'm not a silly girl. I don't need protecting. Take me to him then go and fetch help. Anyway, if I'd a mind to send someone else, there's no bugger here, is there?' She frowned. 'I thought Ethan was with you. Did you leave him with the boy?'

The boy, Frank thought. Her boy, though truth

was Robert was the same age as Ethan and only a little younger than Frank. But yes, he was a boy. Irresponsible and stupid as a child. 'No,' he managed. 'Ethan is . . .'

'Just take me to Robert,' Margaret Hanson commanded. 'You can tell me the rest when I've tended to my son.'

'Missus . . . it's too late for that. I'm sorry, it's too late.'

She stared at him, the colour draining from her face and the fierce light in her eyes fading like a guttered candle. Fading like Robert had done, Frank thought.

'He was drunk, wasn't he? Mazzled again.'

Frank hesitated, then jerked a nod.

'Did he fall? Oh, Lord.' She was on her feet again and heading for the door; Jenny, her eyes protruding frog-like from a sallow face, bustled behind, her mouth twitching with the questions she wanted to ask.

Miss Elizabeth, twelve years old and tall like her father, stood in the doorway and Frank realized belatedly that she had heard it all.

Frank closed his eyes. This could not be happening. Surely he was dreaming all this and would wake in a sweat with the sun streaming through his window and the nightmare would fade and—

Elizabeth came over and clasped her mother's arm. 'I'll go for the doctor anyway,' she said. 'Don't worry,' she added, 'I can saddle Spry.'

She glanced at Frank and nodded. 'You take care of Ma and I'll cut by the top field, get some men back here.'

So calm, Frank thought. Just a kid and yet the clearest headed of them all.

Her mother nodded, rushing now to the kitchen door. Hurrying as though they'd delayed too long and she'd ground to make up.

Elizabeth turned to Frank and laid a small hand on his sleeve.

'What, miss?'

'Ethan's gone, hasn't he?' she said. 'Ethan Samuels. Has he gone?'

Frank gaped at her, not fully understanding why she'd asked or why she should think that. Then he nodded. 'Ethan's gone.' He almost choked on the words. She pushed past him and headed for the stables. Frank scurried after Margaret Hanson and steeled himself to look once more at the battered face of her youngest son.

It was late afternoon and Elijah, Ted and Dar Samuels had returned. The lies still came easy. Easier than he would ever have thought. Perhaps, Frank considered, that was because they weren't really lies, simply omissions, simply small adjustments in the timing. Simply . . .

'I told you, sir.' Exhausted now, worn out by repetition, though each repetition of the story wore the groove of it more firmly in his mind and made it seem more real, more exact, more right.

'We heard a shout and went out. Mister Robert wanted the horse to take the gate – beating at it, he was, urging it on up the hill but dragging on its mouth so the poor beast had no chance.

Mad as hell, Ethan was. You know how he regards the beasts. He was up and racing to Mister Robert before I could say a word.'

He lifted his gaze and met Dar's eyes. Dar stood by the door with his cap twisted in his hands, wrung out between bony, work-hardened fingers.

'He grabbed the riding crop and hit Mister Robert with it. Hit him hard and more than once, that mad, he was. Mister Robert fell and I think the horse must have kicked out at him as he fell. Horse was between me and Mister Robert and I couldn't see so clear. I was running towards them and when I got to the spot, Ethan was leaning over Mister Robert and his face was bloody. Bloody and broken. Like he'd been trampled.'

'You saw the horse trample him?' Elijah Hanson demanded once again.

'I told you, sir, I was on the other side of the horse, running towards them and I didn't see clear, like.' Frank was hoping against hope that the assumption would be that the horse had trodden on the fallen man, though even as he suggested it Frank knew it was unlikely to fool anyone. He didn't want to say he'd seen Ethan punch the man. Didn't want them to think he might have been able to stop him. Didn't want . . . what didn't he want? Frank wasn't really certain any more.

'And then Ethan ran away,' Elijah Hanson said, his voice flat and deathly calm.

'My son wouldn't run.' It was the first time Dar had spoken. 'Ethan wouldn't just up and run.'

Elijah's shoulder's stiffened but it was Ted that replied. 'I'm sorry, Dar, but that's the way it looks just now.'

'When the police catch up with him they'll make him say what happened,' Elijah said. 'But let me tell you, Dar – I seen my boy's face and the damage to it weren't done by no horseshoes.'

'You're accusing Ethan of murder?' Dar said flatly.

'I'm calling it as I see it, Dar.'

Dar Samuels sighed then, abruptly, he stopped twisting his cap, unscrewed it and slapped it back on his head.

'Where you off to?' Elijah demanded.

'Goin' to find my son,' Dar announced. 'No Samuels runs. None ever have and I ain't going to let it happen now.'

For a moment it looked as though Elijah might try and stop him, then he waved a dismissive hand at Dar's retreating back and dropped down on to the overstuffed chair beside the empty grate.

'Someone should tell Helen Lee,' Ted observed. 'Frank, you reckon he'd have gone there?'

Frank shook his head. 'Took off towards Louth,' he said. 'Across the field at the back of the house.' He rose to his feet. 'I'll tell Helen,' he said. 'What there is to tell. Best she hears it from me.'

He glanced back at Elijah Hanson and his family, silent in their collective grief, and he left the farm, knowing he'd have to repeat his story to the police later and that it would be so hard. But first he had to reveal his version of the truth to Helen Lee, and that would be harder still.

179

Thirty-One

Henry's train got in mid-afternoon. Mickey met him at the station and briefed him on the events of the past few days as they walked back to the King's Head.

'And what are your thoughts about this man, Fry?' Henry asked. 'Do you think him capable of getting rid of her and the child?'

'I do.' Mickey hesitated for a moment. 'But I think it would be more his style just to pay them off, to give the woman money to go away and hope that would be the end of it. But I may be wrong.'

'And have you met his partner yet?'

Mickey shook his head. 'No, but I'm reckoning him to be cut from the same cloth.'

'And you're discounting the other two.'

'In as much as I discount anyone, yes.'

Henry told him what he'd read in the letters and that there was another possible name that should be investigated, but that it would mean trawling all the hotels and pubs in the area to find a man possibly called Williams.

'Of course, local knowledge would be of use here but I suspect your Constable Parkin might be better suited for that task than anyone that Carrington might recommend.'

'You really don't like that man, do you?' Mickey said.

'There is nothing to like about some people.'

They walked in silence for a little while, then Henry said, 'And so George Fields is doing his own investigation after all. I don't imagine he'll be dissuaded.'

'Would you be?'

'I think the man feels he has nothing left to lose. In such a mind, *reason* does not come into it. It would have been right to have locked him up for breach of the peace if only for his own safety. I can see this ending badly.'

'Well, it started that way, so why not?'

Henry nodded. Why not indeed.

Thirty-Two

It was as though all colour had been bled from the day, Frank thought. He tramped back down the hill towards the village, feet reluctant and yet seeming to be possessed of their own will, one in front of the other, placed square and deliberate like, taking him down to Helen.

Frank tried to get events in order. He'd taken Mrs Hanson into the field and stood back, watching as she examined her son, turning his face with gentle hands, crooning over him like a new mother with her babe. He and Jenny, the kitchen maid, had stood away, standing close enough that he could feel the hairs rising on Jenny's arms as she grew cold in the heat of the afternoon.

181

Frank had lost track of time.

Later, Mrs Hanson had sent Jenny back to the house for a sheet but she'd kept Frank close by. Not that she'd told him to stay, Frank remembered, just given him that look. That look, so like his mother's 'look' that said, *Don't you move from there, Frank Church. You just stay where I've put you till I tell you different.* And so Frank had stayed and watched and had been relieved when Jenny came back with the freshly laundered sheet and they had laid it over the dead man, covered his ruined face and his bloody hair and his pale, bloodless hands.

Only then had Frank gone to catch Robert's horse. It was standing, quiet enough, close by the gate Robert had tried to make it jump. It whickered in welcome as Frank took hold of the reins and led it to the stables. Frank fed it and rubbed the sweat from its body with an old sack, then covered it with a stable blanket, sensing that the animal felt as chilled and iced up inside as did Frank himself. It was as though the heat of the day could no longer touch any of them. It was deflected, bounced back like rain on a roof.

Frank felt he might be chilled to the bone like this all his life through.

Then Miss Elizabeth had arrived with some men from the top field with the doctor in his car following a few minutes behind and then . . . Dar and Hanson senior and Ted, Robert's brother. Someone had been sent to find the constable and Frank had been taken into the parlour – a place Frank had never done more than glimpse at through the open door until today – and Hanson had questioned him over and over again. And Frank had constructed his story and he'd stuck to it. Stuck so close he no longer doubted the truth. He had seen Robert fall and the horse had been between Frank and Ethan, blocking his view.

He erased from his conscious mind that image, which he knew, despite his efforts, would still surface in his dreams, of Ethan's rage, blind and utterly bent on destruction as he had beaten Robert's face so hard with the crop that it broke in Ethan's grasp and then he'd started in with his fists, hitting and hitting until his hands were bloody and Robert's features all but obliterated.

Had Frank moved to stop him?

No.

Frank closed his eyes, remembering.

Too shocked at first to move, Frank had watched, slack-jawed and horrified and then . . . and then he'd just watched. Watched until slowly it dawned on him, as though the thought came from another place, that he really ought to stop this before it was too late.

Then, as that thought had struck, so had the realization that it was already too late. Much too late. Only then had the panic set in. The shock and the fear. Fear that he was implicated if he didn't at least try to control Ethan now.

Frank groaned. What was he to tell Helen? She'd hate Frank for being the bearer of such news.

Why had he offered to go and speak with her? The truth dawned; Helen would have hated him even more if he'd left it to Hanson or his son.

Frank shivered. He looked up into the blue sky and watched as it darkened to grey. Even though there was not a cloud to be seen, something hid the sun and blocked the warmth of it. Frank clutched his jacket close about his wiry body and stumbled on, feet still with a mind of their own, one before the other, until he found himself rapping hard on the Lees' door.

Helen's mother opened it. Frank saw the question rise to her lips and then the horror in her eyes.

The blood on his shirt, Frank realized. He still had blood on his shirt.

She stood back and Frank passed by her and sat down, uninvited, at the kitchen table.

'Helen!' he heard the mother calling. 'Helen, come quick.'

And Helen came. She hurried through the door, a basket of clean washing tucked beneath her arm. One look at Frank's face and she dropped it to the floor.

'It's Ethan, isn't it?' she said. 'Oh, God, what's happened to him?'

Frank had rehearsed and rehearsed but now, faced with Helen Lee, his words came out all wrong.

'Ethan's gone,' he whispered. 'Helen, Ethan's had to go. He killed Robert Hanson and now he's gone.'

Questions, more questions, and now he was back on track, on familiar ground, it was so easy

184

to lie. He repeated what he'd told the Hansons. Repeated it again when Helen screamed at him that it could not be true. Told it once more when her mother sat down, calm as she could manage and questioned him more closely, clinging on his every word as though a simple change of phrase could undo what he was saying.

Then he told it again as Helen's dad burst through the door. It was news all around the village now and he'd heard, then come back to tell his wife and child before another got to them.

'He had to go,' Frank said at last. 'Helen, they'd have hanged him ifn he'd stayed. I telled him, "Go. She don't want to see you hanged."'

Helen stared at him. Betrayed. Frank tried to meet her gaze but there was so much misery in it, so much pain, he had to look away.

'I'd better go,' he said. 'Mister Hanson's called for the constable. He said I'd best get back to the farm to talk to him.'

He stood. Hanson had told him no such thing but it was the sensible thing to do and Frank was grateful of another half lie to hide behind.

The Lees said nothing. Did not move as Frank crossed to the door and let himself out. Only Helen's mother pulled herself back, as though she didn't want to risk being touched by the man who brought such contamination into their house.

He closed the door softly and replaced his cap, tugged the jacket tight across his shoulders and turned back towards the farm. He glanced down the street towards Red Row and the Samuels' cottage, wondering if Ethan's family knew by now. If Dar had come back and told them.

Frank shivered like a man with fever and once the shivering began found he couldn't stop. His body shook and his feet felt loose and unsteady beneath him. With the greatest effort, he directed them back on to the track that led to Hanson's farm and wondered, his gut twisting with the fear of it as he struggled up the hill, how far Ethan would get before they caught him and if, when they did, it would come out that Frank had lied.

Thirty-Three

Ted remembered what had been said in the papers about the inspector and his sergeant coming up from London. He told his father.

'Get back in the car, get yourself to Louth and bring him back here. I don't want no one else. I want the murder detective.'

Ted nodded and, moments later, was turning the car in the yard and on his way again.

Still later, Dar Samuels returned. There had been no sign of Ethan. He stood in the yard, hesitating until Elizabeth spotted him and came out to greet him. She laid a hand on his arm. 'Come along in, Dar. No one would blame you, not ever. We all know you are a good man. And we don't know the whole story yet.'

Dar looked down at the child who seemed suddenly to have grown up and be standing on the verge of womanhood. 'Thank you, Miss

Elizabeth,' he said and allowed her to lead him into the kitchen. It felt as though his legs were about to give way and he felt sick to his stomach. He knew that there had always been enmity between Ethan and Robert but what had happened that had transformed enmity into intent to kill?

Inside the kitchen he looked around and noticed an absence. 'Where's Frank?' he asked.

'Gone to tell Helen Lee what's gone on,' Elizabeth told him. 'He volunteered for it so we let him go.'

Dar Samuels nodded. Somehow that didn't sound right, that Frank should have offered. There was something here that he did not yet understand, but whatever it was it would make little difference. His Ethan had killed his boss's son and whatever the provocation, there was no remedy for that.

Thirty-Four

The burning in his lungs and the acid ache in his legs eventually felled Ethan. He lay down in a dry ditch, crawled to a place that was overshadowed by long grass and an overgrowth of bramble and then allowed himself to relax.

His mind was numb. Numb and empty. His thoughts refused to form themselves into neat, sense-making lines. Instead they fragmented like worms chopped by a spade, continuing to wriggle and writhe and reach out, one part for the other, but unable to rejoin.

How far had he come?

Ethan was not sure. The position of the sun told him it was now late afternoon. The cheerful brightness of the light and blueness of the sky mocked him.

The police would be at Hanson's farm, Ethan thought. Fat constable Jenkins, who oversaw the everyday troubles of their small community and the villages round about, would have been called.

Ethan tried to imagine Jenkins handling this. Jenkins, whose major challenge to date had been a spot of chicken rustling, now faced with a killing.

Ethan groaned and turned on his side. He braced his back against one side of the ditch and drew his knees tight against the other. Maybe he could just stay here, lie here until the life leached out of him or the ditch filled with winter rain and drowned him.

He lay, listening to the quiet, the buzz of insects and the wind in the tall grass, the call of crows overhead and the sweet, repetitive song of the hedgerow birds, the blackbird always louder and more insistent than the rest.

He thought of that day with Helen, lying in the field, at risk of discovery and yet not caring. Too wrapped up in the moment and in the revelation of Helen's smooth-skinned body to care.

Ethan groaned and the groan brought tears. The tears fell, disregarded, and soaked into the grassy floor of the ditch. Slowly, grief gave way to sleep and Ethan fell into oblivion, hoping that he might never wake.

Thirty-Five

Constable Jenkins had arrived in the village and felt he ought to make a start on his investigation, even though he'd been told that the murder detective from London was being sent for. He now stood by the farmhouse fireplace, feet apart, shoulders squared, drawn to his full height and authority. But despite his repeated questions he wasn't getting very far.

'You say you've not seen him?'

'I told you, didn't I?' Helen was angry now. 'I ain't lying. I saw Ethan late yesterday when we came back home from the fields. I stayed back today to help Ma with the laundry. She takes in extra this time of year – you know that. I've been back and forth all day carrying water from Peter's spout spring to fill the copper and scrubbing shirts and sheets.'

Constable Jenkins nodded. Being a bachelor he was one of those glad to use Mrs Lee's services. 'But you've not seen him today?'

'I'm telling you, not today. Though if I had I'd have told him to run and to keep on running. Come to that, I might have gone with him too.'

'Helen!' Her mother's reproach, sharp as a slap, silenced Helen.

They'd all been summoned to the Hanson place. The Lees, the Samuels, the Churches. They all crushed into the parlour together with the Hansons and were asked the same things over and over again though it was clear from the outset, so far as Helen was concerned, that no one could add anything useful to Frank's statement, the story he had told Helen now formalized and written down by Constable Jenkins in his tight, cramped hand. This was just Jenkins covering his back, making sure he was seen to be doing his job.

'Well, you can tell that again to the inspector when he arrives,' Elijah Hanson told her sternly. 'This is not a trivial matter, girl. It's murder.'

Murder. Helen swallowed hard but continued to look defiant, though she suspected she probably just looked sulky like her mam was always telling her. Her brain buzzed like a hive of bees, buzzed and hummed and tore at the problem but it didn't get any better any way she looked at it.

She found it hard to believe that Ethan could have done this. Ethan, who had always been so gentle with her. Sure, he'd fought with Frank, but they had good reason and no one thought the worse of either of them for it. He'd been known to be a bit handy with his fists and a bit quick with his temper before he'd gone away to sea but no one thought there was anything uncommon in that. It was the way most boys were and the way all men became.

Elijah Hanson had insisted that she view the body, that she look at the face of his son and see what Ethan had done. Even so, her mind rebelled; she could not equate the Ethan she knew with such terrible violence.

'When will this inspector arrive?' Dar asked quietly.

190

Helen shot him a look. Dar had stood by the door since they'd all arrived. He'd been out looking for his son, Helen had been told, but not found him. It occurred to her that Dar might not have looked very hard and then she dismissed the thought at once. Dar would have looked and looked again. Dar would have moved mountains to find Ethan and bring him back because that was the honest thing to do and Dar was as honest as the day.

Helen stared down at her feet, at the expensive red and blue woven carpet that covered the parlour floor, not wanting to catch the man's eye. Not wanting to see the pain-induced grey pallor which seemed to have blanched the sun-browned face.

'He'll be here tonight,' Elijah Hanson said. 'Be here tonight and be staying for as long as it takes.'

He spoke with the confidence of one who knew what service his money could buy, even from a public official.

'He and his team.' Hanson put emphasis on the word, letting all know that the inspector would not be alone. That this was far too important a task for even an inspector to tackle by himself. 'He and his team will be stopping here until Ethan Samuels is found and justice is seen to be done.'

Helen sneaked another look at Dar. She saw him nod sharply and then jerk his head towards his wife.

'You know where I'll be,' he said to Elijah. 'I'm off home. We've left the young un's longer than we should. I'll be out first light after Ethan.

191

Tell the inspector that when he gets here. If he wants to talk to me he'd best be up early.'

Elijah nodded curtly and then dismissed the rest of them. Helen's parents held her back at the door, waiting for the Samuels to get some distance ahead. 'You keep away from them,' her mother said. 'I knew he was a wrong 'un from the moment he came back and turned your head. You've brought enough trouble to our door, lass, now you just keep away.'

Helen could think of nothing to say. Miserably, she followed her parents back down to the village, aware that the Churches trailed along behind them and that they too kept their distance as though Helen herself, by association, was now a threat to them all.

Thirty-Six

Ted had driven as fast as he dared along the winding, hilly route to Louth. The road was not good and was overshadowed by trees and characterized by blind bends and sudden dips. Finally reaching Louth, nestled in the bowl of hills, he parked close by the police station and ran inside, demanding to see the inspector that had come up from London. The desk sergeant finally calmed him down enough to find out what had been going on. He'd been making so much noise that Inspector Carrington came out to find out what the fuss was all about.

Ted gave him the details and explained who he was and who his father was. Elijah Hanson owned a lot of land and was known to be an influential, well-connected man. Inspector Carrington sent a constable to the King's Head with a message for Henry and Sergeant Hitchens to come at once and told Ted to sit down and calm himself.

'Chief Inspector Johnstone will be here presently,' he said.

Looking at him, Ted suspected that there was no love lost between Carrington and the inspector he had named. Carrington seemed to chew on Johnstone's name as though it was a distasteful piece of gristle he had found in a pie.

'I have the car; I could take him straight back there.'

'And I will make sure he goes with you immediately,' Carrington assured him. He seemed pleased with the idea.

Chief Inspector Carrington then withdrew to his office, leaving Ted to wait alone.

It was perhaps half an hour before Inspector Johnstone and Sergeant Hitchens arrived but Ted felt that it had been an eternity and another eternity. Before the London police detectives could question him, Carrington had reappeared. He explained what Ted was doing there.

'You both need to leave at once,' he said. 'Mr Hanson is an important and well-respected man. We wish to extend him every courtesy and concern.'

'And we are already engaged in a murder enquiry here,' Henry Johnstone reminded him.

'One on which you seem to be making very little headway. And besides—'

'And besides she was only a prostitute, her child a prostitute's child, the young man the cousin of a prostitute's cuckolded husband,' Henry said coldly.

Ted looked from one to the other and then stood impatiently. 'Look,' he said, 'I don't hold with any death being seen as unimportant, but my brother was killed this afternoon and we know who did it. We have witnesses to that and now he's run. Ethan ran and he needs catching. So I'd be obliged if you'd come now. Please.'

Henry turned to look at the young man and nodded. 'I'll come back with you. Sergeant Hitchens will stay here and continue with our investigations. I understand you have a car. If you take me by the King's Head I can gather my things. Sergeant Hitchens, I will need the bag, and would you be so kind as to inform Doctor Fielding that I could use his services and send him over in the morning.'

Mickey Hitchens nodded and they all left without another word to Carrington.

Thirty-Seven

Ethan woke when the moon was high and cursed himself for sleeping so long. Stiff and sore, he struggled from his hiding place and then paused to take stock, stretching his back and limbs.

194

He had to his name the clothes he stood up in, an old pocket knife that had belonged to his dad, a hunk of bread his mam had packed for his lunch and a bottle of cold tea. And his father's precious book. Ethan had carried it with him since his father had placed it in his hands.

He paused long enough to drink from the bottle and then, munching the bread as he went, he headed towards where he had spotted the field gate earlier in the day. It was, he figured, probably safe enough to go by road now. No one travelled much after dark and concealment was easy should he by chance see someone on the way.

He had decided now, woken with the knowledge. He'd head for the coast, get aboard ship, either as crew or as un-paying passenger and make his escape that way. They'd look for him there, Ethan thought, but he didn't think he had much other choice.

Reaching the road, he was faced with a choice of right or left and, seeing as he'd spent the afternoon racing across fields, he wasn't entirely sure which way would take him to the coast. Looking up, he scanned the sky. A great fat moon had risen, silvering the hedges and the fields and turning the road into an enchanted river. Searching, he found the pole star and made a guess from that which way was east.

Left it is then, Ethan thought. 'Forgive me, Helen,' he said out loud, his voice seeming overloud in the still darkness. 'I'll send for you. I promise I will. I'll send for you and we'll be together again in no time.'

195

Then Ethan put her from his mind and began to walk, closing his mind to what had been and focusing entirely on what lay ahead. Think of her, he knew, and he'd lose his nerve and will to go on. Think he might never see her again and he'd destroy even the will to live, be turning himself over to the hangman's noose just on the off chance he might get to spend a few minutes in her company before he died.

Don't think, just walk. One step at a time. One step at a time.

Thirty-Eight

Inspector Johnstone was a slender man with a head of unruly curls; one small element of unrestraint that sat at odds with the rest of him, Helen thought. His eyes were grey and stern and hard as river pebbles, and the set of his mouth, half hidden beneath the fox-brown moustache, was straight and tight and uncompromising.

Helen's heart sank. This was not a man who would allow Ethan any quarter. This was a man of the law; a man, she thought, who would have taken Hanson's side even if matters had been reversed and it was Ethan lying cold.

Even though he was not a physically heavy man, Johnstone dominated her parents' small front parlour, his assurance and authority somehow making him seem broader and taller than he really was. Despite the warmth of the evening, he wore a black coat, long and plain and tight across his back.

Her mother fussed about, making tea and her father stood, back to the empty grate, as though he felt the need of illusory warmth even on so close and humid an evening. His hands fiddled with an equally empty pipe and Helen knew he wanted to smoke but wasn't sure of the etiquette involved when being interviewed by the police. Through the window she could see uniformed officers, summoned by the constable, waiting for their lord and master, there being no room for them to squeeze inside, even had he wished them to do so. Helen had the impression he had not but that he had wanted to conduct this interview, as he had called it, in private and beyond other ears.

It was an impression that added to her unease.

'So, the last time you saw him was in the evening. Yesterday. That would be Friday. Late.'

Helen nodded. She had already told him this. 'We work late round here come harvest. I snatched a quick word as he passed. His parents live just down the road.'

'And what time would that have been?'

Helen sighed and glanced at her father for confirmation though this fact, too, had already been repeated twice.

'Well past ten,' her father said. 'As the lass says, we worked late.'

The inspector turned briefly towards her father, long enough to stare him into reluctant silence. 'And that would have been what time, Miss Lee?'

'Like my dad says, well after ten,' Helen said. She scowled at the big man, angry that he should belittle her father. 'That was the last time I spoke to him or laid eyes on him. I told you that a dozen times already.'

'No, Miss Lee,' Inspector Johnstone said. 'You have told me that exactly three times.'

Helen stared.

'Miss Lee, your intended has been accused of brutal murder. Of beating and kicking a wounded man unable to defend himself.'

'He would not.' Helen was outraged. 'He would never do that. He might best a man in a fight but he would never—'

'Miss Lee.' The soft voice rose and the authority in it silenced her as did the look.

Not river pebbles, she thought. His eyes were granite, tombstone hard.

'According to the witness, Frank Church, Ethan Samuels took exception to the way the deceased mistreated his horse. Frank Church states that Mr Robert Hanson . . .' he paused and consulted his notes, '. . . tried to put the horse to a fence too high for it and to jump it uphill and across. A jump Frank Church cites as impossible. He also suggests that Mr Robert Hanson had been drinking.'

Helen nodded, not knowing what to say but feeling some response was required.

'Sounds about right,' her father muttered. 'No care for any of the beasts nor any men neither.'

Inspector Johnstone ignored him but Helen knew he had taken note.

'He was cruel,' she said quietly. 'And he was often mazzled. Too much to drink,' she interpreted.

'I know what it means. Frank Church further states that Ethan Samuels snatched the crop from Mr Hanson's grip and set about his master, beating him about the face and body.'

'Frank Church has no right to say . . .'

'Frank Church has confirmed only what the evidence of my own eyes has told me. There are welts all over Robert Hanson's face and neck.'

Helen looked away. Her throat felt far too tight. She tried to swallow but could not.

'He then states that Ethan Samuels dragged the decedent from his horse, tumbling him on to the ground where he lay, apparently too drunk . . . too *mazzled*,' he leant upon the word as though for emphasis, '. . . to move or to rise. Too dazed, probably, from the fall and the beating he had already received to hope to defend himself.'

Helen glanced at him then tore her gaze away. Her mother, standing in the kitchen doorway with her hand tight to her mouth, was listening with horror written bright in her tearful eyes and her father would not meet her gaze, still fondling his pipe.

'Ethan has a temper,' she said quietly. 'He can't abide cruelty. He was raised to be a stockman, like his Dar – raised to respect the animals he cares for. You don't get the best out of a horse by beating it black and blue.'

'And a man? Do you get the best from a man doing that?'

'A man should know better,' Helen spat. Her anger rose and she could no longer keep her rage in check. 'Robert Hanson weren't worth nothing. He were cruel and spoiled and concerned with no one but himself. Oh, they'll all say the words, all weep at his funeral but there's not one round here who will really grieve that he's dead. Not a one.'

'Helen!' Her mother was horrified. 'Helen, how could you say . . .?'

'Say the truth, Ma? He'd been a bully all his life. He deserved a beating.'

'And did he deserve to be kicked in the head until he died?' Inspector Johnstone's voice, soft but very clear, fell into their midst and silenced them.

Helen stared at him. She shook her head. 'No,' she said. 'Ethan would not do that. Not kick a man already down. Maybe the horse . . .'

'Does the horse wear hobnailed boots, Miss Lee?' He leaned in close, bending over the chair in which she sat. She could feel his breath upon her cheek and his voice, intimate now, whispered softly in her ear. 'Three separate times, so far as I can see. Three prints he left on the face of that young man. One kick might have been aimed in anger, be down to sheer rage or loss of temper but tell me, Miss Lee, to do it twice, three times – perhaps more – speaks to me of cold intent. That speaks to me of murder.'

Thirty-Nine

Morning dawned bright and clear and Helen realized that she must have slept. That she had done so seemed like a betrayal; the tears she had taken to bed should have sustained her through the night. It diminished her that she had given in to exhaustion and escaped her troubles when she doubted Ethan could have enjoyed such peace.

Inspector Johnstone had remained until well after midnight before returning to the Hanson home. He was to stay there, it seemed, until Ethan was caught and the local constables would be billeted in the village. Helen could well imagine the mixed feelings with which the local families would take them in. Resentment that they had been dragged into such a sordid affair would merge with grateful acceptance that the Hansons had promised food and financial assistance to those who cooperated.

Much as she was angered by the prospect of those who wanted to hang Ethan – and there was no other option in Johnstone's mind, she was certain of that – living alongside her friends and neighbours, Helen could not, in her heart of hearts, begrudge them this windfall. Families had come close to starving these last years. Families had been forced into the workhouse at Caistor; children forcibly taken from their parents and fostered out; men kept separate from their wives. Honest, hard-working men and women accused of profligacy and blamed for coming to such a state when any reasonable person knew it was the state of the world and the lack of work that had brought them to such a pass.

Extra food put on the table was a welcome bounty, however it happened to have got there, but it riled Helen to think that Elijah Hanson could afford to offer such assistance now, when it suited his purpose, when he'd previously seen workers laid off from his own farms, thrown on to what passed for parish care and not raised a finger in their defence.

'I'm leaving this place when this is all over,' Helen whispered as she looked from her bedroom window and saw the local constable and his new colleagues already striding down the narrow street. 'Leaving it all and I ain't coming back. I'll find you, Ethan, and I'll get a job and—'

She broke off and bit her lip hard to stop the tears from coming.

If only it could be as simple as that.

Back in Louth, Mickey had been brought news. Children playing on waste ground near the canal had found the candlestick and Constable Parkin had brought it to the King's Head.

Parkin had put it in a large paper bag and he now set it down on the chest of drawers in Mickey's hotel room.

'I asked around,' Parkin told him. 'Asked people to keep a lookout for the candlestick. I thought the killer must have dumped it somewhere close by. I mean, you'd notice someone walking through the streets carrying a candlestick, wouldn't you?'

Mickey, looking at the size of the thing, was inclined to agree.

The stick itself was pewter, set on a square base that had been filled with lead. It was tall and heavy and he could well imagine the impact of it swung at an unprotected head. Damn it, he didn't have to imagine it; he'd seen the effect on the bodies.

Mickey crouched down so that his eyes were level with the base. 'Blood and hairs,' he said. 'And a bit of mud. You say children found it?'

'Kids playing by the canal, yes. It was down in the reeds. I figure the killer tried to chuck it in the canal and missed his aim. They took it back home and the father recognized it from the description I'd given.'

He sounded very pleased with himself, Mickey thought. He allowed himself a smile and, standing up, clapped the young man on the shoulder.

'You think it will help?'

'It might. Trouble is it's been handled by who knows how many people since so I doubt we'll get meaningful prints. Still,' he went on, seeing the look of disappointment on Parkin's face, 'I will try. It's worth seeing if there's anything that matches the prints we found in the house. You've done a good job, lad.'

Parkin went away happy.

Mickey looked again at the shape of the stick. The lead in the base had preserved the shape well but, pewter being a soft material, the stick itself was bent out of shape, dented and scratched.

'You swung it hard, didn't you?' Mickey said quietly to himself. 'Hard as you could against a young man and a little girl.'

Henry had taken the murder bag with him but Mickey, ever prepared, kept a small secondary kit of his own. Gently, he eased the hairs away from the mud and blood on the base and laid them out on a sheet of hotel paper. 'Now,' he said, 'let's see what else you might have left behind.'

Inspector Johnstone had been up and about since dawn. He rarely slept more than a few hours even in his own bed and in a strange house, the atmosphere of which was redolent with grief and anger, rest was slow to come.

Despite his lack of sleep, he felt alert and eager for the day to begin. He had gone out early to survey the scene of crime, only to find that the grass was sodden with morning dew and, instead of needlessly soaking his shoes, he merely stood beside the gate and looked out across the field.

The land sloped downward, away from the farm, and Johnstone could visualize the difficulty of setting even a well-trained horse against such an unwieldy jump. Johnstone himself rode well; he made a point of doing everything well, but *he* would not have attempted it and could only imagine it was the young man's drunken state that led him to think he might succeed.

The field had been left fallow and not been grazed since spring, so Elijah Hanson had told him. The grass had grown long and Johnstone could see clearly where it had been trampled by the frightened horse, the heavy boots of the men and bruised by the impact of the rider when he fell from the saddle.

He could see, also, that there was blood on the ground.

Elijah Hanson came out from the house and stood beside him, a solid, silent presence that demanded answers.

Johnstone resented his company, the emotional implication of which broke into his analytical reverie. He did not speak but, instead, continued with his observation.

'You think he'll be found today?' Hanson said at last when the silence had grown too heavy for him to bear.

'I have sent word and description to the docks and the train stations and the dogs will be here mid-morning. After that we'll have a clearer picture of where he went.'

Hanson snorted. 'Almost a full day will have passed by then. He's long gone. You're town born, man – you don't know how far a country lad could have taken himself in such a time.'

'My colleagues on the docks have a description of him now,' Johnstone said steadily. 'He will be found.'

Hanson snorted angrily. 'I can't believe the lad did it,' he then said softly. 'I knew he had a temper on him but I've never seen it fire off like it must have done yesterday. Can't believe it all turned out this way. If Robert had fallen from his horse or been killed because of drink, well, truth is I'd almost prepared meself for that. He were a bad sort right from being a boy.'

Johnstone looked curiously at this man who

had just lost his son and it seemed to him that he regretted the loss of Ethan Samuels far more. He rated the young man more highly than his kin.

As though Hanson read his thoughts, or it had suddenly come to him how his words must have sounded, he shook his head angrily. 'Robert were still my boy,' he said, 'for all his faults. I'll not have his death unpunished, no matter how or no matter who.'

Johnstone inclined his head in acknowledgement of that. 'Whether *you'd* have punishment or not is of little matter,' he said quietly. 'The law demands it, life for a life, and as the representative of that law it is my duty to see that justice is done. Personal feelings are of little consequence.'

Hanson stared hard at this man whom fate had dictated should be his guest and therefore, under all the rules of hospitality, should be above disapprobation. For a moment, dislike and manners fought it out in Elijah Hanson's brain and dislike won.

'Were you born a sanctimonious fool?' he asked. 'Or did it take learning?'

Johnstone did not favour the comment with a response and Hanson took himself off back to the farmhouse. Death or not, grieving or not, there was work to be done, stock to feed and harvest to bring home, and Elijah was suddenly grateful of that. He could bury his pain and his grief in the routine and the needs of those in his care. Glancing sideways, he was unsurprised to see Dar Samuels striding through the gate, head high but shoulders down as though the weight of the world was laid upon them. He too had work to do and thoughts to bury.

'It's a bad business our sons have got themselves into,' Elijah said.

'I know it,' Dar said. 'And if you don't want me near or the missus can't stand to have me working for you, then I'll be on my way.'

'And you'd go where?' Elijah said. He turned and the two men walked together into the house, pragmatism winning out for now. Dar was useful; Dar Samuels was required for the smooth running of the Hanson farm, but as Johnstone watched them disappear through the kitchen door he could tell from the set of their respective shoulders that the end of their association was close by. Two men had lost their children; one to violence while the other would lose theirs at the end of a rope and, Johnstone knew, because he made a point of being good at knowing, the enmity between them would grow by increments until the burden of referred guilt and continued loss became too heavy for two such basic and honest men to bear.

Forty

As Johnstone had already discovered, Dr Thomas Fielding was no ordinary country practitioner, which was why Johnstone had called upon his services. Robert Hanson's body had been laid out in the small parlour at the front of the house, the room reserved for important occasions and otherwise barely entered. Hanson brides stepped out from this room, leaving the family home; new wives were received here. Christening buffets were laid out upon the mahogany sideboard and coffins placed upon the solid oak of the refectory-style table, pulled out from its usual place against the wall.

For all other seasons the room was kept closed, furniture clad in white dust sheets, carpet covered with a drop cloth and curtains closed tight against any stray ray of sunlight that might fade an unprotected inch of patterned rug.

The dust sheets had been removed from the chairs in case the 'gentlemen' should need to sit down but the sheet covering the oak table had been left in place and now served to protect its surface from the bloodstains on Robert Hanson's clothes and battered face.

Johnstone had opened the curtains and let in the light. He was aware that Mrs Hanson viewed this action as virtual sacrilege; every blind and curtain in the house had been drawn closed, shutting out the life of the outside world and shutting in the dead. It was unthinkable that lights should be lit in daytime and now the house gloomed, stiff and silent and dim as any church.

Only this room, the one place used to existing in such a twilight world, now allowed the sun to stream in through uncovered windows.

Inspector Johnstone doubted that Mrs Hanson, born Margaret Cook and therefore second cousin to the Samuels, would ever forgive him for such insensitivity.

He watched Dr Fielding as the physician examined the body. They would have stripped off his clothes, the better to see the full extent of his injuries, but rigor had not yet passed and his body lay stiff and awkward. Johnstone would have willingly cut the clothes from the body but Fielding had warned him that such action, even in pursuit of scientific ends, would have been beyond the pale. To destroy good clothes and to expose a son, naked, in his parent's parlour; both would be sins in the eyes of the local community, Fielding warned, and Johnstone needed them onside if he was to get anywhere with this case.

'The people here may seem pliant and simple,' the doctor commented, 'but believe me, they can soon turn if you offend their sensibilities. Turn and close ranks and, however much this death has shamed the community, should you be seen to shame it more you'll cease to get help from any of them, the parents included.'

Johnstone might have scoffed, both at the thought that anyone should put traditional respect above scientific demonstration and also that a man of Fielding's education and refinement should take account of such crude emotions, but the voice of Mickey Hitchens in his head reinforced what Fielding had told him. Mickey would have advised in the same way had he been here and when it came to dealing with people Mickey was usually right. The advice fought with Johnstone's instinct and questions. What did mere feelings matter? A murder had been done and the killer must be apprehended. That was the beginning and end of the matter. His sister often joined with Mickey Hitchens and told him that he saw the world in too simplistic a way. Henry respected both of their judgements even if he didn't always agree with them.

The doctor had been adamant, though, and finally they had reached a compromise. The initial examination of the body would be carried out here, such clothing as could easily be undone would be pulled aside and the body would then later be transferred to the infirmary, at Louth, where a more extensive examination could be completed.

Truthfully, Johnstone doubted there was much more to be seen than what could already be observed – the heavy bruising and the cuts to the face and neck. The boot marks, clearly identified to Johnstone's practised eye, that had lain across the cheek, broken the cheekbone and, he suspected, fractured the skull, spoke for themselves.

'No defensive wounds,' Fielding observed, studying Robert Hanson's hands and forearms. 'The initial blow must have rendered him helpless.'

'That and the drink.'

'True. I can smell that on him even now. So he was drunk and foolish, the Samuels' boy lays into him with the riding crop and drags him from the horse, then proceeds to attack him when he's on the ground.' He looked expectantly at Johnstone. 'Is that how you read it?'

'Close enough and it fits with what the witness

told me, though he was at pains to say he could not see clearly – that the horse came between him and the assault.'

'And your witness is Frank Church,' Fielding said thoughtfully. 'You know that he was supposed to have married Helen Lee? Before the Samuels boy came back from the sea and plans changed.'

Johnstone nodded slowly. 'I've heard the village gossip,' he agreed. 'Which in my view makes Church the better witness. He has nothing to gain by diminishing Ethan Samuels' blame in any of this, and yet he seeks to do so by telling me he could not see clearly what passed. He claims to have seen Samuels use his fists but not his boots.'

'And yet, these injuries here. I cannot believe a man's fist could have inflicted them.'

'Nor I, and I've seen enough men mangled in the boxing ring.'

Fielding looked up, interested. As Helen had earlier, Fielding could well imagine Johnstone as a fighter. 'Oh?' he said.

'When I first served as a police officer, bare-knuckle bouts were commonplace, as was the gambling that went with them. A man striking with a gloved hand is able to hit harder, to strike directly at the head and face with little conse-quence to himself, but the marks left are bruising and abrasions on the skin and the unseen addling of the brain, not injuries like this. A man striking bare-handed cannot punch at the jaw and temple with anything like the same ferocity without risking serious injury to his own hands. Mostly, such fighters use body shots. It is in their interest to prolong the fight and the tension for as long as they can and increase their pay by doing so. No, Ethan Samuels might have started with his fists but I doubt he killed Robert Hanson with them. He kicked Robert Hanson in the head. Repeatedly so. Viciously so and with only one intent.'

Fielding was watching him closely. 'I know this village well,' he said. 'I come out to treat the Hansons and the vicar and Thompson, the schoolteacher. By osmosis, I suppose, I've gleaned knowledge of the rest. Dar Samuels raised his children well; I find it hard to believe such a single-minded and vicious attack could have been carried out by one of his children. While it is true Ethan was, like all boys, always getting himself into scrapes, I've never known it said that he was callous. The opposite, in fact, and by all accounts he was in love with his girl and had been promised a house and work by Hanson senior. He had so much to lose that it seems strange . . .'

'Strange that such a boy should be unable to control his passions?' Johnstone shook his head. 'Forgive me, Doctor, but I don't find it so. He took another man's intended, fought him over the matter and it's broadcast in the village that Helen Lee would not have been a virgin on her wedding night.'

'Oh, there is always gossip of that kind. A girl could come straight from a convent to her wedding and the old women would still be looking for signs of pregnancy.'

'I think this is more than gossip. But my point is Ethan Samuels was not a figure known for his self-control and the evidence is there, laid out upon the body for anyone to see.'

A commotion in the yard filtered through the quiet household, reaching them in the parlour. 'It sounds as though the dogs have arrived.' Johnstone headed for the door, leaving the doctor to rearrange Robert's clothing and cover his body.

It seemed as though most of the village had turned out to see the bloodhounds and had followed the van carrying the dogs up the hill to Hanson's farm.

Elijah Hanson ignored them all. Carrying a flour sack in his hand, he strode over to where the handler pulled the baying creatures from the back of the vehicle and called them to him with voice and leash and the deft cracking of a small whip. He did not touch the valuable dogs with the lash, using sound alone to bring them back under his control, but the cacophony of dogs giving voice, the man's harsh calls and the sharp cracking of the cord added a touch of theatre to an already overblown occasion.

The handler, a short-statured, wiry man with a wolfish face, warned Hanson back.

'The beasts are excited, sir. They may snap at a stranger.'

Hanson eyed him and the dogs with deep suspicion.

Johnstone crossed the yard, his gaze sweeping left and right, taking in the crowd of villagers who had gathered in the yard and on the rutted track beyond, eager to see the show.

'Don't they have work to go to,' he demanded loudly as he came to Hanson's side. 'Tell them to get on about their business, Hanson.'

Elijah regarded him through narrowed eyes, his mouth set in a thin line, tight with contempt. 'This *is* their business, Johnstone,' he declared. 'Hereabouts, we like our justice to have a face, to bear witness to its deeds. We don't pass our concerns over to strangers just because that stranger declares himself our better.'

'You called me here,' Henry reminded him.

'That I did, but only because the law does not permit me to take my own revenge. If *you* hang the lad it is seen as justice. Were I to do it that would be taken for vengeance and my own neck liable to be stretched. Believe me, but for that consideration I'd not have brought you within ten miles of my place.'

The handler watched the exchange with interest and called his dogs to heel once more. They did not like to be confined for so long in the vehicle and, now that they'd been freed, wanted action. He knew they would soon become a challenge, even for him. 'We should get started,' he suggested quietly.

'So we should,' Hanson agreed. He handed the sack over to the wiry little man. 'Inside,' he said. 'We took care not to handle it.'

The handler nodded and withdrew a small pillow from the sack that had come from Ethan's bed.

'Will that do?' Johnstone asked.

'Nicely, sir.' He offered it to his dogs. They ceased their baying and fell to silent inhalation,

214

breathing deep of Ethan's scent, learning about the man they would pursue.

'You'll pick up the track in that field,' Johnstone told him. 'Let's be on.'

The gate was opened and the dogs streamed through, pulling their master in their wake. Johnstone, broadcloth coat flying, followed swiftly behind.

Hanson watched as the dogs cast about for the scent so recently learnt. One found it and called to the rest. They sniffed and bayed their satisfaction and then the chase was on, following the trail, invisible but strong, that Ethan had left.

Elijah did not follow.

Dar Samuels stepped up beside him. 'How far can they travel in a day?' he asked.

'I wouldn't know. Far enough, I reckon.'

'Maybe.' Dar sounded bitter. Bitter and terribly saddened by it all.

'Dar, if you want to follow on I'll spare you for the day.'

Ethan's father shook his head. 'If they find my boy I might need time then to do . . . to do whatever I must. Meantime, there's work enough here.'

Elijah Hanson nodded briefly and felt the man leave his side. He stood and watched as the dogs found the gap in the hedge that Ethan had pushed through and then watched longer as they bounded effortlessly on up the hill. The slender figure of their handler dragged along in their wake and the carrion crow in black that was Inspector Johnstone loped effortlessly behind.

* * *

Helen had heard the dogs but could not bear to go up to Hanson's farm to watch. She bent her head over the laundry, hauling hot sheets from the copper and dumping them into the deep sink ready for the final rinsing and the application of the blue bag. Usually her mother would have considered it sinful to be washing on a Sunday but they had lost much of the Saturday because of what had happened with Ethan and Robert and, Sunday or not, people needed their clothes clean and their sheets washed. And her mother needed the money from it.

Anyway, no one felt inclined to go to church or chapel today. She'd even seen the vicar heading up to Hanson's farm.

Nothing seemed quite real. Here she was, dealing with the everyday task of washing and rinsing, mangling and pegging to dry and while she was here, pretending that life was normal and that these simple tasks were of importance, the man she loved was being hunted down by a pack of baying dogs and a man filled only with thoughts of vengeance.

'Please, God, let him be too far away,' she prayed softly as she dumped a fresh load of sheets into hot water. 'Let him be far, far away, even so far that I never see him again. Anything, God. I'll even live with the thought of not seeing him no more so long as he stays safe and they don't find him.'

'Did you say something, Helen?' Her mother stuck her head around the wash-house door.

'No, Mam, I said nothing. Nothing at all.'

Her mother came inside and stood watching

216

her for a moment or two. Helen could feel that she was searching inside herself for the right thing to say. Something helpful, something comforting. Something that would make things right.

For a brief instant she looked up from her task and met her mother's gaze but there was nothing to be said. No help, no hope, no means of comforting. Her mother was the first to break the contact and with a sigh she turned away.

Please, God, don't let them find him, Helen prayed, silently this time. Please, God, let him have run fast and hard and your angels be guarding him. Let him have got away.

Forty-One

Johnstone did not speak, either to the dogs or their handler or to the straggling pack of children and younger folk who kept pace with the hunters for the first mile or so before growing bored or tired or aware of the chores they had left undone and would be punished for neglecting. One by one they dropped away or turned back.

He did not once slacken pace and he did not seem tired, either. When the handler paused for a brief moment for the dogs to check the trace and mop the sweat that ran into his eyes, Johnstone didn't show any signs of fatigue or of being affected by the heat.

They found the ditch where Ethan had lain

217

asleep, followed his steps across the next field and out on to the road.

The dogs milled and circled, checking the trail now filled with fresh scents of car and lorry, horse and van and walker. Then their leader gave voice, his pack confirmed his findings and they were off again.

Johnstone, a stranger to the area, called out to the handler, 'Where does this road go?'

'To the coast eventually. My guess is he'll turn and head out towards Grimsby or Immingham.'

Johnstone jerked his head in what may have been a nod. 'Just as we thought,' he said. 'The word is already out with the dockyard police. It's more than likely they'll have him before the day is through.'

'Maybe,' the handler agreed. 'But it's a fair way, Mister. The dogs can't be expected to run all that distance. Their hearts are willing an' all, but . . .'

Johnstone waved his objections aside. 'Nor would I expect them to. We'll go on a piece until we're certain he didn't take another road, then we'll turn back.'

The handler nodded and let the pack have its head. Johnstone paused to look about and get his bearings, taking note of the curve of the road and the topography of hills and fields. Once he had seen a place and committed it to memory he would know it for all time. He made a point of knowing but he felt relieved now, secure in the knowledge that his assumption had been correct and Grimsby was in all likelihood Ethan's destination. Secure, too, in the expectation that

218

the recently formed dockyard constabulary would be eager to make an arrest and be watching for a young man seeking a fast escape.

Ethan Samuels would be in his custody very soon, Johnstone thought. Justice would soon be done.

For Helen, the day dragged its feet. She tried hard to focus on the tasks her mother set her – the washing and the mangling and the pegging of clean linens on to clothes lines that stretched the length of their garden and into the field beyond so that it looked almost like a crop of sheets and shirts ready for the men to harvest. But her thoughts strayed too often to Ethan.

Her hands were sore from scrubbing stains with the Sunlight soap. Her arms and back ached from the weight of wet cloth and the effort of turning the mangle while her mother took turns at drawing the squeezed cloth through, and her arms and shoulders ached from the many times she had walked to the spring and back. For most of the village the piped spring known as Peter's spout was the one reliable source of water.

For the most part, they worked in silence. What was there to say? The task was so utterly familiar it required neither instruction nor discussion and to speak of what was uppermost in the minds of both women . . . that was unthinkable.

From time to time, Helen snatched a glance along the road. At any moment she expected to see Inspector Johnstone and the bloodhounds returning with Ethan chained or bound, leashed like the dogs.

She caught her mother looking at her, the expression on her round, sun-reddened face so sad and so strained that it tore at Helen's soul. 'Don't, Ma. Please. I can't bear it.'

Silent, the older woman nodded and turned away and Helen followed her, back to the rhythm of the dolly tub, the turn of the mangle, the ache in her arms and the lump of solid pain in the middle of her back. Helen found she welcomed it all. It helped to drown out the silent scream of agony that raged inside her, squeezing her heart until she fancied the blood could no longer flow and she would die from the constriction of it.

They worked until late afternoon and then her mother set her to getting the evening meal for their menfolk. It was early to be about this task, Helen knew. They'd taken bread and cheese with them up to the fields to keep them going through the day and would not be back for supper until it grew too dark to work. She was, though, grateful for the distraction.

Her mother left her in the kitchen and went through into the little parlour. Helen heard her open the front door and knew that, as she had done earlier, she was staring out at the empty road.

For a little while there was quiet in the house, broken only by the familiar clatter of pots and plates. A slight breeze blew through from the open door and Helen was glad of it. The day had been so hot, so dry. Later, she thought, there would be rain.

'Helen,' her mother called to her, softly, anxiously and Helen froze. She knew the reason for it.

She left her task and joined her mother at the

door, grateful for the hand, roughened by washing and still cool from the water, that enclosed hers.

'Oh, Ma.'

The dogs had returned, coming in through the village rather than back across the fields. Less exuberant now, even their great appetite for hunting and sniffing and running satiated. The handler, too, looked worn by the day, limping along behind the pack. Only Johnstone seemed untouched by the exertions, striding before them, his shoulders square and his back straight. His face was set as hard as granite.

'They didn't find him,' Helen breathed softly. 'Ma, they didn't find him.'

'Come away inside,' her mother said, pushing her gently but firmly out of sight. Johnstone's cold gaze fixed on her as she glanced back his way and, despite the heat of the warm summer evening, she shivered.

Johnstone paused at the cottage door.

'You didn't find him, then.'

'But I will. You can tell your girl not to rejoice too much. I set myself tasks and I fulfil those tasks. I complete them. You may be sure; he'll not get away from me.'

Forty-Two

Mickey Hitchens wondered how his boss was doing out in Thoresway village. A gypsy village, he'd been told when he had asked about it in the King's Head bar the night before. He doubted it would be long before news of this new murder was all over the district. He knew that news in country areas travelled surprisingly fast.

Mickey liked to walk when he was thinking; the simple mechanical act of putting one foot in front of the other seemed to free up his brain and he was mulling over what little they had achieved so far in the murder of Mary Fields and the other two members of her family. In the first days after they had arrived in Louth the local papers had been full of the news, the *Lincolnshire Echo* declaring that this was something you would have expected to be happening only in Grimsby or Boston, and the local newspaper, the *Louth Standard* practically proclaiming that the world was at an end and that justice must be done. Both had now fallen quiet and moved on to other events, and Mickey could not help but wonder if that was due to the influence of men like Inspector Carrington, who had made it very plain that this was not the kind of thing the town should be known for and that such headlines were upsetting its more respectable cohort.

Mickey despised such hypocrisy; the same hypocrisy that had led to Henry Johnstone being called to attend what was evidently considered a much more important murder. Mickey knew, because Constable Parkin had told him, that Carrington had been furious that he had not accompanied Henry but had chosen to continue with the investigation in Louth. Mickey also knew that Carrington had telephoned Scotland

Yard and insisted that the pair of them be removed. He gathered that he'd been given short shrift.

It was not uncommon for local police to resent their presence, to feel that it undermined their authority or called their skills into question, but it had been a while since he and Henry had run into such blatant opposition, particularly as Carrington was responsible for them being there in the first place. Mickey was wondering what had happened that now made Carrington so anxious. What pressure had been put on him and from where? Who was upset by their investigation? The names Fry and May came to mind.

It was now six o'clock and the church bells were ringing to announce the end of evensong, though Mickey was not quite sure which church they were calling from. As he turned the corner he ran into a group of people dressed in their Sunday best who were headed out of St Mary's and now seemed to be on their way to the outskirts of town to enjoy the calm summer evening. Mickey was of a mind to follow them anyway, having nothing better to do, but what really decided it for him was catching a glimpse of a man he was sure was George Fields also headed in the same direction. The man was a little ahead, and while he could not be absolutely sure, the clothes and the slightly heavy shouldered gait, head thrust forward, looked to be the same that he had noticed before.

A little further on Mickey realized where they were headed when he saw a sign for Hubbard's Hills. He had been told this was a local beauty spot, donated to the town some decades before by one Auguste Alphonse Pahud and which was now a popular Sunday walk.

He followed the knots of people down Crowtree Lane, through a kissing gate and then on to a rough path. It was certainly a pretty place, Mickey thought as he continued to wander, keeping his eyes open for George Fields and whoever George Fields was interested in. Mickey was not of a mind that George was just here for a Sunday stroll.

A little stream ran through the bottom of the valley, hills climbing on either side with more level areas that would be good for picnicking and a great many trees. Stepping stones crossed the stream and children played, running back and forth across them while their parents gossiped and others set out picnics. The women wore soft summer pastels and shady hats while the men dressed in lighter jackets and panamas. It was a mixed crowd, Mickey noticed. Those more well-to-do and those for whom Sunday was obviously the one day of the week when they had time off and whose Sunday best had most likely been their Sunday best for a decade. It seemed to Mickey that the two groups studiously ignored one another, apart from one man. George Fields stood in the shade of a small clump of trees and appeared to be watching one particular party with great attention.

Mickey circled up behind him and stood for a few moments watching what George was watching before he spoke.

'And who might they be?' Mickey asked.

George jumped then turned, his face reddened

224

and angry and his fists raised before he realized who Mickey was.

'No need for that,' Mickey said. 'I was just curious, George, as to what brought you up here on a sunny Sunday evening.'

George turned away from him, his attention returning to the group of picnickers who sat in the shade of another clump of trees.

'Me and Mary – we did our courting here. Then we used to bring our Ruby up here – sometimes bring a picnic too. Though it were never as grand as theirs.'

Mickey looked at the picnic being laid out on a tartan blanket. Food had been removed from wicker baskets and hampers and for the first time he noticed that there were servants in attendance; they must have come up before and brought the supper.

'No,' he said. 'I don't suppose it would have been. The likes of you and me, we don't get to go on picnics like that. We bring our sandwiches in a paper bag and our tea in a thermos and if we are lucky we might have a nip of something in a flask.'

George glanced at him as though uncertain whether or not Mickey was being patronizing. It appeared that Mickey was not.

'So who are they, then?'

'It's the Mays,' George said.

'Business partner to Mr Fry?'

'That'll be the one.'

'So what's your interest in them? Was he seeing your Mary?'

For a moment George said nothing and then

he nodded. 'Reckoned he was. Mebbe. Walter says he thought he'd seen him hanging around but he couldn't be sure.'

'Didn't mention him in the letters, though, did he?'

'No. And I'll want those back.'

'And you'll be getting them, I promise. So why follow them up here? You planning on harassing the man? I really would have you for breach of the peace then.'

'Just wanted to see what the bastard looked like,' George said.

'If you don't know what he looked like then how do you know it's him?'

'For one thing I got someone to point him out to me, and for another thing that's his wife in the blue, sitting with Fry's wife, the one in the pink, and there's Fry just coming up now, see?'

Mickey looked to see where George had indicated and indeed spotted Mr Edmund Fry making his way up to the group. In addition to the wives there was an older couple and another woman and four children running around, skipping back and forth across the stepping stones.

'George, you'd best come away with me now,' Mickey said. 'Let's the two of us go and have a drink and put our heads together over this one. I'll buy you a pint and you'll do the talking.'

George didn't move.

'It's either that or I get you arrested here and now.'

'I've done nothing.'

'Like I said before, I see it as preventive action. Now put your sensible head on and come

226

with me. A pint on a sunny evening – what could be better?'

'Problem with that round here,' George said. 'Local bylaws – no pubs open.'

'No, but the hotel will be. The King's Head isn't the Wheatsheaf but it still serves a decent pint.'

Reluctantly George Fields turned and followed Mickey back down the little path and into town.

Forty-Three

Contrary to expectations, Ethan had not headed for the coast but turned back inland. His first intention had been to get aboard ship in either Grimsby or Immingham but eventually he thought better of that. They would be looking for him there; his description would have been sent out and there was a very good chance he'd be picked up. He had started on a journey now and he wasn't about to stop and get sent back to the hangman's rope. He needed to get away, to put as much distance between himself and anybody that might know him as was possible. And that meant going somewhere else. That meant looking for work and passage to a place a long way from here.

It crossed his mind that it would be easier to get work somewhere like Liverpool and he was not deterred by the fact that this meant crossing an entire country. He'd sailed out of Liverpool

227

before and knew that the sheer scale of the place gave him a better chance of either finding someone to take him with few questions asked or of sneaking aboard and hiding until they were well out to sea. He knew the way this worked; stowaways were usually just made to labour for their passage and although they would be threatened with being handed over to the authorities the next time a ship reached port, in practice that was rarely enforced.

Anyway, Ethan decided that he didn't have much choice in the matter.

He had tried to remember if a photograph of him existed. Of the people in the village only the schoolteacher and the vicar owned a camera. And Miss Elizabeth. Before Ethan had left to go to sea she had been given this very expensive gift for her tenth birthday and had delighted in going round the fields and the village, taking photographs of everyone she could persuade to pose for her. Ethan remembered that he'd been photographed at the harvest festival that year, along with most of the other young men and women in the village, but he'd never seen the image and didn't know if Miss Elizabeth had even managed to print her photographs. It was a risk but not one he could do anything about.

That aside, any description put out for him would have been so general as to fit many other men of his age. He was of average height and build and the only unusual thing about Ethan was that, despite having dark hair, his eyes were blue, an anomaly that appealed to Helen and which cropped up in the family from time to time. But he doubted that would really set him apart. He hoped not anyway.

And so, Ethan walked. And walked and walked some more.

Forty-Four

Edmund Fry had spotted George Fields as he'd walked up towards his friends and he quietly pointed this out to May. The two men watched as George strolled away with Sergeant Hitchens.

'Has he arrested him?'

'Doesn't look like it, old man,' May responded.

'So what the hell do they want?'

'Edmund, don't be such a bore. What are you two gossiping about? You look like a couple of maiden aunts with your heads together like that.'

'Just business, dear. And I'm sorry – we shouldn't be discussing that on a Sunday. Particularly not in such delightful company.' He took a glass from his wife and a plate of food from the maid and leant back against the bole of a tree, stretching out his long legs.

'I thought I saw that poor man a moment ago,' Celia May said.

'What poor man, dear?' Delia Fry asked her.

'You know, the one who came home to find his wife and child murdered. Mrs Henderson pointed him out to me one day in the marketplace. Mr Henderson, you know he's a magistrate, and the man was up in front of him for punching a police

229

officer. Would you believe it? They let him off with a fine because the police officer was kind enough to say that the poor man had suffered enough.'

'Henderson is too soft,' Fry declared.

'Edmund, I'm quite sure he's not. I'm sure he was just showing a little compassion.'

'Compassion should be shown to those who deserve it.'

'The man had just lost his wife and child. To violence.'

'And a woman who lived the way that she lived, well, sooner or later violence was bound to find her.'

'But the child,' Celia insisted. 'She can't be blamed for the way her mother lived.'

'If you ask me it probably spared the child much future pain.' May drained his glass.

'What on earth can you mean?'

'I mean, dear girl, that the apple never falls far from the tree. It would only have been a matter of time before the child was as corrupt as the mother.'

Celia look shocked. 'You can be such a hard, cruel man.'

'I'm just a realist. These traits get passed down the generations and there is nothing the likes of you or I can do about it. It's only a surprise that it wasn't the husband himself who killed her. In his place, who could have blamed him?'

The children chose that moment to come running back and the conversation shifted in a more suitable direction. May poured himself more wine and smiled at his sons.

Forty-Five

Henry had arranged for the body of Robert Hanson to be removed to Louth where a proper post-mortem could take place. Elijah Hanson had been in great opposition to this and so had the boy's mother. It seemed to them like a final insult that he should be cut open and examined when it was very clear what had killed him.

Henry himself decided that he would return to Louth as well; there was little to keep him there and the investigation would be better served once they had news, as Henry was sure they would have soon, from the dockyard police.

Before he left, Ted Hanson having promised to drive him back, he went to the Samuels' cottage on Red Row with the intention of examining any possessions Ethan might have left behind.

Dar Samuels let him in and invited him to take a seat at the table. The cottage was sparsely furnished with a scrubbed table, four wooden chairs and an old dresser that looked as though it was built into the cottage itself. On the dresser were plates and cups and glass jars filled with dried beans and lentils and flour. There were flowers in another jar and Henry was reminded of Mary Fields' house and the flowers on the mantelpiece.

Cooking was evidently done over the fire and a Dutch oven sat on the hearth. Henry had seen

231

poverty in town but it seemed to him that here he could be stepping back fifty or a hundred years and only the clothing the occupants wore would have changed. There were candles on the mantelpiece and one paraffin lamp. A stack of newspapers sat beside the hearth.

'You like to keep abreast of the news, Mr Samuels?'

Dar frowned. 'When I can. Ted . . . Hanson, he's good enough to keep me supplied. He's a good lad is Ted.'

'Not like his brother,' Henry said.

Dar gave him no reply. Instead he sent the children to play outside and took a seat opposite Henry Johnstone. His wife stood close by the door, almost as though she wanted to escape from him and would rather have been sent outside with her young ones.

'Do you have a photograph of your son?' Henry asked though he knew it was a stupid question.

'Do we look like a family that can own a camera?' Dar asked him impatiently.

'No, I'm sorry. It was a foolish thing to ask. I should have asked if you knew of one existing.'

'Mr Thompson, the schoolteacher, bought a camera some years back and he took a class photo. I think Ethan was probably in that but he'd have been no more than nine or ten.'

Henry nodded. 'I'd like to see where your son sleeps,' he said. 'See if there're any belongings he might have left behind.'

'He sleeps up in the children's room. The wife and I have the other. You can go up and look but you'll find nothing. There's two old shirts and a couple of collars that he wore on Sundays when he needed to look respectable but that's all you'll find. Everything else he owned he was wearing or he carried in his pack. But that was little enough. We are not folk who own things, Inspector.'

Henry went up the narrow stairs and into the first bedroom. This evidently belonged to the parents. Rag rugs decorated the floor, as they had done downstairs, and as had been the case in Ruby's bedroom a clean one had been laid across the foot of the bed to provide extra warmth when the weather got cold. There were two wooden chairs and a chest of drawers in here, and on the chest of drawers a moulded bowl of orange carnival glass and two little candlesticks. He opened the drawers, found clothes inside and folded sheets. Everything smelt of lavender. In the bottom drawer was a store of soap and blue bags and washing stuff, so evidently Samuels did not make use of the Lee's laundry service. There was a Book of Common Prayer and a Bible. When he opened it he found the names of the family inscribed, generation upon generation, inside. He closed it and put it back.

In the second room there was a single bed and a mattress laid out on the floor. The younger children must sleep top to tail, he thought, looking at the pillows – one at the head and one at the foot. Everything was clean and neat and cared for but no, the Samuels were evidently not people who owned things. The small tin chest at the end of the bed held a doll, a toy car and some carved wooden toys. He wondered if Dar

233

had made them. And there were winter clothes layered up with lavender to keep the moths at bay. The shirts Dar had mentioned had been folded and placed upon a shelf. A newspaper had been folded up and placed beneath. Curious, Henry moved the shirts and took the paper down. It was just a single page, recording the deaths of Mary Fields and her kin and folded over so the story was the only one visible.

Henry frowned, puzzled. He started to put the shirts back when he noticed the buttons. One was dissimilar from the rest.

Henry went back downstairs and lay his finds down on the kitchen table.

'Did your son know Mary Fields?' he asked.

'He did, yes. He was at sea with the husband.' Dar Samuels frowned at Henry. 'What of it?'

'I found this in his room.'

'He was upset at the news.'

'And he had a button missing from his shirt,' Henry pointed at the offending fastening. 'When was it replaced?'

'I don't recall exactly,' Mrs Samuels said. 'He lost one and I found another from the button box. We always keep buttons even when the clothes are worn through.'

Henry nodded. 'I need to take this shirt,' he said.

'And why would you need to do that?'

Henry paused, reluctant to pile grief on grief. 'Your son – when did he last see Mary Fields?'

'I wouldn't know. Inspector, what are you saying?'

Mrs Samuels had come to stand next to her husband now. 'You can't be suggesting that Ethan had anything to do with . . . with that?'

Henry considered then decided to tell them the truth. 'A button was found at the murder scene. The button matches those on this shirt.'

'And probably matches half the shirts in Louth,' Dar Samuels protested.

'Probably so, but your son has shown himself capable of violence. I can't ignore this, Mr Samuels. You must understand that. I'll be going now,' he said. 'Mr Samuels, I don't have to tell you – if you hear from your son you must let us know.'

Dar Samuels nodded. 'I'm hoping I don't hear from him,' he said. 'That way I won't have to lie to anyone.'

Henry let the comment pass. He walked back up to the Hanson farm where Ted was waiting with the car.

George's presence in the lounge of the King's Head had caused some raised eyebrows but no one had said anything. The police officers were foreigners and therefore would have some strange habits. But they were also police officers and no one wanted to challenge them.

George looked uneasy; this was not a place that he should be but Mickey hoped the unease would actually loosen his tongue. He brought them both beers and took them back to the table in the corner where George sat.

'So tell me,' he said, 'what your Walter told you about May.'

'Not much to tell. Walter said he thought he saw that man talking to our Mary. That she seemed uncomfortable. That Ruby was there,

235

fidgeting around and Mary got cross with her because she wouldn't stand still. Our Mary rarely got cross with Ruby – there was no need. Ruby was a nice, calm little thing. She caused no trouble to anyone and our Mary knew that. I never saw her raise her voice.'

Mickey was of the opinion that no child was ever that good. 'And your Walter thought that he'd said something to upset Mary? I thought it was May that made sure you and Mary got your bequest?'

'It was but you can be sure with a man like May that there were always strings attached. He was as bad as that partner of his, Fry. Neither of them really saw any reason why we should have anything even if the old lady had left it to us.'

'And yet May took your side?'

'May said that the will was watertight, that it would only make their firm look bad if Fry went ahead to try to fight it. After all, it was only a little bit of money. Not enough to make a difference to a man like that but enough to make all the difference to people like us.'

'And yet he doesn't seem to have made a difference to your condition. You are still poor as church mice.'

'At the time it did. We managed to rent somewhere half decent but I had problems finding another job and it soon went. We couldn't ask the parish for help – they'd have said we had money and when we'd run out they'd have said we couldn't look after Ruby. The parish is the ruination of families; it would have been the ruination of us. Eventually I went back to sea and Mary, well, Mary went back to her old ways.'

'And May knew all about this?'

'Of course he did. Fry had tried to blacken her name before. He said he'd take us to court, say what kind of a woman she was, make sure we didn't get the money we were owed. He threatened to say that Mary had been stealing. Mary had never stolen anything in her life and neither had I.'

'And when you went away to sea you left Mary and Ruby unprotected. I'm not blaming you, George, I'm just telling it how was. The pressures that must have built upon them, on Mary especially . . . A woman on her own, with a reputation and very little money – it must have seemed like an easy way out.'

George nodded slowly. 'I should never have gone. I should have stopped here with her, with them. We should have gone down to where her family were, Newark or Nottingham. I think she must have been lonely but she never said. I think she would have been better off somewhere else but my pride wouldn't let me say I'd failed. But I did fail, didn't I? Failed them in the worst way.'

'Your father doesn't like me,' Henry Johnstone said to Ted as they drove out of the yard and on to the main road.

'Well, for a start you don't make yourself very easy to like,' Ted said frankly. 'And secondly I don't think he would like anyone who came from the outside at the moment. We're used to handling things ourselves and it irks him that he can't handle this.'

'I think it irks him more that your brother was a bad lot and that a more useful man killed him.'

'You have a strange way of putting things,' Ted said. 'Not one I can like.'

'But, nevertheless, you recognize some truth in it.'

Ted shook his head and Henry knew it wasn't something he could admit out loud anyway. 'What will it do to the village community?' he asked.

'Hard to say.'

'I hear that Ethan coming back shook things up. That he was a disruptive influence, becoming involved with Helen Lee like that.'

'Love isn't something that can be controlled, Inspector. That had all been settled. They'd have got married and moved just a little bit away so no one's nose got rubbed in it but they were still part of the community and by the time the next generation had come along and were set to be married, well, the chances are some arrangement would have been made to draw the families back together again. It's always been that way.'

'And has an arrangement been made for you?'

'Arrangements don't apply to the Hansons any more. You could say we've moved beyond that.'

Henry nodded; that chimed with what he'd already thought. 'The world is changing,' he said. 'Too fast for some, not fast enough for others.'

He was silent for a few minutes and then he asked, 'Would you have believed Ethan capable of this?'

'Capable of giving Robert a beating, yes. They would have come to blows sooner or later but we would have dealt with that. No one thinks badly of two men facing one another in a fair fight. But I'd not pegged Ethan for someone to hit a man when he was down.'

'What do you think will happen to Helen Lee now?'

Ted shrugged. 'The families will work something out,' he said. 'That's the way it's always been done.'

Forty-Six

By the time Ted dropped Henry off, George had already gone on his way and Mickey, after his evening meal had been taken, had now returned to the lounge bar and was waiting for his boss to get back. Henry went to join him, dropping gratefully into the big fireside chair and closing his eyes.

Mickey studied him thoughtfully. 'Tough day?' he asked.

'I followed the dogs about a dozen miles. My mind is unchanged – that he'll head for the docks and try to get on a ship. It's a life he's used to – no doubt he'll have contacts he can use. But the word is out and the dockland police will catch up with him.'

'And the body has been brought back here?'

'It has. I'll attend the post-mortem tomorrow – you too if you wish.'

239

'I may as well; I'm making little progress else-where. I spoke to George Fields at length today.'

'And did he have anything useful to say?'

Mickey apprised Henry Johnstone of the day's events and what George had told him. Also about the candlestick that Parkin had brought to him.

'Any usable prints?'

'The only clear ones belong to the children who found it. There are a few partials but nothing very useful.'

Henry brought his sergeant up to date on the events of the day, the shirt and newspaper.

'I'll compare the buttons,' Mickey said. 'Does this mean we have ourselves a suspect?'

'A *possible* suspect. But I'm not discounting other options,' Henry said thoughtfully. 'We should keep a close eye on George. I can see him turning impatient.'

'I doubt patience was a virtue he ever had, but you can understand the man's frustration, both with his wife and with whoever finished her off. It's a bad business any way you look at it.'

Henry nodded then leaned back and closed his eyes. He was tired, he realized. Weary after a long day. He guessed it must have seemed an even longer day to Ethan Samuels.

Seeing George Fields at Hubbard's Hills had unsettled May far more than he would have cred-ited. It was probably the sight of George going off with that policeman, he thought as he sat in his favourite chair cradling his brandy glass. Fry had noticed his unease, of course, but no one else seemed to have done so. He remembered the first time he had seen Mary Fields; such a pretty woman with such a happy smile. The sunlight had caught the gold in her blonde hair and for a moment it had seemed as though she was wearing a halo around her head. But that had been then and he'd learnt different since. The woman was no angel.

She had still been working for old Mrs Fry at that point and it had been another year before he'd had any real contact with her – that had been in the dispute over the will. He had been astonished by Edmund Fry's intent to try and do Mary and her husband out of their little bit of a bequest. It had seemed so petty. It was only when he challenged Edmund that it had emerged that his fit of pique had nothing to do with the money, not really, but more that the woman had rejected his advances and told him that she didn't do that sort of thing any more.

May had immediately been interested. 'You mean she did before?' he had asked.

'Oh, but she certainly did. Had quite a reputation did Mary.'

'I take it your grandmother didn't know anything about it?'

'That's the devil of it – she did know. Came out with some claptrap about everyone deserving a second chance. She was always a little soft in the head. But our little Mary said she had promised my grandmother that she would behave and she wasn't going to break a promise.'

Fry had laughed, as though he could not quite believe the words. What right had any woman to turn him down, especially one like Mary Fields?

And so, when May had been dealing with the dispute over the will, he had approached Mary with the proposition. At first she had refused him but over time he had worn her down. Her situation had worn her down and she had given in.

It had even been fun, for a while.

Forty-Seven

The post-mortem on Robert Hanson had been scheduled for two p.m. on the Monday afternoon and Henry and Mickey had planned to spend the morning going over the evidence and discussing what direction they should take next. They were interrupted, however, by the arrival of Constable Parkin. Inspector Carrington had sent him to get them both and, Parkin said, Carrington was in a right fury.

'It's George Fields,' Parkin said. 'He's been going from hotel to hotel and pub to pub looking for a man called Williams who he says slept with his wife. He's been making a right lot of noise and there have been complaints from landlords and members of the public he's upset. Inspector Carrington thinks it's all your fault.'

'Of course he does,' Mickey said. 'Who else's could it be?'

'He says you put George Fields up to this, upsetting respectable people just going about their daily business. He says you should have given up the enquiry by now because you ain't

242

getting nowhere. He says a lot of things but I should probably not have been listening.'

'Probably not,' Mickey agreed. 'But sometimes it's hard not to, isn't it, lad?'

They accompanied Constable Parkin back to the police station. Carrington heard them arrive and came out into the reception; he was bristling with anger, red in the face and blue about the gills. Henry sent Mickey to speak to George Fields and suggested that he and Carrington should go back into Carrington's office and discuss matters quietly. Inspector Carrington did not feel inclined to do so but, nevertheless, he turned and strode back through his door, sat down behind his desk and glowered at Henry Johnstone.

'Do you know what that man has been doing? He's been going from one establishment to another, standing in the lobby or pacing up and down in the reception and shouting at the top of his voice for someone called Williams to come out and face him. Five different establishments. Five. Can you imagine how many people he has upset and distressed?'

'A few, I expect,' Henry said. 'It appears that he thinks someone called Williams—'

'I know exactly what he thinks. The whole world knows exactly what he thinks. But was there a Mr Williams to answer his challenge? No, there was not. Just a lot of very distressed customers and very put out employees. And it's you I blame for all of this. You have no control over this investigation and even less over George Fields.'

'I never claimed to have any control over George Fields,' Henry observed.

'And from what I hear you've also upset the Hansons. Do you know how much land Mr Hanson owns hereabouts? What influence he has?'

'No.' Henry shrugged. 'But I've no doubt you could tell me.' He got up. 'I'll go and speak to George Fields,' he said. 'See if he has any idea where to look for this Mr Williams. His methodology thus far leaves little to be desired. It may be that Sergeant Hitchens and I will have better luck.'

Carrington had taken a deep breath, no doubt to deliver a new tirade, but Henry left, closing the door behind him, and went down to the police cells to join Mickey.

George Fields had the grace to look shamefaced but he was clearly unrepentant.

'I've read your wife's letters,' Henry said. 'Once you're out of here I can give them back to you. Do you really think this was the way to proceed?'

'Do you really think *you're* making any progress?'

Henry thought about it for a moment and then shook his head. 'Truthfully? Very little as yet, but sometimes that's the way of things. The case will break. We will find out who killed your family. But you do have to trust us and let us do things our way. George, all this will achieve is more trouble for you, and though you may not think you care right now, you have the rest of your life to live.'

'But no one to live it for,' George said sullenly.

'You think I can just walk away from this and start again? It doesn't work like that, does it? You don't just walk away and start again.'

'Sometimes there is no other choice,' Henry told him. 'George, do you remember a young man called Ethan Samuels? You were shipboard with him?'

'Of course I do. The gypsy boy. He was nice enough, came back home with me a time or two but . . .'

'But what?'

George looked a little shamefaced. 'He was a bit too cosy with our Mary,' he said. 'I wasn't sure I liked the way he was with her.' He looked puzzled. 'Why do you want to know? I heard about the death out at Thoresway. Hard to believe the boy would do something like that.' He looked from Henry to Mickey, expecting some kind of explanation but receiving none.

There wasn't a lot else that Henry or Sergeant Hitchens could do for George Fields and so they left soon afterwards. 'Well, he might have stirred things up a bit for us,' Mickey observed. 'Someone somewhere might remember something just because George Fields has made a bit of a noise.'

'The trouble is,' he added, 'we're on the back foot here. Back at home we'd have our snouts and snitches and would know the way things worked but a place like this, it's like a giant, exclusive club you have to be part of. Never did like country towns or country politics. Give me a straight city villain any day.'

Henry nodded. He might not have quite put it

that way but he understood what Mickey meant and agreed with him.

News of George Fields' rampage had spread across the town and reached Edmund Fry's wife. She told him all about it when he came home to lunch.

'Celia says that's the man that was up at Hubbard's Hills yesterday. That he was watching us. His wife worked for your grandmother, didn't she? Before we were married? That's what Celia says.'

'She did, for a while. My grandmother could not always be trusted with good judgement. Anyway, it's nothing for you to be concerned about. The man has been locked up and won't bother you again.'

'He didn't bother me in the first place,' she said. 'I only mention it because there was a connection in the past and because the police are investigating and so it would be natural if they came to talk to us.'

'I've already spoken to them,' her husband said. 'That inspector came to the office on Saturday morning.'

'You didn't tell me.'

'And why would I tell you? It was of no consequence. They merely wanted to know the circumstances.'

'What circumstances?'

'What I knew about the woman,' he said impatiently. 'Which was little enough. Certainly nothing to bother you with and certainly nothing Celia should be gossiping about.'

'She wasn't gossiping. She just told me, that was all. Apparently everyone thought the man must be drunk or mad. Both perhaps. She said—'

Edmund cut her off with a wave of his hand. 'I don't want to hear any more. It's a sordid business and not the kind of thing we should be discussing over lunch.'

She looked at him in some surprise but when he changed the subject she followed his lead. 'I didn't mean to upset you,' she said later as he was about to return to work.

'You didn't upset me. I just don't wish to discuss that kind of woman in our house. Or that kind of man. Those people have no place in our lives so I'd be really grateful if—'

'Of course,' she said, but he could see the puzzlement in her eyes and had no doubt that as soon as he had gone she would be on the telephone to Celia.

Forty-Eight

Sergeant Hitchens and Inspector Johnstone had both attended the post-mortem with Dr Fielding. It was the first time that Mickey had seen the body and Henry stood back so that he should get a better view as Dr Fielding pointed out the main injuries.

'If you help me roll the body so that you can see the back of the head . . . Yes, that's right; look, my thought is this was the first injury, beyond some superficial lacerations to the face, of course. The witness says that Ethan Samuels seized the crop and set about the rider with it and that he then fell to the ground.'

'Looks like he hit his head on something,' Mickey observed. 'A rock, maybe, though if he fell hard, just hitting the ground with his head would have rendered him helpless.'

'And might have killed him but most likely it didn't. You can see where the toe of the boot made contact with the temple, and we're assuming this was the last of the injuries as there was still some bleeding around the wound. Of course, none of this is a certainty. It is possible that all but the wounds from the boots were made before he fell from the horse, that he then hit his head and this was the cause of death. That he was kicked as he was dying.'

'Whatever the order,' Mickey said, 'I would suggest there was intent to kill or at least intent to wound heavily. There was no restraint that I can see.' He indicated the wounds of Robert Hanson's face and neck. 'This speaks to me of blind fury.'

'And fits with what Frank Church told us.'

'I doubt any jury would be content with anything less than a murder conviction,' Dr Fielding commented. 'Especially any local jury. The Hansons carry a tide of influence in this county and have friends that do well beyond it. Whatever the circumstances, it's likely they'd be lining up to tie the noose.'

Henry Johnstone nodded and they resumed their examination. There were bruises consistent

248

with the fall down the young man's back, most of which had developed since his death and had now become visible. He had fallen very hard.

'See here,' Henry Johnstone said. 'Where the body had been lying on the table in the Hanson house there is no post-mortem staining on the shoulder blades or the bones of the spine where it's been touching the hard surface, but there is bruising. For the rest it's hard to distinguish, visually, between the two. The redness bleeds into the purple and it would require a section putting under the microscope to tell the difference. But I'm satisfied that he hit the ground hard, falling flat on his head and back and made no attempt to break his own fall.'

'There are marks from the riding crop on his face and neck and one stripe on his right hand, but he seems to have made little attempt to defend himself.'

'From what we've all heard he was blind drunk,' Henry Johnstone said. 'In no position to do anything. If Ethan Samuels had merely grabbed the horse and held it hard and Robert Hanson merely fallen, even if he had then hit his head, the three of us would not be called into this mess.'

'And it is a mess.' Dr Fielding nodded sadly. 'This is going to have repercussions across the community and not just in that little village.'

'More than the death of Mary Fields and the others?' Mickey Hitchens asked.

'Long term, yes. The town is in shock but there is also a frisson of excitement. Brutal murder, detectives brought up from London, gossip about who her clients might have been and which men took their pleasure with her. There will be a fair few in this town looking over their shoulders for a while but ultimately the shock will die down and only the frisson will remain. The murder of Mary Fields and Ruby and Walter is too big for people to comprehend and at the same time too small. They lived on the outskirts of our society; Robert Hanson was at its heart. His father continues to be at its centre. And his murder is at once shocking and terribly banal. No excitement or frisson there, just cold fact.'

'I think you are as cynical as Mickey,' Henry Johnstone observed. 'But there may be a complication.'

Briefly, Henry told Dr Fielding about the possible connection between Ethan Samuels and the death of Mary Fields.

'Oh, my dear Lord,' Fielding said. 'Are you serious about this?'

'I'm looking at it as one possibility.'

Fielding shook his head. 'I feel so sorry for the Samuels,' he said. 'They are good people and this . . . this is not something that can be easily healed.'

The post-mortem had told them little they could not already guess. Robert Hanson's brain had been dislodged and badly bruised, and had he survived then his liver would no doubt have finished him off well before his time. As they walked away from High Holme Mickey was unusually quiet and it was Henry who finally broke the silence.

250

'Nothing yet from the dockyard police,' he said. He sounded disappointed.

'It could be that you've misjudged this – that he headed elsewhere.'

'And I plan to go back and speak to the family again. The Samuels and the Lees stay put but many of their kinsfolk still travel and it's quite possible they would help a fugitive escape if it was one of their own. Probable, even. We must spread the net wider and away from the coast, I think.'

'And his family are right, what Dar Samuels said – you've no notion of how far a young man could travel in a couple of days with the devil at his heels.'

'Meantime, we focus on what must be done here,' Henry Johnstone said.

Forty-Nine

It was a little after eight o'clock in the evening when word came to Henry Johnstone that someone wished to speak to him but did not want to come into the hotel. Collecting Mickey, he went down the stairs and into the reception area. The young man at reception pointed him towards the front door. 'A young woman, sir. Didn't want to come in on her own.'

Henry and Mickey went outside and the girl stepped out of the shadows. 'Are you the detectives?'

251

Henry made the introductions and invited her to come inside but she shook her head. 'No offence, but I don't want to be seen with you. Apart from it wouldn't be proper, it would be awkward, see, if anyone seen me talking to you.'

'Perhaps we should walk down to the churchyard,' Henry suggested. 'It will be quiet this time of night and the church may still be open. If you want to go a little ahead and wait for us?'

They waited for the woman to walk off and then followed a few minutes later.

'She'll probably be gone,' Mickey said.

'I don't think so. I think she's made her decision – she just doesn't want to be seen making it.'

She was sitting in the church porch when they got there and Henry and Mickey took a seat opposite. 'You know our names,' Mickey said. 'Am I allowed to know yours?'

She looked embarrassed and then said, 'Mabel Atkins. I work at . . . one of the hotels where that man came today, shouting for Mr Williams to come out and show himself.'

'I'd like to know which hotel,' Henry told her. 'He disturbed the peace at several today.'

'Well, I suppose it would be all right, I suppose you'll find out anyway. It's the Belmont. I work there as a chambermaid but I was passing through to the back room where we store all the cleaning stuff when he arrived and started shouting.'

'And so . . .'

'And so I know the Mr Williams he was talking about. But he's gone now – left a while ago, three, four months. Something like that. He were asked to leave, you see.'

'And do you know why he was asked to leave?' Henry asked.

Even in the dark he could see that the girl's cheeks flushed scarlet. 'He had a bit of a reputation, if you know what I mean. He was undermanager and the girls all kept out of his way if we could. Or at least, most of us did. One of them, young Martha, fell for his, well, you know, his charms. Believed he really wanted to take her away with him.'

'And was Martha dismissed as well?'

She nodded. 'Well, she couldn't hide it, could she? Even behind her apron you could see. And the manager's wife saw and she said that Martha couldn't carry on working looking like that. And they said she had to tell who it was that had, you know. And she thought that Mr Williams was going to marry her, silly little thing. So she told.'

'And do you know where this Mr Williams went to?'

She shrugged and shook her head. 'No, but I know where Martha ended up, poor little scrap. She tried to go home but her mum and dad wouldn't have her and in the end I hear she got pulled out of the river. Her and the baby.'

'And so I can imagine Mr Williams is not your favourite person,' Henry suggested.

She bristled at that suggestion. 'I ain't lying.'

'I never said you were.'

'And where might he have gone?' Mickey asked. 'Are there friends still here that would know?'

She shook her head. 'No one liked him. And

253

we all warned her. But she wouldn't have it. But there's another thing.'

'And what would that be?'

'It's about that woman, that Mary. I never knew her, see, but someone said as she used to work in the hotels round here. I mean, maid work, not the other. And one of the older women who used to work with us, but now she's married and moved off – they reckon she used to take care of little Ruby. That she sometimes used to have her overnight when Mary was away. I seen her with Ruby a couple of times – Phyllis, she were called. Little thing she was, Ruby. Such a nice, polite little girl. Phyllis said she were no bother.'

'And does this Phyllis have a second name and an address?' Henry asked.

'She does, and I spoke to her. She will talk to you but only somewhere private and not if you come to her house. If the police come to her house . . . She's a married woman and the neighbours might think, well, you know. Policeman going to her house . . . So you see she's willing to do her bit but you got to be discreet.'

Henry took a decision. There was no chance to consult with Dr Fielding but he was the one person in town whose home might serve as neutral ground and who could be trusted not to gossip. And Dr Fielding had a housekeeper who could be called upon to chaperone if the need arose.

He gave Mabel the address and told her that she should bring or send Phyllis to their house at ten in the morning. Did she think that would be a suitable solution?

Mabel Atkins nodded. It would do.

She left before they did and they watched her walk back through the churchyard and disappear from sight before they left the porch.

'It's been suggested before that Mary sometimes saw men outside her home, that she sometimes left Ruby with other people.'

'Well, we shall see where it leads. It won't mean that this Phyllis knows who she was seeing. It could lead to another dead end. So where now – warn Doctor Fielding that he will have a visitor in the morning?'

Henry nodded. 'That would seem like a sensible idea.'

Helen could not seem to settle anywhere. In the end she'd gone walking even though her body ached from another day of hard work. Her mother seemed intent on keeping her busy and in some ways Helen was grateful though the repetitive tasks still gave her too much time to think.

Where was he? Was he safe? Was he thinking about her, was he regretting ever having come home?

She walked past the cottages of Red Row. There was a light on in the Samuels' window and she caught a glimpse of Dar sitting at the table. There was a newspaper spread out in front of him but he was not reading it – he was staring into the distance. His heart is broken too, Helen thought, but she couldn't go to speak to him. That would have been unthinkable. She wondered if in some way he blamed her even though she'd been nowhere near Ethan and Robert Hanson

255

that day. Somehow everything felt intertwined and tangled, and Helen could not help but think that if she and Ethan had walked away from each other that first night, not danced together, not talked, not fallen in love, that the world would be a different place.

She wandered up into the churchyard, not a place she usually frequented, her family being chapel. Both she and the Samuels had ancestors buried here. Old Mother Cook's grave was still fresh and covered in flowers. Helen knelt beside it. 'If you'd still been here you'd have been able to sort this out, wouldn't you?' But even as she knelt there Helen knew that that was a stupid thing to say. Even Mother Jo would have been defeated by this problem.

Fifty

At ten a.m. the following morning Henry and Mickey were waiting in the front parlour of Dr Fielding's house for the mysterious Phyllis to arrive. Dr Fielding's house was in a quiet street where any stranger would have been very evident and Henry was hoping that Phyllis was not going to be put off by this.

At 10.05 a.m. the door opened and Dr Fielding's housekeeper came in, attended by a younger woman. Henry commented that he'd not heard the doorbell ring.

'No,' the housekeeper said, 'I kept an eye open

for her coming round the corner and then went out and suggested she come in through the back garden. There is a little path that runs at the rear of the houses, so that seemed like a good idea. I'll bring your tea now.'

She left the door ajar and the younger woman stood uncertainly on the threshold until Henry invited her to sit down. She was neatly turned out in a blue print dress that made a nod to the drop waists of the latest fashion but was longer at the knee than his sister Cynthia would have worn and her stockings were thicker. At first Phyllis was reluctant to give her second name but eventually she told them that it was Miles and that she no longer worked in the hotels because she was a married lady now and her husband had a job that did well for both of them. And besides, she now had a child.

'You used to know Mary Fields and sometimes look after her daughter?'

Phyllis pursed her lips and looked a little uncomfortable. 'I feel she lied to me,' she said. 'She told me sometimes she had to go away because she was offered a bit of work. She led me to believe it was cleaning work or serving work. She was trained as a silver service wait-ress, you see, and then she did chambermaid work. Or in the silver pantry, like she did when she first moved away from home. It's usually young girls that work in the silver pantry. It lets the housekeeper keep an eye on them while they settle in, you see. So I used to look after Ruby, let her get a few hours work here and there.

If there was a big party on at one of the big houses they always wanted extra staff.'

'And some of the hotels – do they do external catering?'

'Not so much. But sometimes they would hire staff on behalf of those that needed it. Staff they had already got the references for, you see, and they'd go off to one of the big houses hereabouts, help out for the evening then get brought back. A lot of the big places, they used to employ twenty or thirty or more all the time but these days no one can afford the staff – not like they used to. And people don't want to be in service no more. Not when they can earn more in a factory and not be told what to do all the time.'

'How often did you look after Ruby?'

'Oh, I don't know, maybe a dozen times in all. Then I began to realize that she wasn't doing what she said she was doing, Mary. She let slip one time that it was a different kind of work altogether. I didn't take no notice. I didn't want to take no notice. But then the rumours started. People said she was doing things with men while her husband was away and in the end I talked about it with my mother and she said I should be keeping clear of women like that and I should tell her that I couldn't look after Ruby any more, especially not with me being married to a good man with a good job.'

'And when was this – when did you tell her?'

For the first time Phyllis looked really uncomfortable.

'I'm right in thinking that you didn't take your mother's advice straight away?' Henry asked.

'I felt sorry for her. She'd had a really bad time what with that Mrs Fry dying and leaving her money that she then couldn't get and all the trouble that came from it. So I carried on looking after Ruby, from time to time, but I told her it would have to stop. Told I couldn't keep on doing it.'

'And eventually, when did you stop?'

Phyllis took a deep breath. 'When things . . . things I couldn't . . . things I couldn't approve started happening. I mean, I turn a blind eye to a lot of things because I know how hard it is for people like Mary Fields and for little Ruby. And if you want to know the truth, I did love that little girl. But Mary was getting in . . . getting into things she didn't ought to have done. I mean, apart from the obvious.'

'What kind of things? Phyllis, I know this is hard but it's really important. Mary and Ruby are dead and so is Walter, their cousin. We think somebody should pay for that, don't you?'

Phyllis nodded. 'Look, I don't want to make it sound as though I'm passing judgement on a dead woman but I think she brought some of it on herself. Mary thought she was cleverer than she really was and she got Walter involved. And she should not have done that, not a young man like that.'

'Involved in what?' Henry asked, but he suspected that Phyllis was set on telling the tale in her own time and he was not going to be able to hurry it along.

There was a pause in the conversation as the housekeeper brought the tea and set it down on

259

a little table. She glanced at the three of them and then withdrew but Henry didn't think she would go far. He hoped she was as discreet as Dr Fielding reckoned her to be.

Mickey got up. 'Shall I be mother?' he said. 'Sugar, is it, Mrs Miles?'

'Oh, yes, one, please.' She watched Mickey intently and then settled herself with a cup and saucer, declining the offer of biscuits.

'You were saying that Mary had got involved in something deeper,' Henry prompted.

Phyllis took another deep breath; it seemed she had to be well oxygenated if she was to tell her story effectively. 'You know perhaps about old Mrs Fry, about her leaving some money. And about the grandson saying that shouldn't have happened and about Mr May, his business partner, making sure that it did.'

Henry nodded. Mickey had sat back down again and was helping himself to biscuits.

'Well, she told me that she'd got herself involved with this Mr May. That she was seeing him, regular like, going away overnight sometimes. And him booking a hotel.'

Henry nodded in what he hoped was an encouraging manner. That fitted with what had been rumoured; that May had made approaches to Mary and that George Fields had been under the impression that she had rejected him. Or perhaps that was just what he wanted to think.

'And how long ago was this?' Henry asked.

'A year or more ago, it started. She said she'd been helping out at a party somewhere. She said they put them all in these black uniforms with

260

frilly white aprons and frilly little caps. She said they were all drinking champagne. I don't mean the servants, of course, but she said the guests were all drinking champagne for hours. Dancing on the tables, they were.'

'And Mr May was there?'

'And his wife too.'

'And this was when their . . . liaison started? After that?'

'Soon after that, I think. But anyway, she got involved with him. She said he paid for every-thing when they were away and gave her some money to bring home with her. But Mary, well, she wanted more out of it. She reckoned he had enough to spare for her. She said she wanted the best for Ruby and that the likes of May didn't deserve it anyway. She said it was his wife's money, most of it. That his wife's father had paid for Fry and May to set up in business or maybe it was for him to join the business or something. I don't remember. But that's when she had the idea, you see?'

'The idea?'

'And that's when she started to involve Walter.' She sipped her tea and looked appeal-ingly at Henry Johnstone, as though he should draw the right conclusion and she not have to say it.

'Are we talking blackmail here?' Mickey asked, helping himself to another biscuit.

'Well, yes. Like I said, she had an idea. She thought she could threaten him. Tell his wife.'

'Did she have any hope that his wife would believe her?'

'Of course she did. She'd have had the pictures, wouldn't she?'

'Photographs. You mean she got Walter to take photographs?'

'And where would Walter get a camera from?' Mickey asked.

Phyllis shrugged. 'That I don't know. But she reckoned he could. She reckoned she could make good money out of him. I reckon she were a bloody fool, excuse my language, but a man like that isn't going to just lie down and take it, if you see my meaning.'

'And how long ago was this?'

'Three, four months ago maybe. It was then that I went and talked to my mother . . . Again. And she was furious with me for not taking any notice of her the first time. And I told Mary then and there that I'd not be looking after Ruby for her. She needed to stop before it got too bad. She needed to think again. A man like that . . .'

Phyllis Miles left soon afterwards, slipping out of the back door again and Mickey and Henry, having thanked the housekeeper for her help and impressed upon her the need for secrecy, left by the front.

'This begins to make sense,' Henry said. 'Now we need to know if Walter managed to get the camera and if he took the pictures. If so, where are the pictures now? There was no sign of the house being searched, not that there was much to search – just a quick rummage through the drawers would have done it. So it's possible, of course, that whoever killed Mary and the others took the photographs away.'

'It draws May into the frame, though, doesn't it? Though whether he'd do the deed himself or get someone to do it for him is a moot point.'

'But he'd surely not want to admit to anyone that these photographs existed and perhaps lay himself open to further blackmail.'

'Well, we don't know that yet or whether Mary followed through with her plan. Walter may have been unable or unwilling to assist. We need to talk to George Fields again, find out where his cousin might've got a camera from. Or if he'd any inkling this was what his Mary was planning.'

'Even if he had, he'd have put it from his mind,' Henry said. 'George Fields has this image of perfection in his head where his wife and child are concerned and it's an image he's going to be reluctant to shift from.'

'Well, it's a picture he's going to have to redraw if we're going to catch the man who did this.'

'And now we have two possible suspects – May and Ethan Samuels. Do you favour one over the other?'

Henry nodded slowly. 'Yesterday,' he said, 'I was halfway to being convinced that the Samuels boy was responsible but now I'm drifting in the other direction. May has a lot to lose and a long way to fall.'

George Fields was in a recalcitrant mood when they had him brought back up to the interview room. He listened in thunderous silence while Henry told him that information had been received that indicated his wife had been having

263

an affair with Charles May and that she may even have been trying to blackmail him.

'Whoever it is, they're lying,' George insisted. 'I told you before – he tried it on with her and she told him where to go.'

'She may have had the strength to tell him that when you were around but when you were no longer there she may have decided that what you didn't know couldn't hurt you.'

George Fields shook his head and would no longer meet Henry's gaze.

'Just tell me one thing,' Henry said. 'Where would Walter have got a camera from?'

George sighed deeply but it seemed that was a question he could answer. 'We have a relative, assistant to one of the promenade photographers in Cleethorpes. It's possible he might have got one from him.'

Henry remembered the photograph that he'd found in the drawer, the one of George and Mary and Ruby taken on the promenade. He nodded. 'Thank you, George. You can go back to your cell now.'

The door to Carrington's office was closed so the man must be inside, but neither Henry nor Mickey felt like disturbing him and it seemed that Carrington wanted nothing to do with them.

'So what now?' Mickey asked.

'I think we leave things over until morning and then we bring Charles May in for questioning. We don't have enough evidence to charge him with anything but we do have enough to unsettle the man.'

Mickey nodded. 'We going to do it quietly or with all the bells and whistles?'

'I think with a full brass band if we can find one,' Henry replied. 'This is a man who needs to keep up appearances. It seems to me that the key to breaking him is public display.'

'And if he's innocent, we stand to ruin his reputation.'

'Then we'll offer an apology,' Henry said.

'Why wait until tomorrow?'

'Because I want to find out more about him before we jump, gather what ammunition we can. If his money is really his wife's fortune, how widely is that known? I want to go in as well armed as we can.'

'Newspaper offices, then,' Mickey guessed.

Fifty-One

Charles May had been brought to the police station at nine o'clock the following morning. He had been escorted from his house, put into a police car and driven through the streets at a time when the town was fully awake and active and many could see. A quiet word had been dropped to the local newspapers that this was happening and that Mr Charles May was helping the police with their enquiries concerning the murder of Mrs Mary Fields and her child.

The tipoff had been anonymous, of course, but a journalist had been on the scene ready to photograph events as Mr May was led through the front door of the police station.

It was underhanded, of course, and Henry was under no illusions. He had little evidence against May and, if asked, would be at pains to insist the man had come voluntarily and the police car had simply been sent to pick him up as a courtesy. Actually, he would probably have left Mickey to say all that, his sergeant being a far more convincing liar than he was.

He fully expected a hurricane of protest from Inspector Carrington when he finally arrived at work and the vilification of polite society in Louth and beyond, a prospect which, frankly, worried him not in the slightest. Henry Johnstone was never concerned about treading on corns.

Charles May was fuming quietly. He sat in the interview room across the table from Johnstone. 'You do realize that you will pay for this. I have influential friends who will take a very low view of me being dragged here. So I suggest we get this over and done with and I leave. I have work to attend to.'

'I'm going to put it to you that you were having a relationship with Mrs Mary Fields, a relationship that was getting troublesome.'

'And I put to you, that though I knew Mrs Mary Fields in a professional capacity, I had no dealings with the woman outside of that. Why would I? I have a wife, and should I want to have an affair there are many other young women willing enough. Why should I have to scrape the dregs from the barrel?'

'Where were you on the night of the murder?'

266

Henry asked. 'That would be the twenty-third of June.'

Charles May began to laugh, very softly. 'Inspector, you should have asked me this before and I could have saved you a lot of trouble. I, my wife and Mr and Mrs Fry were attending a midsummer celebration out at Willingsby Hall, in the company of perhaps sixty others. It was a big party that spilled out on to the lawn under a marquee. We took over the house, Inspector, and we danced the night away. I have many witnesses to the fact that I was there. And if you had troubled to ask me, in the privacy of my own home, I would have told you this.'

'You don't have to be present to have commissioned a murder,' Henry Johnstone said. 'We have reason to believe that Mrs Fields was trying to blackmail you, to reveal the details of the affair to your wife who, I believe, actually controls most of your fortune. I'd consider that a good motive.'

Charles May's face twisted into a look of disdain but Henry could tell that he had hit a sore spot. 'My wife's fortune is mine,' Charles May said. 'There is no difference between what I own and what her father has given to her.'

'I understand you are given an allowance,' Henry Johnstone said. 'I understand that the bulk of your wife's fortune will pass purely to her on her father's death and is tied up in a trust fund that cannot be touched.'

'How dare you involve yourself in my personal matters!'

'It's a matter of public knowledge,' Henry

267

Johnstone said. 'My sergeants and I spent yesterday afternoon searching through the archives of the local newspapers and they had quite a lot to say about your marriage to Celia and the, some might say, unusual financial ramifications.'

'Did you find the photographs?' Mickey Hitchens asked. 'Or were you yet disappointed?'

'What photographs? There were no photographs. There was no relationship beyond my dealing with a small matter of Mrs Fry's bequest. And believe me, it was a small matter. Fifty or a hundred pounds, I don't remember now, but nothing significant. I could never understand why Fry made such a fuss over it. It was nothing in the greater scheme of things.'

'It was to Mr and Mrs Fields, though. It was of great matter to them.'

May gestured airily. 'I've no doubt it was,' he said. 'And it was dealt with satisfactorily. I then had nothing more to do with the woman. To suggest that I might have had any kind of relationship with her . . . and I resent the idea that this might have been an affair, Inspector. People have affairs with their equals and she was certainly not that.'

A knock on the door and the constable told them that Mr Fry was insisting that he see Mr May, his client.

'So you're a client now,' Mickey Hitchens said. 'Is Mr Fry also an expert in criminal law?'

'You can tell Mr Fry not to fret,' Henry Johnstone told the constable. 'Mr May will be with him directly.'

Henry exchanged a look with Mickey. There

268

was nothing more to be gained from keeping Fry waiting or keeping May here. Seeds had been sown and all they could hope now was that they would take root and grow swiftly.

Edmund Fry had his car waiting and Henry watched as the pair drove away. Carrington had arrived in time to see this event and was now demanding that Henry explain himself.

'Information was received that Charles May was having an affair with Mary Fields and that she sought to blackmail him over this. Mr May therefore becomes a suspect. A legitimate suspect. And so we brought him in for questioning. I take it there are no objections.'

Neither Inspector Johnstone nor Sergeant Hitchens waited around to see if there were. As they walked back to their lodgings, Henry confided that he was still frustrated at there being a lack of news from the dockyard police. He had arranged to borrow Dr Fielding's car and drive back out to Thoresway. Mickey Hitchens planned to take the train up to Cleethorpes and track down the photographer and his assistant there.

'What do you think May will do now?'

Henry Johnstone shrugged. 'I imagine that he will try to consolidate his alibi,' he said. 'And by this time tomorrow his friends will be falling over themselves to assure us that he was at this party, all night, and in full view of them for all that time.'

'And the more versions of the story there are, the more likely they are to contradict.'

'We have to hope so. And we also have to

hope that the photographs exist and that you can get your hands on them, or at least on the negatives. Once we can prove a direct link between May and Mary Fields, a link he may not wish to have exposed elsewhere, we're one step further on to proving that he murdered her. And I'm now even more inclined to favour him over Ethan Samuels.'

'Inclining and proving can be a whole field apart. They'll close ranks against us. Like I said, it's a club we don't belong to.'

'And in any club there is a central clique and there are the hangers-on, the ones who have to try hard just to keep a fingertip hold. Then there's the staff who see everything and servants brought in from outside who have no loyalty to anyone and the chauffeurs left to gossip among themselves outside, who would notice if somebody drove away. No, Mickey, we don't belong to the club and so we concentrate on those who don't belong either but who are in a position to see the way it works.'

Fifty-Two

Back in their offices, Charles May and Edmund Fry had cancelled all the day's appointments and were in conference together. The effect of the police action was already being felt; two of their clients had called to ask questions, one informing Edmund Fry that he would be taking his business elsewhere. It might be a difficult few weeks, Fry thought, but eventually it would all blow over.

He had questioned his friend, going over and over exactly what the police had said to him and what they had wanted to know, and now he felt somewhat relieved. 'There is nothing whatsoever that they can do,' Edmund said. 'You were elsewhere on the night of the murder so how can they suspect you? We'll speak to our friends, get our stories straight. My advice to you would be to forget about it.'

'And I suppose Celia is going to forget about it too, old man. You know what she's like – she'll be sucking up every little bit of gossip, ready to use it against me with her father.'

'No, she won't. Think about it, Charlie, just for a moment. She won't want to do anything that draws any more attention to this. The best thing the pair of you can do is go away for a few weeks. Take a trip – I can manage here. Go away until this has all blown itself out. People forget in no time.'

'They won't forget something like this,' Charles May said bitterly. 'Edmund, I plan to make a complaint. A formal complaint to the highest authority I can find. That man will find himself out of a job.'

Edmund Fry shook his head. 'Look, Charlie. You once advised me to leave well alone when I was ready to go out all guns blazing. When my grandmother died I couldn't believe that she had done something so stupid as to leave that woman money. But you pointed out to me it would do our reputation more harm if—'

271

'The two things don't even compare and you know it.'

Charles pushed himself out of the deep, button-backed chair and crossed to the console table set against the far wall. He poured himself another drink.

'I've never seen you so rattled,' Edmund said.

'I've never been hauled into a police station and accused of murder before. You should try it – see how you feel about it.'

'He was fishing, that was all. He knows he has nothing and no doubt your name just came up somewhere.' Edmund Fry hesitated for a few moments and then said quietly, 'But you *were* seeing her, weren't you?'

'What the devil do you mean?'

'Charles, you were spotted. Let's just say a mutual friend mentioned it. I've said nothing, of course, but it did strike me at the time as being damnably stupid.'

Charles May swallowed his drink and then slammed the glass down on the console table. 'I'm going home to face the music,' he said. 'And you can tell our mutual friend, whoever it might be, to keep his or her bloody mouth shut. And I'll thank you not to interfere. Keep your nose out of my life, Eddie boy.'

Dr Fielding owned an Armstrong Siddeley Tourer, a two-litre, four-cylinder car in a deep, dark blue that purred happily up the hills but was a little skittish on the bends. Henry thought about the events of the morning as he made his way out to the village. He and Mickey had stirred things up but what would rise to the surface? He should be further on with the investigation by now and that grated terribly.

As he entered the village he saw a team of horses on the hill ploughing an awkward slope; he had just overtaken a small tractor with bright red wheels tootling along at not much more than walking pace. Manpower, horsepower and the mechanical seem to sit side-by-side in this landscape but he wondered how long that would last.

He parked beside the church and walked back along to Red Row. He didn't expect Dar Samuels to be in but thought that Mrs Samuels would be. She must have seen him drive past because she had the door open before he knocked and for a moment he could see that she expected news.

He watched the hope fade in her hazel eyes. 'I'm sorry,' Henry said. I've nothing new to tell you.'

She was alone in the cottage. She invited him in, told him to sit down and offered to make him tea but she did not take the seat opposite. Instead she hovered uncertainly between the kitchen sink and the fire.

'He'll not be back for a time yet,' she said. 'But the children will be.'

'Home from school?'

She shook her head. 'No, there's no school just now. There's the first harvest to be brought in. Hay and the second early potatoes. Then they'll go back for a bit and come out again for the main harvest. We will all have to pitch in for

273

that, work up in the fields. The women fetch and carry for the men and the children help out with whatever they are of an age to do. No one can stand idle then, not even the little ones.'

'Where could your son have gone to? There's been no news of him at either Immingham or Grimsby.'

He saw the relief on her face but she just shook her head. 'He's worked on the boats – used to trade horses with his father back when we still could. His granddad was a horse dealer as was his granddad before that but that's all by the by now. He's worked down on the south coast, did a little time with a boat builder down there, but I doubt he'd have headed that way.'

'You still have family that travel. Could he have joined them?'

'If he has I've not heard of it. Look, this time of year there are itinerant labourers all over the country. Plenty of work and no questions asked. He could be anywhere, and I hope he is.'

'You hope your son escapes justice.'

'I hope my son escapes the noose. Of course I do. I don't agree with or condone what he done but I don't agree with a lot of things and they still happen.'

'I'll be off up to the Hanson's,' Henry said. 'And I'll be talking to others in the village too.'

'I've no doubt you will. I've no doubt there'll be some who make suggestions, even give you names. But if Ethan has a mind to disappear then Ethan will disappear. I just hope he stays gone.'

* * *

It was the same answer everywhere – people made half-hearted suggestions and Helen Lee could not hide her delight at the fact that Inspector Johnstone was getting nowhere with his investigations. Even Elijah Hanson gave him short shrift.

'His mother wants to know when she can bury her son,' Elijah said.

'The body will be released in a day or two.'

'That's just it, isn't it? The boy is just a body to you.'

Henry thought about protesting but realized that the man had read him correctly. He had no particular feelings for Robert Hanson beyond the vague sense that he may not have liked the young man.

As Henry Johnstone drove away he had the sense that the entire village was watching – even those whose doors were closed and could not be seen through their windows. He was an outsider here in an even deeper sense than in the market town. He had come to realize that Elijah Hanson had called him in only for the look of things. Elijah had been completely straight with him about that, and had there been a way of taking care of this business themselves the community would have done so. He found it unsettling – not their suspicion, which was commonplace enough – but the sense that he was not really needed, that his version of the law was a mere veneer. Civilization applied as a thin whitewash to the village walls.

Sergeant Hitchens was having a slightly better time of it. He'd found the photographer without any real problems and managed to get a few minutes to chat to the assistant, Thomas Fields. The photographer knew all about the tragedy that happened in Louth and was openly curious. Mickey made a lot of sympathetic noises, said that he was trying to chat to all of the family just in case Mary might have mentioned something that could be of use to the police in their investigation.

He and Thomas Fields stood round the back of the shop and Thomas – 'Call me Tommy' – lit a cigarette. He looked to be about the same age as Walter or perhaps just a bit younger. He eyed Mickey warily.

'Not sure why you'd want to talk to me,' he said. 'Mary was only related through marriage and I didn't know her very well. Only met her a couple of times so there's not much I can tell you. It's not like she'd have confided in me.'

'No, but we know she did confide in Walter. And I'm sure you'd rather your boss heard the excuse I gave than have me ask if you've ever lent Walter a camera. I can't imagine that would go down too well.'

Tommy glanced around nervously and his face grew pale. 'I'd lose me job. I can't afford to lose me job. You can't tell him.'

He hadn't sought to deny it at all, Mickey noted with satisfaction. 'I've no intention of getting you into trouble – I just need to know what Walter told you and if he actually borrowed the camera and took the pictures.'

Tommy Fields shuffled his feet. He'd finished his cigarette and dropped the butt to the ground.

'He came to me, said he'd got the opportunity to earn a bit of money. He said he needed a camera to take pictures for a . . . gentleman, like. I didn't like the sound of it so I pushed him a bit and he admitted it was for Mary.'

'Did he tell you what kind of pictures? Did he tell you what they planned to do?'

'Didn't so much tell me as *not* tell me, if you know what I mean. I figured it out. I told him he could have a camera just for a couple of days. I told him I didn't like what he was doing but family is family and he told me that this man, this gentleman had been threatening our Mary.'

It was *our* Mary now, Mickey noted.

'And that she wanted some insurance.'

'And did you believe him?'

'Like I said, I worked out what he didn't say.'

'You thought he intended to blackmail this man or that Mary did?'

'Mary, more like. Walter would never have thought of it.'

'What did you think of Mary Fields?'

'I thought she was not the kind of woman who should have married George. No matter what he did it would not have been good enough. Mary always wanted more. That's what me mam said anyway. Like I say, I only met her twice or maybe three times.'

'And when he'd taken these photographs, did you process them for him? Did you develop them?'

Reluctantly, Tommy Fields nodded.

'And did you keep copies for yourself? Did you keep the negatives?'

Another nod. He moved restlessly now. 'I'd best be going in. Boss will need me.'

'And *I* need those negatives.'

'I got a room at a boarding house. I left them there. But I can't go now, can I? Boss will want to know what's going on.'

'Do you have a key?'

'Got a front door key. But the landlady, she's a right old battleaxe. If she sees the police go into my room, what she going to think? Be out on me ear and the boss will want to know why and I'll lose my job and—'

'Give me the key, tell me where they are and she'll never know I was even there.'

Tommy Fields looked around desperately but he didn't think he had any options left. He dug in his pocket, found the key and handed it to Sergeant Hitchens. Mickey Hitchens pointed to one of the dustbins standing out in the backyard. 'See that bin? I'll slip the key underneath it when I've done. You can pick it up when you finish for the day. Believe me, lad, you'll feel better when this is done and those negatives are gone from your life for ever.'

Tommy Fields looked far from convinced but he went back inside, having given Mickey directions to his lodging house.

The street was a few back from the main promenade and Mickey stood on a corner watching the house for a few minutes to see if anyone went in or out. It was a large Victorian terrace, three storeys high, with a basement beneath and, fortunately for Mickey, the less fortunate

Tommy Fields had a room in the basement. Apparently it was divided into two and four young men shared Tommy's half. They had a tiny kitchen, a washbasin in one of the rooms and access to the privy out back. Tommy had described this quickly along with the information that his landlady had put proper bathrooms in the main house. 'Two of them, but she said they were for her decent guests.' The ones who could afford to pay more than the bare minimum that Tommy and his ilk were able to shell out each week.

Mickey crossed the road and glanced around but it was practically empty and there was no one to take any notice of him. He went round the area railings and down the four steps to the basement door then slipped the key in the lock. The basement smelt of damp and cooked food and young men who didn't wash very often, though to give Tommy his due he hadn't smelt too bad. Mostly of carbolic soap and hair oil and developing chemicals. Mickey had inhaled far worse.

Tommy shared the left-hand room, off the tiny kitchen, or what passed for a kitchen in that it had a sink and a two-ring burner. It put Mickey in mind of the first place he had lived when he left home. He hadn't actually had a separate bedroom and three of them had shared the single space that was not much bigger than a closet.

He stood and listened for a moment but could hear no noises from outside or upstairs in the main house, so he went through to Tommy's bedroom and found a loose floorboard beneath the bed that Tommy had said was going to be there and took out the envelope from beneath it. The corner had been chewed by something that looked bigger than a mouse and the envelope was covered with droppings. Rats, Mickey thought as he shook the droppings off back into the hole. Quickly, he checked inside the envelope. Photographs and negatives. He poked around inside the hole to make sure there was nothing else there and then left the way he'd come. Only when he was back on the promenade did he have a proper look inside the envelope, sliding some of the pictures out just far enough to satisfy himself that they showed what he had been told they would. Mickey gave a low whistle, then smiled to himself and tucked the envelope back inside his jacket pocket.

True to his word, he returned to the back of the photographer's shop and slipped the key beneath the bin. Circling back to the front of the shop, he caught sight of Tommy speaking with a customer. Tommy spotted him and Sergeant Hitchens gave him a slight nod of acknowledgement. He saw the relief on the young man's face.

Hopefully this would be the end of it for Tommy Fields, Mickey thought. Hopefully they wouldn't have to call him to the court to give evidence. That certainly would put the cat among a lot of pigeons.

Fifty-Three

Edmund Fry received a visit from Chief Inspector Carrington in the middle of the afternoon. He had come, he said, to apologize personally for the inconvenience caused, and asked if he could speak to Mr May to reassure him that this would go no further.

'I have no control over the behaviour of the London detectives,' Carrington said. 'I believe they have behaved abominably.'

'If you have no control over them then it's difficult to know how you could assure either of us this will go no further.'

Carrington frowned. 'I'm sorry,' he said. 'I thought a personal visit might be appropriate. I certainly have no wish for this to continue. Your father and mine were friends for years. Mr May senior was part of the same circle.'

'And I do appreciate the sentiment, believe me. But I think the damage has already been done. And now, if you would excuse me, I still have clients to see today.'

Carrington flushed red at the abrupt dismissal. He took up his hat and left.

Edmund Fry sat quietly in his office after Carrington had gone. In truth they had cancelled all appointments for that day but he couldn't abide the man's presence any longer. He had begun to wonder, the thought growing in his mind, that his friend might not be as innocent as he claimed. What if Mary Fields and Charles May *had* been involved, properly involved, and she had sought to benefit from that? He really could believe that of her. He knew that she had stolen from his grandmother. His resentment of the woman was not so much because of his grandmother's bequest but because he knew that she had been taking and selling small items long before his grandmother had died. The old lady had been slightly less than mentally acute in the last years of her life. Forgetful and occasionally just a little dotty – and he knew that, more than once, when she had missed an item that he believed Mary had taken, Mary Fields had simply used that elderly eccentricity against her, telling her that she must have forgotten where she'd left something. Or didn't she remember, she'd given that away. He'd been furious when he'd realized what was going on but there was nothing he could do. Relatives had simply been glad that somebody else was dealing with the old lady, who had quite a temper and could be very difficult at times. The result was that Mary Fields had free rein and Edmund Fry could do nothing to change that.

But what if Charlie was lying to him? What if he really did have something to do with those three people being murdered? Truthfully, if the opportunity had arisen then Edmund could quite easily see a situation in which he would have done away with Mary Fields. But not the child or the young man, come to that. They, it seemed, were just in the way at the wrong moment.

Charlie had been at the party, right enough, but Edmund had been far too preoccupied to know where he was or what he was doing and, if he was honest, far too drunk anyway to have taken any notice of anyone. Charles could have left, conceivably, and no one would have noticed. He allowed himself a wry smile. It had been one hell of a party.

Fifty-Four

Sergeant Hitchens arrived back at the hotel just after his boss. He went straight to Henry's room and knocked on the door. He didn't mind sharing crime-scene photos in the bar of the Wheatsheaf but this was something else.

He shook the photos out of the envelope and laid them on Henry's bed.

'Photographs and negatives,' he said. 'And a very athletic young man he is too.'

Henry studied the photographs dispassionately. 'We have proof of infidelity,' he said, 'which is slightly more than we had this morning. And the implication is that Mary Fields certainly meant to use blackmail. The question is does it also prove that Charles May was involved with the murder?'

'Prove it, no. Take us further down that path, certainly. Now all we need to do is break his alibi for that night.'

'I drove back via Willingsby, took a look at the

hall and then timed how long it would take to get back here. He would be gone perhaps ninety minutes in all. That would give him time to commit the murder and get back. The problem is finding somebody who will admit to seeing him leave.'

'Or to seeing his car back in Louth when he was supposed to be there. That's always assuming he drove himself and didn't go with his friends, in which case seeing *their* car back in Louth when it wasn't supposed to be here.'

'So our next move will be?'

Mickey gathered the photographs together and put them back in their envelope. 'Seems to me our next move must be to go and see the wife, show her the evidence and see if she'll still vouch for her husband.'

'I suppose that depends on how persuasive he is already being,' Henry said. 'I don't imagine she'll welcome us anyway.'

Fifty-Five

On the Wednesday morning Henry went to visit Mrs May. He was told that the lady was out but he'd come prepared. He had put one of the photographs in a small sealed envelope and now he sent that with the manservant to give this to the lady of the house.

A few minutes later he was told that she must have returned and that she would see him in the morning room.

His hat in his hand, because no one had bothered to take it from him, Henry went through as directed. Celia May, in a yellow dress with matching headband, sat on the window seat. The sun streamed through into the cream, green and gold room and Henry guessed she must have chosen this room as a perfect setting for herself. It was a very feminine space; no sign of Charles May in here.

Celia May held the envelope in her hand and when he came close enough she tossed it on the floor at his feet.

'You are the most disgusting man.'

'I don't feature in the photograph. I'm merely the messenger.'

'And no less disgusting for that. I told you I don't wish to speak to you. I told my servants to say I was out.'

'And then you changed your mind.'

'Something I am now regretting.'

Henry had not been invited to sit down but he did so anyway, seating himself on a high-backed chair which he pulled out from the wall.

'I don't wish to distress you but I am conducting a murder investigation and I *do* believe your husband to have been involved.' He held a hand to silence her as she began to speak again. 'No, please wait. Your husband had an affair with Mary Fields. Mary Fields arranged for them to be photographed *in flagrante*. We have reason to believe she also intended to use these photographs for blackmail, though whether things progressed that far we have no way of knowing. It's likely she told your husband that this is what

285

she planned to do – perhaps threatened to send the pictures to you or to your father. He must have known that the pictures had been taken. I don't imagine Walter Fields would have been discreet and anyway, from the look on his face in that one he must have been very much aware.'

She got up and drifted across the room to a little side table, the yellow silk of her dress floating about her. It was the kind of dress that Cynthia would have liked, Henry thought. Soft and light and expensive looking. His sister enjoyed being rich but she also enjoyed being generous. Celia May took a cigarette from an ivory box and inserted it into an amber holder. She didn't offer one to Henry. And she didn't light her own either. He guessed she just wanted something to do with her hands.

'My husband made a mistake,' she said. 'He became involved with that woman and yes, I can accept that she tried to blackmail him. I can even accept that he must have been glad when she was killed and was no longer a problem. But you are accusing him of a triple murder. Can you imagine, can you understand how absurd that sounds? A man like Charles?'

'Men like Mr May kill all the time. There is no group within society that is exempt. Murderers are found everywhere, in all classes and places.'

'I pity you,' she said. 'You spend your life mired in such filth you cannot believe that there is anything clean.'

'I think your husband is far from clean. I think your husband is far from innocent. I think your husband believes himself to have an adequate

286

alibi but that with sufficient probing we can break it. You were with your husband at the party on the night Mary Fields died?'

'We were all there – you know that already.'

'I didn't ask if you were there, I asked if you were *with* him. If you can account for his movements for the entire evening.'

'You're being ridiculous,' she said. But he could see the beginnings of doubt in her expression. 'He played billiards for a while and he spent time with his friends. We all did. Charles doesn't like to dance and I do, so no, I wasn't with him every minute. But there were plenty of other people who will tell you where he was every second of the night, I'm sure. We left after breakfast the following morning. And none of us had much sleep, I can tell you that.'

'Did you drive there in your car?'

'Yes, of course.'

'And your husband drove himself. You don't have a chauffeur?'

'No, we've never bothered. He likes to drive and so do I. If we need to go any distance and need someone else to drive then I borrow one of my father's people.'

She finally lit her cigarette and waved it in Henry's general direction. 'I would like you to go now. You should also know that I'm leaving for a few days. I'm spending time with friends. I'd rather not be here until this awful business is out of the way.'

'And is your husband going with you?'

She exhaled a long stream of smoke and then pursed her lips. 'No,' she said. 'We talked about it last night and decided we had better have a little time apart. You must understand that I am . . . very angry with him.'

She rang a small silver bell that was set beside the cigarette box and a servant appeared in the doorway. 'The inspector is leaving now. Please see him out.'

As Henry exited, Charles May crossed the hall. He scowled when he saw Henry but did not speak to him. Instead he went into the morning room.

The manservant was holding the front door open but Henry paused before passing through. From the morning room issued raised voices, and it sounded to Henry like an argument that had simply picked up where it had left off earlier. The door was closed so the words were muffled but he could guess what was being said. He'd left the photograph, in its little envelope, lying on the floor. He had no doubt this was now being used as further ammunition.

I keep thinking about Haydn Symmonds and his reasons for finally admitting his guilt. What will it take to break our Mr May? We are beginning to build our evidence – the affair, the blackmail – but the final resolution depends upon our ability to destroy his alibi and that may be more problematic.

May's social circle will protect him – for a time, at least. They will believe, as a matter of course, that no one in their circle could commit such a murder – certainly not to kill a child, but the doubts will surface, I hope, and May's unease will grow.

Rather in the way that Symmonds could not agree to confess his guilt until his confederates had been found guilty and were sentenced, when that final objection had been removed, only then did he feel he could acknowledge his own guilt. It was almost a matter of principle on some very twisted level.

May, I feel, will slowly disintegrate – if he is in fact guilty. It won't be a simple case of gathering the evidence and laying it out and hoping that he will crumble under the weight of it. The disintegration will come about by other means, from the slow withdrawal of support and belief. His wife has left him – how long before his friends desert him too?

Fifty-Six

It took several days to obtain a guest list and several more to begin the interviews of those who had been present at Willingsby Hall on the night of the murders. In all, including servants, both those who resided at the house and those who had been brought in, there were almost eighty people on the list. And a good number of those were not local but had travelled for the party.

Henry managed to hive off some of the interviews to police in the areas from which they had come, and others he and Mickey conducted themselves.

The story was consistent; yes, many of them knew Charles May, if only in the sense that he was a friend of a friend and a good number recalled seeing him on that night, but the evening had been fun, chaotic, a little lively and it was impossible to know where anyone was at any given time.

To be truthful, Henry had expected nothing else. He and Sergeant Hitchens had faced a great deal of resentment from those that they interviewed. A common complaint was 'Why on earth are you asking us? You can't possibly think that any of our set would have anything to do with those murders.'

The most common response that Henry got was, from those who actually knew Charles May well, 'I'm sure I saw him about. He was with . . .' Followed by a list of guests who had, at some point in the evening, been seen chatting to or drinking with Charles May.

The interference with the county's rich and influential had of course upset a great many people, including Chief Inspector Carrington, and had also duly been noted in the local newspapers.

Inspector Johnstone was asked to give an interview; he declined.

Mickey had observed that it was likely that the murderer would have had blood on his clothes even though he'd strangled Mary Fields. It seemed like a safe bet that he'd traded blows with Walter before delivering the final killing strike, and it was entirely possible that there would have been cast-off blood from that. The party had been informal, many of the guests

290

being in fancy dress, and Charles May had apparently been wearing a dark blazer. Someone recalled an incident when wine had been tipped over him in the crush and he'd been forced to change. A maid remembered offering to take his jacket and sponge it down but he'd declined; he'd simply taken it off and cast it carelessly into a corner of the room.

Was that significant? Henry wasn't sure. He applied for a warrant to do a forensic search of Willingsby Hall but it was slow going. It was also likely that all traces of blood that had ever been on the jacket, and had been transferred to anything in the room, would have been cleaned away by now.

He felt he had been clutching at straws. He had not even been able to take Charles May's fingerprints because, despite him having brought May in for questioning with as much possible noise, the man had never actually been charged. Henry had known that he was overreaching himself and that it was now coming back to bite him. The great and the good of the county were, as predicted, closing ranks.

He'd had Sergeant Hitchens take a photograph of Charles May's car and then show it around the streets close to where Mary Fields had died, but nobody remembered seeing it at all and certainly not on the night of the murder. It was a substantial car; it would have been noticed.

'If he left the party,' Henry concluded, 'it was not in his own car.'

Finally, the owners of Willingsby Hall announced that they were going down to London and that

291

the police could therefore 'wander around their estates to their heart's content as they would no longer be in the way'.

'And as there will no longer be anything to find,' Mickey said acidly.

'Robert Hanson's funeral is scheduled for tomorrow,' Henry said. 'We will attend that and then go on to the hall.'

'I'm sure we'll receive a warm welcome at both locations.'

Once again they had made use of Dr Fielding's car but this time Dr Fielding himself was present and in the driving seat. He had decided that he ought to go and pay his respects but Henry also realized that he was curious. Henry had agreed that Dr Fielding should drive them out to Willingsby Hall; he knew the countryside around and he might be useful.

It was a bright morning when the car turned down into the little valley and parked some distance away from the church. The coffin was being carried down from the Hanson farm on the broad shoulders of half-a-dozen farmworkers. Elijah Hanson and his wife walked in front and Ted behind. Villagers lined the route, watching one of their own brought home and put into the ground.

Henry saw the Samuels standing outside their cottage and the Lees a little bit apart. When the funeral procession had passed he crossed the road to talk to Dar Samuels.

'I take it you've had no news or you would have been in touch with me.'

'I've heard nothing. And I'm glad of it.'

'We are leaving here, after the harvest is in,' Mrs Samuels said. 'This is no longer a home to us.'

'The Hansons want you to go?'

'The master never said that but it's for the best. He has asked about and found us a position with a cottage up at Boggle Hill. It's sheep up there. Not much call for horses but I can handle sheep and the cottage is solid enough. And it's off his land. Seems right, that.'

'And Helen Lee? What becomes of her?'

'Frank Church did what he should have done months ago – spoke up for her. It's been agreed. They'll be married in a couple of weeks' time. That's for the best too.'

'And will they be leaving?'

Dar Samuels shrugged. 'Frank's mother won't want to share her kitchen. I doubt Frank will want to move in with the Lees. I've not asked what they are going to do. Not my concern now, is it?'

His wife nudged his arm. The procession had gone into the church. The Samuels drifted away to join the other villagers standing in the churchyard. Not family able to go and witness the funeral service but close enough that they must be present when the body was put into the ground.

'I think we should leave now.' Dr Fielding came across to join him. 'I had a quick word with Ted and he was polite enough to suggest that we go up to the Grange and have a bite to eat after the funeral. But we're not wanted there – not if he's honest about it. So we should get about our other business.'

293

Inspector Johnstone nodded. Fielding was probably right and there was nothing to be gained by hanging around in the village. They waited until the rest of the villagers had gathered in the churchyard, Henry noticing that the Lees were not among them, then they drove away up the steep hill out on to the Croxby road.

'The Samuels are leaving the village,' Henry said. 'Sometime after the harvest, he said. For somewhere called Boggle Hill?'

'Out Caistor way, I think,' Dr Fielding said. 'Going to be a shepherd then. I imagine it's going to feel like a long time before Michaelmas.'

'Michaelmas?' Henry asked.

'When the labourers traditionally move farms. Twice a year, Michaelmas, and usually around Candlemas, though some switch to Easter and get moved in before Good Friday. Round here Good Friday is their day for getting their garden started. Most of the farmers still keep to that tradition. If Samuels doesn't stay until Michaelmas he won't get paid what has been agreed for the year. No one would expect him to leave until then, not even the Hansons, not even after what's happened. It would make them look bad in the eyes of the wider community and that matters. At least the Samuels have a place to go to – they won't need to visit the hiring fairs.'

'What are the hiring fairs?' Mickey asked.

'Pretty much what they sound like. Men wanting jobs – usually their families too. They go and stand in the market square. Places like Louth and Spalding. Those who want workers go round and choose the best. I've seen men standing

294

with placards round their necks, saying what skills they've got and where they worked before. Looks like the pictures you see of slave markets but many don't have a choice. It's that, travel elsewhere or go to the parish for help. An increasing number are heading for the towns or off to sea like young Ethan. If it keeps on like this the countryside will be empty within a generation.'

They drove in silence for a little while and then Henry said, 'It feels like parts of this county have not yet reached the twentieth century.'

'I sometimes wonder,' Dr Fielding nodded, 'if parts of it have even reached the nineteenth.'

The house was built in a mix of old red brick and mossy grey stone. Lighter stone framed the windows and the large front door and a gravel drive circled a lawn at the front of the house. It was not a particularly grand house but it did look solid and settled in the landscape. They were escorted through to the housekeeper's room. She was seated at a table going through her ledgers but she set them aside when Dr Fielding and the police officers came in. It was clear that she knew Dr Fielding and welcomed him enthusiastically. Inspector Johnstone was glad that he had decided to bring the doctor along; anything that could break down the barriers and get people talking to him.

'Well, bring us all some tea,' she told the maid who had brought them in. 'Gentlemen, are you comfortable enough here . . .'

'This is a lovely room,' Mickey said with a broad smile.

'Mr and Mrs Saltby said you could have the run of the place now they were gone,' she told them proudly. 'And anything you want to know, I'll do my best to tell you.'

She turned her attention to Dr Fielding and began to ask about mutual acquaintances. Mickey raised an eyebrow. 'Mrs Haddon,' he said, 'I wondered if you'd mind us maybe having tea afterwards, and we could leave Doctor Fielding here to have a chat while we get business done. We don't want to inconvenience you any further than we have to.'

She looked momentarily doubtful and then pleased. It seemed, from the conversation, that Mrs Haddon was well acquainted with Dr Fielding's family. Sergeant Hitchens and Inspector Johnstone took themselves away.

'According to eyewitness statements,' Mickey said, 'our Mr May tossed his jacket into the corner of the red billiard room. Do you suppose that means they have two billiard rooms – one in another colour?'

'I would guess this house is big enough to accommodate two billiard rooms,' Henry said, 'but what anybody would want to do with two billiard rooms I couldn't guess.'

It turned out that the red billiard room was just off the hallway. Everything was covered down with white dust sheets, the family being away, and what servants were left were busy scrubbing and polishing and cleaning every surface to within an inch of its life. Henry's heart sank; the small hope he had of some tiny scrap of forensic evidence remaining had diminished to nothing. In the red billiard room the table was set on a deep maroon carpet, laid on broad wooden boards which were exposed round the edges of the room. He could smell at once that they had been newly polished.

'So,' he said, 'we talk to the servants, we see what recollections they have of that night and if any of them know Charles May and could shed more light on his whereabouts. If I take care of that, Mickey, you go out and see if you can find the chauffeur. Unless he's gone with the family to London, of course.'

Mickey nodded and wandered away, and Henry took himself on a tour of the hall. He soon understood that it would have been impossible to keep sight of anybody for a full evening. Rooms led off to other rooms, broad steps led down on to a lawn. There had been a marquee pitched on the lawn, on one side of which was a small coppice, on the other the entrance to a walled garden which led in turn to another gate down to the river.

He returned to the housekeeper and asked if he could speak to the servants. They were duly lined up ready to be interviewed but after another hour it was clear that most of them didn't even know who Charles May was. He was not a regular visitor – just another of the gentlemen that had been there that night.

Henry asked about the incident with the wine and found that it was one of several. 'There was a lady who got champagne down her dress – that wasn't so bad because champagne don't stay the same way. Then there was a gentleman who got whiskey on his jacket and we sponged it off and gave him his jacket back, then there was the man with the red wine he got down his blazer. Dark blue it was, with shiny buttons on. But he just took it off, tossed it to one side and said it didn't matter. And to leave it alone.'

'And you think this might have been Mr Charles May?'

'Not if he was a younger gentleman, no. This was an older gentleman with grey hair.' She leaned a little closer to Henry. 'To be truthful, he'd been drinking so much I don't think he knew where he was or even if he'd got a jacket.'

Henry sighed. This, he thought, was a waste of time.

A few minutes later Mickey came to find him.

'I've been speaking to one of the gardeners,' Mickey said. 'The chauffeur had driven the family down south, but the gardener says that on the night of the party what was happening was the cars were all parked around in the back field. The owner of the house didn't want his lawns messing up and it seems he didn't trust his guests to park. So his chauffeur and a couple of the others were given the job of moving the cars round the back then fetching them around again when people were ready to go. The gardener reckons there were maybe twenty cars or more parked up on the same field so anyone would have had access, and with the amount of noise that was going on he reckons no one would have heard a thing. They'd got a string quartet playing in the marquee and two gramophones blaring from the house. Later on someone fetched

298

one of the gramophones out on to the terrace, so you can imagine the racket.'

'But anyone leaving would have been seen, surely, from the front of the house? Presumably at least one of the chauffeurs would have been left on duty in case anybody wanted to get their vehicle.'

'Ah,' Mickey said. 'But I've got a solution to that one. You need to come and look.'

Henry followed Mickey out to the back of the house and down to the side of the walled garden. The gravel drive took an extra curve around here and led into what had been a stable yard. Beyond that was an open field. This was where the vehicles had been parked on the night of the party.

A young man was waiting by the gate and they followed him across the field to another gate. 'Follow this'n round,' he told them, pointing to a rutted track. 'She brings you back on to road.'

Mickey thanked him and the gardener took himself off. 'Have you followed the path yet?' Henry asked.

'I waited for you. Shall we?'

Henry led the way. The path was narrow and rutted and in places high hedges rose on both sides. There was evidence that something had broken off the thin branches. 'It would scratch the car,' Henry observed. 'But probably not that badly. The owner might not have noticed it at once.'

'Especially not if they'd been drinking or were hungover,' Mickey agreed. 'But it seems to me, just to be certain of him not being found out,

299

May would need to know who was staying overnight and whose car he could safely borrow. And it would need to be a smaller vehicle, which narrows things down even more.'

Unexpectedly the path broadened out and the road was just ahead of them. Neither Henry nor Mickey were quite sure what road they were on, but that could be easily established by asking the gardener.

'So this opens up a new set of possibilities,' Henry said. 'A new vehicle to look for witnesses to.'

'And the housekeeper will have a list of overnight guests.'

They turned and walked back towards the house.

By the time they left they had a list of those who had been planning to stay overnight and also those who had remained as impromptu guests. There were twelve in all, and on the list was also the registration number and make of car. The chauffeurs had been required to write the names of the guests and which car was theirs on a list just to make things easier on the night. And they had one small snippet of information in addition to this: the gardener recalled one of the chauffeurs being puzzled.

'Boss had allowed us all some beer,' he said, 'so we all sat around drinking and chatting and the chauffeurs went to fetch the cars as they were needed. One time one came back and said that he was sure he'd parked another way, but when he went to fetch the car it was pointing towards the house and not towards the hedge. We wanted to know how much beer he'd had but he said it had been no more'n a pint.'

Dr Fielding drove them round to where the track came out on to the road. It was clear that his own car would not fit but something smaller would. Something like an Austin or a Sunbeam might fit the bill and, looking at the list, Henry narrowed his search down to a possible three. The car the chauffeur had been puzzled over was an Austin seven, and thinking about the car that Ted drove – same make if not exactly the same model – Henry was pretty certain that it could have been driven through the gate and down the narrow track.

Driving back to Louth, he finally began to feel that they might be getting somewhere.

Fifty-Seven

Heath House was two miles outside of Boston and the owner of the car in question was Melissa Heath, sister to Toby Heath, both of whom had been at the party that midsummer night. Henry had spoken to them both on the telephone and the following morning he and Mickey had caught the train and gone down to Boston. Toby Heath met them in his car and drove them back to the house.

'Sis loves to drive,' he said. 'I have to say,' he laughed a little uncertainly, 'I like to have myself a drink and she says I don't drive well when

I've had a drink or two. And like all women, she fusses. And so, if we go anywhere like that, nine times out of ten Melissa drives. This brute is far too big for her so we went out in hers that night.'

'And you stayed overnight? You had been intending to?'

Toby Heath laughed again. 'Too busy drinking and dancing and having fun, old man. Didn't notice the passage of time, you might say. Next thing we know the sun is coming up. So I crash on some sofa, in the billiard room, I think, just for an hour or so. Don't know where Melissa took herself off to. Have to ask her that.'

'And what time did you leave?'

'Ah, it would have been just before eight, I think.'

'And when you left did you notice anything unusual about the car? Scratches to the doors, perhaps?'

Toby turned to stare at Henry, taking his eyes off the road for what felt like a dangerously long time. 'How the devil did you know that? Melissa was furious and tried to blame the man who'd done the parking for us, but like I pointed out to her, she couldn't be absolutely certain that it happened on that night. Melissa drives like a mad woman sometimes, takes the corner so tight she takes half the hedge with her. Anyway, it didn't seem worth making a fuss over.'

Mickey had brought the camera with him and spent some time photographing the car and also the damage to the doors and sides. The scratches were not deep but were consistent with being driven along the narrow pathway, the hedge catching on either side. On its own that meant nothing. But Henry felt that it was another link in the chain.

Melissa stood beside Henry and watched as Mickey took his pictures.

'Do you know Charles and Celia May?' Henry asked her.

'Only casually. We're part of the same crowd, I suppose.' She smiled at Henry again. 'We've heard all about what you've been doing, though. You've been making a lot of waves, Mr Policeman. A lot of very big waves.'

'It's difficult to do my job without upsetting someone,' Henry said. 'Is he well liked?'

A little moue of disgust answered that one. 'He seems pleasant enough,' she said. 'But he has, shall we say, a bit of a reputation. Celia has, I'm told, threatened to leave him two or three times already.'

'Do you think she will now?'

'I thought she already had.' She tipped her head to one side. 'From what I hear, Celia May and her children have taken themselves off to Nice. Her father has a property there. I hear,' she leant in closer to Henry, 'that there are lawyers involved.'

'And what do you think will happen?'

She shrugged delicately. 'I imagine Celia's father will make him an offer and the marriage will be quietly dissolved. He'll get a settlement, I suppose. That's unless' – a small, sideways look at him – 'you arrest him first, of course.' She laughed then, as though this was an impossibility.

'And do you think he could be guilty?'

'Oh,' she said. 'How on earth would I know? It's sad though, isn't it? Three people being killed like that. Sadder than what happened to Robert, in a way.'

'You knew Robert Hanson?'

'Of course. The old families tend to stick together. We all know one another. I know your Chief Inspector Carrington, too. He married Elsie Marris – she's Canon Marris's niece. Nice woman but I'm not so keen on him.' She giggled. 'I don't suppose I should tell you that.'

Mickey had finished his task and Henry said that they would need to leave if they were to get the next train back.

'Toby will drive you,' she said, and Henry had the impression that the novelty of the police visit was already wearing off. 'Of course,' she added, 'the Hansons and the Marrises and the Carringtons aren't really in the top set, are they? But our paths cross. You know how it is.'

Henry didn't but he thought he could probably guess.

'And are Fry and May in the top set?'

'I suppose.' She smiled slightly. 'By marriage anyway.'

'And did you have an opinion of Robert Hanson?' he asked.

'One really doesn't like to say.'

Toby drove them both back to the station and Henry half listened as Mickey chatted to him about cars and horsepower. He guessed that news of their visit was halfway round the county by now and that it would eventually get back to May.

Fifty-Eight

Chief Inspector Henry Johnstone and Sergeant Mickey Hitchens had taken up their accustomed seats in the snug of the Wheatsheaf. They still had the space to themselves but, Mickey reckoned, it was a sign of their acceptance that the locals were slower to move away and didn't shift so far. Another week and they'd be accepted as a normal part of the scenery, ordinary enough that he and the boss might have to move their 'office' elsewhere.

Mickey hoped they would be gone before he had to test that theory out. He took a long drink of his pint and then set the mug down on the table. 'So,' he said, 'what do we have?'

Henry took a mere sip in comparison then set his glass aside. 'A clearer picture, perhaps. Though I'm not willing to discount anything as yet.'

He ticked off the points on his fingers. He had long, rather slender hands but Mickey knew they were surprisingly strong.

'Ethan Samuels. The button found at the scene matches. The boy admitted to his father that he knew the Fields and George Fields told us that he thought Mary and Ethan might have liked one another a little too much, so . . .'

'So it's possible he visited her with thoughts of sex rather than killing on his mind. He's not off the hook, though. He's shown himself fully capable of violence. If she caused him to lose his temper, well, there's not much evidence that he can keep a rein on it once it's lost.'

Henry nodded agreement. 'Robert Hanson's face was beaten to a pulp,' he said. 'The punishment meted out had rage behind it, not merely the loss of temper. Then we have the candlestick.'

'There's a partial that might match one of the unknown prints from the house but frankly it's so partial I'd be reluctant to put it forward as proof. No, the usefulness of the candlestick will come when the case finally gets to court. You can imagine the effect it will have on the jury. A tiny girl like Ruby Fields attacked with a weapon of that size and swung with the intent to smash out her brains.'

Henry allowed himself a wry smile. 'You should have become a prosecuting counsel, Mickey.'

'I think I'd have needed a different set of parents if I'd any hope of bringing that about. And then we have our Mr May. Technically a man with motive but no opportunity.'

'Technically a man who could have created his opportunity. He could easily have taken Melissa Heath's car, driven back here, killed Mary Fields and her family, driven back again and picked up his champagne glass without anyone being the wiser.'

'And he had a good motive, at least in his own eyes.' Mickey frowned. 'I wonder how much or, should I say, how little cash it would have taken to have shut Mary's mouth for good. My guess is a couple of hundred pounds and a train ticket back to her family and that would have been an end to the matter.'

306

'You're probably right,' Henry agreed. 'But she could just as easily have kept him on the hook. He'd not have risked that. My conviction is that he didn't risk that.'

'He must have had blood on his clothes.'

'So he went home and changed. It's a big enough house – he could have slipped in the back way or he could have taken a change of clothes with him. One blazer and one pair of lighter-coloured trousers look pretty much like another and I doubt our Mr May has such a restricted wardrobe that he owns only one of each.'

'His valet would notice an absence?'

'And his valet would accept an excuse. Valets generally want to remain in employment.'

Mickey nodded. 'So, now we wait. We let the gossip do the rounds and its job. May will know that we're closing the noose.'

'And when the pressure has built sufficiently, we bring him in again.'

'There's still the missing key,' Mickey reminded his boss.

'Which most likely went the way of the candle-stick but didn't land in the weeds.'

'True,' Mickey agreed. 'But I did wonder if the landlord might still have a spare.'

Celia May and the children had barely contacted Charles since they had left. He had received a postcard from the boys and a brief phone call from his father-in-law, informing him that his wife planned to take an extended holiday but that was all.

Charles May could feel his entire life sliding away from him.

He poured himself another whisky, this time without the soda, and remembered a happy day, just a scant two weeks before, when he had joined Celia and the children at the seaside. They had walked together along the promenade and then watched the one-armed man dive off the end of the pier and tossed some coins into his cap. It had been a relaxed and happy afternoon, so different from the previous visit he and his family had made there.

The difference was that he had known Mary Fields could not interrupt their visit this time.

A few months before, at Easter, on a blustery but sunny day, they had gone – Celia and Charles and the two boys – to blow the cobwebs away after the long winter.

Charles remembered that the wind had been blowing off the sea but the sun had been shining and he had been happy. Celia had been happy too. And then he had seen her, Mary Fields. And for a distressing moment he was certain that she must have followed him there.

She was standing with her own little girl and with a younger man that Charles now knew was Walter Fields, and she was smiling at Charles. A knowing, spiteful smile and Charles knew, just knew that she planned to destroy him.

A small knock on the door. 'A telephone call for you, sir.'

Charles went to his study, hoping it might be Celia telling him she was on her way home.

It was Edmund Fry. 'I heard,' he said, 'that

308

the police visited Toby Heath. They were asking about Melissa's car, suggesting that you might have borrowed it on the night of the party and driven back here. I just thought you should hear it from me.'

Charles thanked him but a chill settled in the pit of his stomach.

'I've been thinking of joining Celia for a week or two,' he said, attempting to sound cheerful and normal. 'You were right, of course, telling me we should both go away for a while. I should have listened to you.'

There was silence on the other end of the phone, then: 'Charles, I don't think . . . I don't think that's such a good idea. It might have been, of course, but now . . . now I think it would just look . . . guilty.'

Guilty. 'You think I did it,' Charles said flatly.

'No. Of course not. Of course I don't think—'

Charles set the receiver back into its cradle.

Edmund believed he might have killed her, Charles thought. Edmund no longer believed him.

Fifty-Nine

In small communities it is difficult to hide anything, and when the letter came it was impossible for Helen to keep it secret. Helen Lee rarely received mail.

She knew at once that it was from Ethan. She recognized his writing – a pencil scrawl. She ran from the house and up to the copse of ash trees on the ridge above Vale farm and there, sitting on a fallen tree, she opened the envelope and read the short message within.

It was written on a piece of rough paper that looked as though it might have been a flyleaf from a book. The envelope bore the mark of a seamen's mission and she knew, because Ethan had told her, that they sometimes made envelopes and stamps available for those who could not afford to buy but who needed to get a message home.

She looked at the postmark and was only faintly surprised to find that it was Bridlington – a port she vaguely recalled was somewhere in Yorkshire.

Ethan had headed north.

The letter was brief and also written in pencil.

My Darling Helen,

I am so sorry, sorry more than words can say. I didn't want any of this to happen. I never planned to fall in love with you and I never planned to hurt anyone and now I have and it means I have to go away from you.

I want you to be happy, my darling. I want you to be happy because I can't come back to you and I can't ask you to wait for me to get settled somewhere and send for you because I'd be asking you to run away with a guilty man and I've got nothing I can offer to you.

I know no one will forgive me and I'm not asking you to either. I love you and it breaks me up that we can't be together.

I don't know where I'll be going and I couldn't tell you anyway. You understand that, don't you.

I will always love you, my dearest darling.

Please tell my family that I love them too and I always will.

Yours, Ethan

Helen read it twice then couldn't read it again because her eyes were too blurred with tears. Dimly, she was aware of two people coming up the rise towards her. One was her mother and the other was Robert's father, Elijah Hanson.

They were arguing but Helen couldn't quite focus on the words until Elijah Hanson towered over her, demanding that she hand over the letter.

'No,' Helen said. 'It's not for you. It isn't anything to do with you.'

'Helen.' Her mother's tone was like a slap. 'Show it to me, please,' she asked more gently.

Reluctantly, Helen placed the precious note into her mother's hand.

Then she broke down and wept, her heart breaking all over again.

Sixty

The following morning the letter was given to Henry, delivered with the full weight of Carrington's fury.

'You harass a pillar of our community, you ruin his business and interrogate his friends when you have a murderous gypsy running free, probably having fled the country by now.'

'Perhaps so,' Henry agreed. 'But that doesn't make Charles May any less guilty.'

Waiting outside the King's Head, Henry saw George Fields.

'I wanted to catch you, Inspector,' George said.

He looked older, Henry thought. Old and tired but no longer angry. He seemed to have passed beyond that, or perhaps he no longer had the energy.

'I wanted to tell you that I'm off back to sea. It seems like the best thing. I've nothing keeping me here and I'll gain nothing by hanging around longer.'

'I hope it works out for you, Mr Fields. And I'm sorry I've not brought things to a better conclusion.'

'I hear talk about Charles May,' George said. 'Do you think he's guilty?'

'George, I can't tell you that.'

George Fields nodded. 'Truth is, Inspector, if I stayed here I know I might get drunk one night, get myself a bit riled up like and, well, our Mr Charles May might end up . . . no longer in the land of the living.'

'And I would know who was responsible, George.'

'I know that too. I've been asking around, talking to people about my Mary and . . . I've learnt a few things. But that don't make me feel any different, Inspector. And it don't excuse what was done to my little Ruby. So I think the safest thing for everyone is if I go away, back on the boats for a bit. Leave you to do your work. I don't want to have to hang for something I know I might be tempted to do.'

'George, can I ask you something? How easy would it be for someone to get work on the boats?'

George shrugged. 'Depends, don't it. Grimsby and Immingham, your papers have to be in order. You get checked or the master of the ship has to vouch for you. Other places, it's easier. Crews change all the time, and in the smaller ports it's easy enough to get yourself on to a boat, especially one of the bigger boats, and hide until you're out to sea. Chances are they'll just make you work it out.' He shrugged again. 'You're thinking of the gypsy boy?'

'Ethan Samuels, yes.'

'I hear rumours that he might have killed our Mary too. But I don't see it.' He looked thoughtfully at Henry. 'Those rumours true?'

'A button was found in the bedroom,' Henry told him quietly. 'It matched one from Ethan Samuels's shirt.'

'So he came to visit Mary.' George shook his head sadly. 'I knew he . . . wanted her. He had that look about him, you know? So I discouraged him, thought I'd warned him off but . . . He'd not have killed her. I don't believe he had it in him.'

'We know he killed Robert Hanson. He had *that* in him.'

For a moment both men fell silent, then George said, 'If I was him, I'd go down the coast a ways

313

to one of the little fishing ports. King's Lynn, maybe. Boston, even. Ships come down river from all over the world – mixed crews always in need of deck hands. It's no harder to get a place than it is to get field work come harvest.'

'And few questions asked.'

'Not if he's young and strong and willing.'

George twisted his flat cap between his hands then set it straight on his head. 'I'd best be off. I've a way to go.'

Henry nodded. 'Good luck, George.'

'Good luck to you too, Inspector. Seems to me we're both in need of it.'

Sixty-One

Charles May was dreaming. It was actually more in the nature of a nightmare and, worst of all, it was a nightmare about actual events.

He woke with a start and lay staring at the bedroom ceiling. Light filtered in through the summer curtains, bathing the room in soft, crisp morning. He listened to the sounds of the household moving around him, servants clattering and a car driving up the road outside the house.

He'd been remembering, he supposed, and that had filtered into his dream.

He turned over on to his side and stared at the window. It was slightly open and the curtains billowed. They had been Celia's choice, embroidered with flowers and little birds. Duck-egg blue, like the bedcover. He knew that Celia would never be coming back. That he would have to leave this house, his business and go somewhere else with whatever allowance his father-in-law decreed he might deserve.

He'd be generous, Charles thought. It would demean him to be anything else, but that was scant compensation.

And all because of *that* woman. If she'd been content just to have some fun, earn a little cash. Earn a substantial amount of cash compared to what she could glean elsewhere then all would have been well. But no, Mary was greedy. Mary was unreasonable.

He'd been horrified when that young man, Walter, had let himself into the hotel room. Mary must have unlocked the door. Charles recalled the shock of looking up and seeing him there with the camera in his hand.

But she had warned him in a way, Charles acknowledged. There'd been another time when he had booked them both into a hotel. Mary had been pleased, preening herself, making believe that she was a lady when all she was really was a little slut.

They'd been leaving when Walter had suddenly appeared on the hotel steps and Charles realized he must have been waiting outside.

'Take a good look,' Mary had said, taking Charles's arm with a possessive air. 'Take a very good look, Walter, because this is a very important man.'

He should have known, then. Should have followed his instincts and broken off all contact.

But he'd been stupid and Mary had made certain that he paid for that stupidity.

And now it was all too late.

Henry and Mickey had been showing the new photograph of the car round the streets that backed on to the canal. They had focused on those areas where the car could have been parked quietly or even hidden on the waste ground, close to where the candlestick had been hidden.

So far there had been little result.

'You don't see many cars parked at this end of town,' one woman told Henry.

'Which is why it might have been noticed. Why someone might have seen.'

A shake of the head. 'I might have seen a car but I can't be certain of the day. I see a man come down to that bit of waste ground between here and the canal. Can't be sure of the day.'

Someone else had heard, or thought they had heard, a gate crash closed on the evening Mary Fields and her family had died.

Then, one small breakthrough.

'I was up, late. The baby had colic and I'd been pacing the floor with her for a good hour. Every time I laid her down she'd start with yelling again and my Fred, he had to get up for work at five, so I just stood there and rocked her in the other room. The front room. And I think I saw a man over at Mary's place. I think it might have been that night.'

Nora Mason was a very young woman. Married a year and with her first baby just a few weeks old, or so she told Mickey Hitchens.

'Why didn't you tell anyone this before?' he asked.

'Because I've been over at me mam's. I wasn't coping very well and I've no one here but my Fred and he's no help. What man is when it comes to new babbies? So I went home to mam for a bit. She sorted me out.'

Mickey nodded his understanding. 'And you saw someone come out of that house?'

She shrugged. 'It weren't that unusual. Men would hang about till they thought no one was looking and then they'd knock on the window and she'd let them in. She were discreet about it, waited till it were late and most people round here would be in their beds. But I've been up nights with our Linda. She just wouldn't settle. Fred moved into the back room so he could get some sleep and I took her in with me most nights.'

'And this night, you were up with her. With her colic.'

'It must have been that night because I went to visit mam the next day. I was at the end of my tether, if I'm honest. You know what it's like with a baby that won't stop crying for hours at a time, not even if you give her the gripe water?'

'It must be really hard,' Mickey said gently.

She nodded and he could see that she was very close to tears. 'So I'm standing in the bedroom and watching the street, just for something to do. I sometimes see a fox come trotting down the road, sniffing round the dustbins.' She smiled awkwardly. 'You can imagine how lonely it feels when you're standing there rocking a baby and the whole of the rest of the world feels like it's asleep? Seeing a fox is, like, the height of entertainment.'

She laughed and Mickey laughed with her. 'And this man. Can you describe him?'

'It was dark. He knocked on the window and Mary opened the front door but there was no light on. He was tall and well built, I suppose, and he was wearing a dark jacket and some lighter-coloured trousers. But I couldn't see him very well.'

'Nora, did you see a car? Was he driving a car, do you think?'

She shook her head. 'I didn't see him get out of one but I saw a car drive down the end road just before he arrived. It was a small car, sit up and beg style, you know? Dark coloured. I don't know if it was his.'

'And what happened then?'

'I tried putting Linda down for a while and she settled for a bit but then she woke up again and started screaming her head off once more. So I stood with her looking out of the window again and I saw the man leave. When I came home and heard all the talk about what had happened I said to our Fred, "That must have been the night before I left to go to Mother's". He said I ought to say something.'

'I'm glad he did,' Mickey told her.

The night of the party Charles May had been wearing light trousers and a dark blazer.

'Do you think you'd recognize the man again?'

She shook her head. 'I didn't get a proper look.'

'And the car.' He took the photograph of Melissa's car from his pocket. 'Did it look anything like this?'

318

'I think so,' she said. 'It wasn't open top, more of the sit up and beg, like I said. It could be that one.' She looked hopefully at Mickey as though he might provide her with the correct response.

'Thank you,' Mickey said and saw the disappointment as she realized that this interview was over. That it was time to go back to the crying baby and the husband who needed his sleep. 'I hope she gets over the colic,' Mickey offered. 'I'm told they usually do after the first few weeks.'

She nodded gratefully, as though he'd offered much more than casual reassurance.

As Mickey walked back down the street to where his boss was waiting, he was aware of her, standing in the bedroom, the child cradled in her arms, watching him leave.

Charles May was not best pleased when Inspector Johnstone and Sergeant Hitchens turned up on his doorstep in the early evening. It was time, Henry had decided, to increase the pressure, even if that meant a little bending of the truth.

'A man fitting your description was seen at Mary Fields' house on the night she and her daughter and Walter Fields were murdered. A car belonging to Miss Melissa Heath is known to have been, shall we say, borrowed from where it was parked at Willingsby Hall that night and seen close by the house where the murders occurred. Yes, you were at that party; yes, you have witnesses but, Mr May, my sergeant and I have been to the hall and we have seen that it would have been perfectly possible for you to leave, unobserved, in the borrowed car.'

'And if you're so sure of yourself, why not have me arrested? You have nothing, Inspector. It's all circumstantial. You are playing a very foolish game.'

Henry nodded thoughtfully. 'I hear that your wife is filing for divorce,' he said. 'Or is that just a rumour? It seems that your wife may well have her doubts.'

Charles turned on him, furious. 'That's low, Inspector, even for a policeman. She's gone away for a while because she is, understandably, very upset by all this. My wife and children are staying with family in France. And that is all. All.'

He was shaking, Henry could see that. Barely suppressed rage and what more? A little fear, perhaps.

Henry knew he had scored points.

'I may be joining them,' Charles said. 'Some time away would be a good thought.'

'I'd advise against it,' Henry told him.

Sixty-Two

Edmund Fry had spent the previous day in a state of anxiety. The feeling had grown, overnight, that something was terribly wrong. That Charles might be guilty of more than just having an affair. The upshot of this anxiety, that had interrupted his sleep and troubled his dreams, was that he confided in his wife over the breakfast table.

Delia's eyes widened as she poured his tea from the forget-me-not blue pot. 'You can't be serious. Can you? Charles and Celia are our friends.'

'And Celia hasn't contacted him since she left for Nice. She has her father's lawyers involved. She's looking for a separation.'

She looked down at her plate, suddenly guilty.

'You knew that already?'

'Oh, dear. I didn't want to mention it, not until . . . You already seemed so upset by all this.' She took a deep breath and reached across for more toast.

'You want the marmalade?'

'Please. We talked, just before she left. She said that she was furious with him because of the affair. I think she was offended, if you must know, that he'd chosen a woman like that to . . . well, anyway.' She paused, scraped butter across her toast then added a spoonful of marmalade. 'She didn't want the boys to overhear anything. Young Robbie is off to school next year; he's old enough to ask questions.'

'And does she think he . . . did anything else?'

Delia looked sternly at her husband. 'You mean, does she think he might be a murderer? No, of course not.'

'You don't sound so certain. Delia?'

She dropped her toast back on to the small, square plate. 'Edmund, I don't want to think he could do anything like that, really I don't, but I've been talking to our friends, people who were with us at the party and, well, we all want to think that we knew what Charles was doing all

321

evening. That we can give him an alibi. In good faith, I mean.'

'And you think we can't.' It wasn't a question.

'Darling, I know she was, well, a prostitute, but she was still a woman.'

'Not a very nice woman. But no. I do take your point, personal enmity aside. And believe me, dear, I'd never wish anything to have happened to the child.'

He sat back and studied the breakfast table as though the eggs and toast, dishes of preserves and the forget-me-not pattern on his wife's cup could provide him with solutions.

Delia retrieved her toast then put it down again.

'And what do they all think?' he asked her. 'I don't know how much . . .'

She sighed. 'Oh, dear. Well, the fact is we did our best to put it together, to find out who'd seen him and when and what he was doing. There's a great big gap when no one seems to have known where he was.' She looked slightly shamefaced and then added, 'Toby suggested he might have been otherwise engaged with a woman. He could have slipped up to one of the bedrooms and no one would have known. I mean, with a woman we know, rather than a woman he . . . paid.'

Edmund nodded, his appetite suddenly fading. 'Let me think about this,' he said. 'Delia, I need to think about this for a while.'

She nodded. 'Do you think he was as desperate as all that?' she asked.

'If Mary Fields threatened him with blackmail I think he would have been very desperate,' he told her candidly.

She shrugged impatiently. 'Then he should have just given her the money, shouldn't he? Made her go away. A woman like that, he could have paid her off. He didn't need to . . . not that I'm saying he did.' She looked across the table at her husband, noting for the first time how pale and worried he looked, how . . . creased.

'Oh, dear,' she said again.

By early afternoon Edmund Fry had made up his mind. Charles had not come to the office again that day. In fact, it had now been three days since Charles had last come to the office and the days before when he'd actually arrived he hadn't stayed for long. And he'd been drinking. Properly drinking, not the odd, sociable whisky in the office.

He called his partner at home but was told that Mr May didn't want to speak to anyone. So at half past two, his last appointment of the day dealt with, Edmund Fry went to call on his friend and see if he could get any sense out of him, face-to-face.

'He's sleeping, sir. He had a bad night, I believe,' Charles's man told him.

'Then I plan to wake him up, Evans. I have business to discuss.'

Evans nodded, stood aside and directed Edmund to the study.

Charles May lay sprawled on the day bed in the study. A glass sat on the floor beside it and he looked as though he must either have slept in his clothes or forgotten how to dress himself.

'Charles.' Edmund Fry shook his friend. Eventually Charles opened his eyes.

'God, man. You stink of booze. What are you doing to yourself?' He took Charles by the arm and hauled him into a sitting position. 'Evans, bring some coffee. Make it good and strong. Charles, what's got into you? Look at me, Charles. What are you doing to yourself?'

Charles May looked at his friend with something close to despair in his eyes. And then they hardened. 'I've nothing to say to you,' he said. 'Want nothing to do with you.'

'I'm your friend, Charles. Talk to me.'

Slowly, May shook his head. 'Nothing you can do, old man,' he said. 'Not a bloody thing anyone can do.'

'I feel like a traitor, Inspector. I truly do.'

Edmund Fry looked pale and anxious. He wrapped both hands around the plain white cup containing over-strong, sweet tea. 'But I'm very much afraid that he may . . . may have had something to do with the deaths.'

Henry listened carefully as Edmund Fry explained, telling him what he feared and what his wife had found out. What had happened when he had gone to confront his friend.

'He was so drunk. So utterly . . . I've not seen him like that before. He's not himself, Inspector, and I'm very much afraid of what that might mean.'

Henry Johnstone nodded. I'd like you to tell Chief Inspector Carrington everything you've just told me,' he said.

'Of . . . of course.' Fry looked puzzled but nodded his head emphatically.

Henry summoned Carrington and then beckoned Sergeant Hitchens to follow him. 'We bring him in now,' he said. 'I think our stirring has finally caused the scum to rise to the surface.'

Charles May looked rough and smelt worse, and Henry wondered just how much he'd had to drink in the past twenty or so hours.

He was charged and asked if he wanted legal counsel.

Charles May looked at Inspector Johnstone as if he didn't quite understand the words.

'Take him to the cells,' Carrington urged. 'Let him sober up overnight. 'You'll get nothing from him yet.'

For the first time since they had met, Henry found himself agreeing with the man. He nodded at Constable Parkin. 'Ensure a watch is kept,' he said. 'Checks on the quarter hour. Ensure his tie and laces and belt are taken.'

Carrington stood at Henry's side and watched as Charles May was taken down. 'You're certain of this?' He sounded shaken.

'I'm sure,' Henry Johnstone said. 'He'll confess. Just give him time. He has no choice left to him.'

'And now?' Carrington asked.

'We search his home,' Henry said.

Sixty-Three

Ethan's hands had been calloused since boyhood and the skin grew harder daily as he hauled the ropes and swabbed the decks, his bare skin lashed by wind and the cold, driving rain. Rounding Biscay, the weather had turned on them and he felt he had not been warm or dry in days.

But he was still alive and he was moving steadily and surely away from the threat.

He was also moving further and further away from Helen Lee and that grieved him more than hard work or pain or rough weather ever could. He saw her face every time he closed his eyes, remembered the softness of her skin and the smell of her, warm and womanly and perfumed with lavender.

He grieved for her. Sore of body and heartbroken, Ethan felt that nothing could hurt him further or more deeply than life already had.

The one thought he held tight to was his love for Helen Lee. The one he tried hardest to put aside was the guilt mixed with anger he felt when Robert Hanson came to mind.

He blamed Robert as much as he blamed himself. Robert Hanson had died that day but Ethan felt that he was the one that had been buried.

* * *

'I love my wife, do you know that? And I love my boys. She threatened that. All of it.

'I helped that woman, you see, and then she . . . she inveigled her way into my life.'

'And into your bed?' Henry asked.

'You are a crude, uncouth man.' May lashed out but then seemed to regain a measure of control. 'Yes,' he admitted, 'I was stupid and weak and allowed myself to be led. She took advantage of me. Of my good nature. She blackmailed me. She—'

'And so you killed her,' Henry said flatly. 'What happened that night, Mr May? Did the child interrupt you? Did Walter Fields try to stop you? What did you hit them with, Mr May? What did you do with the murder weapon?'

'You can't prove anything.'

Henry slipped a hand into his pocket and withdrew a key. He laid it on the table in front of Charles May. 'This was found in your home,' he said. 'It's the key to the house where Mary Fields lived.'

For a moment, May scowled at him and then began to bluster. 'She gave me the key,' he said.

'Then why were you seen knocking on the window, waiting to be let in? There's enough evidence to bring this to court. You need to convince a jury of what you did or didn't do, not me.'

Charles May stared at Henry then dropped his head into his hands. 'She had the boy take photographs,' he said. 'She threatened everything I had – everything. Pushed me into a corner. Pushed me too far. What else was I to do?'

'And so you killed her. Killed them.'

327

'What does it matter any more?' Charles May said. 'What does any of it matter now?'

An hour later and Henry had a written statement, confessing to the crime. May hadn't expected the child to come into the room. Mary had told him that she was spending the night with friends. And he had no idea that Walter had a key to the front door.

'Where did you find the key?' Carrington asked him.

'In the pocket of the jacket he'd been wearing. I think he just forgot that it was there.'

'I'd never have believed it,' Carrington said. 'Not Charles May.'

As Henry and Mickey walked back to the hotel Mickey fished in his pocket and produced another front door key. 'I'd better get this back to the landlord,' he said.

'Insurance policy, Mickey?'

'Didn't need it in the end, did we? The man was stupid enough to hang on to the one he'd taken from Walter. Reckon we can go home now, boss?'

Henry nodded. 'I think I'd welcome that,' he said.

Sixty-Four

'Well, one out of two isn't a complete disaster,' Mickey said cheerfully as they boarded the train and began their journey back to London.

'Ethan Samuels is long gone,' Henry agreed. 'Mickey, none of this has turned out well. Broken families and communities that are torn apart. This will resonate for a long time to come.'

'Murder always does,' Mickey said. 'At least George Fields will have his justice.'

'His wife and child are still dead.'

Mickey looked speculatively at his boss. 'You're in a fine mood,' he said. 'Me, I'm just glad to be heading home. We can't change the world, Henry. All we can do is fix what we can.'

Extract from *The Murder Book*:
I heard the news this morning that Mr Charles May has been found dead in his cell. He had evidently decided not to wait for the executioner and hanged himself with his bedsheet.

It occurs to me that most deaths are banal, ordinary, and murders often the more so. Death by violence often has such small and ridiculous beginnings. The need or desire for money, for status, for sex – often not even for love. I can comprehend these needs, especially if, as is so often the case, the perpetrator has little to begin with; is lacking for all of those things and so just seeks to take what he or she can. Human impulse leads to us seeking comfort in whatever form is appropriate. To be recognized, to be comfortable, to be valued.

Most death by violence grows from the actions of a single instance. A man who feels his wife has nagged him once too often or a woman who lashed out against a man who is hurting her or a parent who strikes out at a child or a man

329

*who sees a horse beaten and takes the crop
against the owner. Charles May had none of
these excuses. Perhaps a man who is so used to
buying his way through life simply finds it incom-
prehensible when he realizes that can't always
be the solution. Perhaps he realized, or assumed,
that Mary Fields would never cease to blackmail
him, though I suspect, strongly, that he could
simply have paid her off. She cared for her child.
Her husband thought that most of Mary's misad-
ventures stemmed from that root and about that
I'm not so certain. I suspect that Mary simply
liked the adventure of it all and thought little
about the true consequences.*

I wonder if Charles May's wife will miss him.

*Doctor Fielding sent word that he'd had reason
to go out to Thoresway and that Frank Church
and Helen Lee are married now and he's heard
rumours that she's in the family way. Whose
child? I wonder. Frank's or Ethan's? The old folk
will be counting the days, no doubt, but I have
the feeling that no one will count them too loudly.*

*He tells me that Frank has been raised to the
position of stockman at the Hanson place so I
suppose the Samuels must have left or be leaving
soon.*

*I wonder if Helen Lee will continue to miss Ethan
Samuels. He's as good as dead to her now and,
though it goes against the grain, there is a small
part of me that is glad he escaped the hangman.*

Henry reread what he had written and allowed
himself the ghost of a smile. Then he crossed
through the last lines.

A foolish sentiment, Henry Johnstone thought.

330